EVENING FLOWER

BY

R. ELIZABETH MIGLIORE

PublishAmerica

Baltimore

ISBN: 1-4137-0282-1
PUBLISHED BY PUBLISHAMERICA, LLLP
www.publishamerica.com
Baltimore

Printed in the United States of America

To my parents, Willi and Leny Mohler.

All the information and facts in this book are from letters and diaries, and from countless hours talking with my parents and their friends about the years in Indonesia during the second World War. Some is from my own memory. The names of towns, cities and countries are those used during that time. The names of persons appearing in this story have been changed to protect their privacy; my family's names are real.

REM

Contents

EVENING FLOWER

VOYAGE TO THE ISLAND OF BORNEO

Willi and Leny stood by the railing of the Dutch steamship, Sibajak, waving at the figures slowly disappearing from view. They were on their way to Batavia, the capital of Netherlands East Indies, and from there on to the island of Borneo where Willi was going to work as a geologist for a large oil company.

It was September 30th, 1938. They had been married for only eight months and were now on their way to a foreign land and a life filled with new adventures.

Willi's arm rested on the shoulder of his petite bride. He stood about twelve inches taller than Leny, he was six feet, she only five. Willi had curly dark brown hair, brown eyes, a straight nose, and a dimple in his chin. Leny was a brunette with dark brown eyes. They were childhood sweethearts who grew up in a small village nestled in the Jura mountains of Switzerland near the Rhine. Willi was born in 1911, and was an only child. Already, when he was a young person, he decided to be a geologist. He and Leny had known each other all their lives; Willi was a friend and classmate of one of Leny's brothers. They decided to get married as soon as Willi had completed his doctorate in paleontology. His parents wanted him to be a doctor or a teacher, maybe even a minister as they did not think that a geologist had a future. But Willi stood his ground. Leny always supported him as did her large family; she had three sisters and two brothers.

They married the end of January 1938, and immediately left for The Hague, Holland, where Willi was being trained to go overseas. Holland soon became their second home and they learned to speak the Dutch language. During those days, the Dutch did not like to hear German because of Hitler and the German threat. Every free moment they spent exploring the sights and towns of Holland. They went to the nearby beach, they drove to Utrecht and to Soesdijk, where Princess Juliana and Price Bernhard lived in a huge palace amidst beautiful forests. They went to the Zuider Zee where women wore long dresses with white epaulets and bonnets, and men dressed in black trousers, blue shirts and wooden shoes. The sails of old windmills slowly moved in the ocean breeze. They admired field after field of colorful tulips and daffodils, and visited Amsterdam and Rotterdam. The months in Holland flew by, and before they knew it, they were on their way to Southeast Asia.

The sea voyage was fantastic. All they did was eat, drink and sleep. Coffee was served in bed, then they had a delicious Dutch breakfast consisting of various breads, cold cuts and cheeses, at ten they were served a hot and spicy beef broth, at 12:30 they ate lunch, followed by tea and biscuits at four, and at 6:30 they ate an incredible dinner consisting of many courses. Finally, between ten and eleven at night tea and sandwiches were served by their cabin steward, Kalam. He was a young man from Java, was very attentive, and always made sure that everything was in order. He tidied up, made the bed, put fresh water in the pitchers, and everything in the cabin was cleaned and polished until it shined. There were dances and games at night, and during the afternoons they played tennis, or lay lazily in lounge chairs on the deck enjoying the cool ocean breeze.

All they saw was the endless water of the ocean. They sailed through the Suez canal to the Red Sea. From there they entered the Gulf of Aden, passed Cape Guardafui, Italian Somaliland, and soon were on the Indian Ocean. On the open sea the ship began to rock. Leny became very seasick. Thankfully, after two weeks at sea the ship anchored at the harbor of Colombo on the island of Ceylon.

For the first time in their lives they set foot on tropical soil. Leny was happy to stand upon firm ground and began to feel better immediately. Willi was enthralled by the foreign fragrances, unfamiliar people, animals, plants and huge trees. He was amazed when he saw first one and then other flying foxes; fruit eating bats the size of a small dog. During the day they hung from the branches of the trees. At night the creatures detached themselves and flew silently into the dark night. Street scenes were enchanting. Vendors offered clothes, food and gems, and women cooked meals on the side of the dirt roads on small cooking stoves. Smoke smelling of roasted meats, spices and coconut oil entered their nostrils as they walked by. It was very tempting to taste the spicy food, but they had been told not to buy any roadside prepared foods because they could contain dangerous bacteria.

Willi was full of delight over this exotic place. It seemed like a beautiful dream or a fairy tale from "1001 Nights". A taxi drove them to a hotel at Mount Lawinia. The vegetation was lush with thousands of shrubs, flowers and palm trees. Nature was free-giving and offered its fullest beauty. The palm trees lining the shores hung full of coconuts; further inland were banana and breadfruit trees, and thousands of shrubs with colorful blossoms lined the streets.

They slowly drove through streets filled with people and rickshaws and carts pulled by oxen. At the hotel Willi quenched his thirst with a cool beer and Leny enjoyed an aromatic Ceylon tea. They sat on the hotel terrace surrounded by huge planters filled with tropical flowering shrubs. The leaves rustled in the cool breeze from the ocean. At six in the evening the sun lowered itself toward the ocean's horizon, touched it briefly, and then sank into the water. For a moment the sky and ocean were of a red-orange color, then the darkness of night set in. All around they heard the songs of night insects and frogs. The passengers had to return to the ship. During the slow drive back hundreds of mosquitoes buzzed around their heads. They left Ceylon at around nine at night, at first cruising parallel along the island and then heading east toward Netherlands East Indies. Colonies of luminescent organisms lit up the shores, turning the dark water into a bright, blue-green, brilliant color. Jelly fish lit up like small ghosts in the murky water. Willi and Leny stood side by side watching with utter fascination the phenomenon in the black waters.

The first harbor they reached in Netherlands East Indies was the island of Sabang on the northern tip of Sumatra. The farmers grew rice, coconuts, pepper and rubber trees. Willi and Leny spent a day on the island, undertaking small excursions by taxi. For the first time they truly felt the humid tropical heat; sweat poured from their bodies even though they did not exert themselves. A strange smelling smoke permeated the air, and with every breath they took they inhaled the musty smell of the mangrove swamps. The coconut palm fronds rustled in the light breeze blowing from the ocean. The ship anchored in Sabang for two days, so Willi and Leny had ample time to take in the sights. Their next stop was Belawan. Again, Willi and Leny took a taxi and drove to Medan, the capital of Sumatra. The roads were excellent, they were paved, and wound along the coast, through the jungle and past native villages. They could not make up their minds what to look at first; the native houses built on stilts, the colorful birds, or the large butterflies fluttering in the tropical breeze.

Once again they boarded the ship and headed toward Singapore where they arrived in the afternoon of October 18th. The sun was shining, the ocean blue, and all around were green islands covered with coconut trees and shrubs. Singapore was surrounded by a huge fort. Vendors sold their wares, everything could be bought. The first thing Willi and Leny bought were tropical helmets as the sun shone mercilessly on their heads. The merchants were mostly Arabs, Chinese, Armenians and Malays.

They drove to the botanical garden with its tropical trees, shrubs and flowers. Lakes were covered with beautiful water lilies. Brilliant dragonflies flew silently over the water's surface, and, as if doing a dance, occasionally dipped into the water leaving tiny ripples. Shrubs with large flowers emanated a sweet smelling, intoxicating aroma. The garden was like a jungle; screeching monkeys jumped around the canopies of the trees.

Their driver was a Chinese man who spoke some English. After the botanical garden he took them to see all the attractions and interesting places. They entered a Buddhist temple. The interior smelled of incense, and when they stepped into the darkness inside they saw a huge statue of Buddha. It was almost thirty feet tall. Next to his feet were numerous under-gods. Amidst incense and sweet smelling flowers lay the sleeping Buddha. Small children and old women dressed in ragged clothes begged for money. Willi and Leny also stopped at a Chinese temple which was decorated with numerous dragons. A monotonous sounding chant reached their ears but, unfortunately, they were not allowed to enter. Then they went to a market where the stores were under an arcade. Every imaginable merchandise was offered. Sometimes the odors emanating from within Chinese food stores brought tears to their eyes and made their noses run. There were meats, dried fish, shark fins, half rotten eggs and more. The exotic market was fascinating to see, and they could have spent hours taking everything in. At six in the evening they left Singapore heading south. At three in the morning they passed the equator and were now on the southern side of the globe. The ship cruised past the Banka Strait toward Batavia.

A car drove them to a hotel. The next morning they ate breakfast and then Willi had to go to the office. Leny returned to the cozy room of their bungalow. She did not stay inside very long; she was anxious to explore the beautiful garden. She walked up to a hibiscus bush, her hands gently touching the delicate red petals. She strolled around for a while, admiring newly discovered plants and insects. Willi returned in the late afternoon. They took a nice long nap, then dressed for dinner. Finally, Leny was able to enjoy a meal without feeling sick to her stomach. The food tasted good, they ate a local dish which was very spicy hot, but the fluffy white rice, cool slices of cucumbers and fried bananas sweetened the taste. After dinner they strolled around the gardens and then sat on the front porch, enjoying the cool tropical night. Crickets sang high pitched tunes and frogs croaked from a nearby pond. Leny felt refreshed and happy, and she was delighted that she was off the ship.

BORNEO

Their journey continued on a small steam ship heading for Balikpapan on the east coast of Borneo. Balikpapan was their final destination, an oil place on the Bay with a large harbor. They debarked the ship, Willi with a hunting rifle slung over his shoulder, a box of ammunition under his arm. It was the rifle his friend Anders had asked him to bring. Willi and Anders were old friends, they had studied geology together. Two police officers immediately surrounded and escorted him to the police chief. The officer addressed Willi in Dutch with a heavy German accent. He was told that it was strictly forbidden to import weapons and ammunition into Netherlands East Indies without a permit from the Governor General.

"You are here not in Switzerland where everyone goes target practicing on Sundays," he said.

Willi knew that he could not contact his friend because he was working somewhere deep in the jungle and could not be reached for several months. The gun, a Drilling, and the ammunition were confiscated by the customs officials. Willi asked if he could apply for the import license on behalf of his friend, but it was denied.

A car picked them up at the harbor and drove them to the hotel, a simple white wooden building on stilts amidst a green lawn at the edge of the ocean. Their room was large and pleasant. They were tired and soon went to bed. The next day Leny was still feeling a bit shaky from the long voyage, but she accompanied Willi to the dining room where they ate a delicious breakfast. After Willi left for the office Leny took her writing pad and pen and went downstairs to the lobby. She looked around and saw some rattan chairs and a table by a large window and sat down. Immediately a native waiter dressed in a white uniform wearing a turban approached her quietly in his bare feet. He placed a tray with glasses and a pitcher of cool lemonade next to her. She was finally able to write a long letter to her family. She was so happy that the incredibly interesting, but very long voyage was behind them.

Balikpapan was large and spread out, the houses of the Europeans were very nice and were built on hills surrounding the area. The house that had been assigned to them was also high up on a hill. It was surrounded by large trees. For the time being they had to stay at the hotel until their house was ready. Everyone was very helpful and nice. A Swiss couple, Christian and Flori, immediately befriended them. Flori told Leny how things were done, she instructed her about daily routines and took her shopping. Anders was still somewhere deep in the jungle and was not scheduled to return until sometime around Christmas. There were about ten Swiss families in Balikpapan and the wives quickly became friends. Willi's work started at seven and he returned home at noon. They ate lunch, and then he went back to the office until 4:30. In the mornings after Willi had left for work Leny went for a walk before it turned too hot. She never went far, the heat was very intense. She mostly strolled over the beautiful lawn of the hotel and club and walked down to the beach. The vastness of the area surprised them, especially in comparison to Switzerland and Holland. Along the shore were all the factories. Right behind the homes was the immense jungle. There were a total of about three hundred European employees and about a thousand military personnel. The homes were quite a distance from the office and a bus picked up the employees to take them to and from work.

Willi and Leny's new home was surrounded by trees, shrubs and flowers. It was still being painted and some minor repair work had to be done. The ceilings were very high, the rooms airy. The floors were made of terrazzo, which were cool and easy to clean. The main house was connected to a back house with the kitchen, bathroom, pantry and the rooms of the servants. All the houses were built about three feet off the ground on stilts and a set of stairs led up to a small porch.

Christian and Flori helped interview servants. After talking with several they decided on a married couple. The wife was the cook, "kokki", who cooked the meals and took care of Leny's clothes and laundry. The husband, "djongos", served the meals, cleaned the house and took care of Willi's laundry. He also did some of the yard work. Their house was now ready, their trunks were brought over, they had bought all the necessary furniture, and their new servants had moved into the quarters at the back of the house. Leny was thrilled to finally be able to furnish and decorate their first new house together.

Willie

The following Sunday Willi took his writing pad and pen and went into the back yard after they had finished eating their dinner. It was around one o'clock.

They had a table and chairs under the large tree. He did not get very far with his letter. The air turned still, the heat became intense. He began to sweat and the paper stuck to his hands, so he went inside and joined Leny for a nap. They soon learned why everyone rested after lunch. Later in the afternoon, after a nice long rest, they took a bath. The bathroom was huge and in the middle stood a large cement container filled with water. It was scooped out with a small bucket and poured over the body. Their drinking water was quite clean, but for safety reasons it was boiled and filled into bottles which were kept in an ice box. Twice a week a truck delivered a large chunk of ice which was placed in the bottom of the box. At six at night it turned dark and immediately thousands of mosquitoes buzzed around their heads.

The early days in Balikpapan were fascinating. In Willi's office there were Dutch employees as well as Indo-Dutch, people of Dutch and Indonesian origin. The Indo-Dutch lived like the Dutch, but their skin complexion was darker than that of the Europeans and they had dark eyes and dark hair. Politically and culturally they sided with the Dutch, but the Dutch still rejected them and considered it to be of bad taste to socialize with them.

Soon after they arrived Willi was already reprimanded. He had an Indo-Dutch assistant, Silatus, who often gave him good advice on how to associate with the native population. The two got along great and one day Silatus invited them to his home. They had an interesting evening together. Silatus and his wife, both well educated people, recounted many stories and Willi and Leny listened to them intently. Before they left they reciprocated by inviting their new-found friends to their home a few days later. Early the next morning the director's errand boy came to Willi's office and informed him that the director wished to see him immediately.

When Willi entered the office the director looked at him, and said in a dry voice, "Who did you visit last night?"

Willi, of course, responded, "My assistant."

"Well," the director said, "we Europeans do not visit these apes, I demand that you not make such a faux-pas again."

Willi ignored the order and a long-time friendship developed with his assistant Silatus.

The Indonesian population was very diverse. On the coast lived mostly the Malays, also called Bandjarese. They were strict Moslems and wore the black fez. Many had on the white cap of the Hadji, the Mecca pilgrims. Willi's draftsman, Halani, also wore the head cover of the Hadji, and Willi asked him when he had been to Mecca.

He answered, "I do not remember, at that time I was still in my mother's stomach when she took part in a pilgrimage to Mecca."

Halani had two wives, and frequently he complained that it was difficult to live according to the rules of the Koran which required that each wife be granted the same amount of love.

"This is so hard, I cannot stand it any longer," he often lamented to Willi.

Some of the personnel were Javanese. Officially they too were Moslems, but they still lived according to the Hindu-Javanese culture and traditions. During days of celebrations they wore the Javanese headdress and the kris, the Javanese dagger. They were polite and friendly, but it was difficult to penetrate their world.

Their two servants were also from Java. Some of the new customs made Willi and Leny feel uncomfortable. If one of the servants wanted to talk with them they approached on their knees, bowed, assured that they were telling the truth, and then stated their concern or request. Every morning at exactly six the bedroom door opened, the "djongos" entered silently, bowed, and brought a tray with two cups of freshly brewed coffee.

Willi and Leny had a good relationship with the natives who were extremely polite, conscientious, and truly concerned for their welfare. Thefts were rare even though they had access to the entire household. Every week Leny went to the store, picked out and ordered the groceries which were then delivered later to the house. Coffee and sugar were very reasonable. When the merchandise arrived she gave each of the servants a portion for their own use. They cooked their own food which consisted of rice, meat, fish, eggs and vegetables. They did not touch the European food, it tasted too bland. They consumed no alcohol, but quenched their thirst with coffee and tea. Every Sunday the "kokki" prepared the traditional rice table. The meal began with chicken broth, then they had rice with chicken cooked in a yellow sauce, fermented duck eggs, shrimp, meat on skewers called "satay", fried bananas, "krupuk", a thin wafer made of shrimp meal, a thick spicy sauce made of crushed peanuts, grated coconut, and many different vegetables. There were various hot sauces which were poured over the food. When the "kokki" went to the market to purchase all the ingredients she usually needed no more than a guilder. Eggs cost just a few cents as did a chicken or a bag of rice.

In November Leny was four months pregnant and she had to see the company doctor who confirmed her pregnancy. He told her that she was in great shape. As they were living in the hot and humid tropics it was required that she see the doctor once a week. They were getting the nursery ready and she had already bought some furniture. She was feeling great and looked forward to having her baby.

When someone moved into a house a celebration was held by the natives called a "slamatan", to wish the new owners of the house good fortune and to keep bad spirits away. The master of the house treated the families and friends of the servants with a meal. On the chosen day two cooks began preparing the food early in the morning. They cooked all day long. At around 8:30 that night the guests arrived silently and sat in a circle on the floor around a priest. Most of the guests were other servants of the neighborhood. Willi also sat on the floor between his and the neighbors' "djongos." The priest then informed the guests that they had gathered to wish the "tuan," the master of the house, and the "njonja", the lady of the house, good luck in their new home. Willi thanked the guests for coming and for their wishes. He then invited them to begin with the meal. Each received a portion wrapped in a banana leaf. They only ate a small amount and took the rest home to their wives and children. These celebrations were attended only by the men, according to Moslem traditions and the "adat", the law. The priest then stood up, bid farewell to all present, and the guests departed. They left as silently as they had arrived. Only the hush of their bare feet on the stone floors could be heard. Moslems did not consume alcohol, the people were always predictable. Even at large celebrations they remained calm and dignified.

Their house was now fully furnished to Leny's satisfaction. On the porch were four easy chairs made of Rattan, a round table and a tea table. In the late afternoon, when Willi returned home from work, the "djongos" carried the furniture outside under the trees where they took their afternoon tea in the shade of the large "waringin," a ficus tree. The branches spread out over them and the canopy was like a gigantic umbrella. The natives considered the trees to be sacred. Ficus trees were abundant throughout the entire archipelago and there were more than eighty different species.

The porch led into the dining room. In it stood a large, expandable dining table, six chairs, two china cabinets, a serving table and two small round tables. The bedroom had a large bed with a mosquito net, a "klambu", a large dresser and an armoire. In one of the stores they had seen an old, hand-carved camphor chest from Formosa standing in a corner. The art work was beautiful, the entire chest was covered with carvings of trees, animals and people. It was an exquisite piece so they bought it. Leny used it to store some of her linens. The back house, which was behind the main house, had the kitchen, bathroom, pantry and the rooms of the servants. The hill on which it stood was called Klandasan and it overlooked the Bay of Balikpapan and the Strait of Macassar which connects the Java Sea and the South China sea.

During the day when the sun stood straight above, the heat was so intense that the ground remained warm until midnight. As they were so close to the ocean there was always a nice breeze which brought some relief from the intense heat. Every day during the late afternoon Willi and Leny strolled around the yard, admiring the yellow acacias in bloom, and shrubs with violet flowers. Butterflies floated through the air and red dragonflies danced in the warm breeze. Willi was fascinated with the beetles, crickets and other insects. At night geckoes called "tjikdjak", came out, scurried along the walls and ceilings of the house, catching insects that somehow had found their way inside. These house lizards were about six inches long and Willi and Leny soon became accustomed to them, especially as they were very beneficial to have around the house.

The "kokki" was happy that the young couple liked the local food she prepared, so she made another dish called "nasi goreng", fried rice, and with it she prepared chicken "satay". When she went to the market she bought the chickens alive and the animals were butchered in the back yard prior to cooking. The animal's throat was slit and then it was thrown on the ground where it fluttered around until it died. It was difficult for Willi to see this, to him it was animal cruelty, but the belief of the natives had to be respected. They told him that it had to be done that way so the animal's soul could escape. If the head were cut off the soul was then trapped inside the body and she refused to cook the animal. Often she also brought home a duck and the left-over meat was given to the servants. Occasionally, Willi and Leny ate pork, but when the meat was offered, the "kokki" declined politely, telling Leny that Malays did not eat pork.

On Sunday afternoons their friends always stopped by. They sat under the trees enjoying tea and cookies or cake which Leny had baked. Two of Leny's friends were also pregnant, so the women had a lot to talk about. The men's conversation was generally about their homeland far away and the terrible war that was brewing in Europe. They were concerned about what was happening there and hoped that their loved ones were safe.

Willi was conducting research on foraminifers (single-celled sea animals. They form deposits on the ocean floor and are the main component of chalk and many deep sea oozes). This was his specialty and he had done his

Leny

paleontology thesis on foraminifers. His office building stood amidst oil tanks and refinery factories. The oil was pumped into huge tankers which transported it to Europe. He also began to study the flora and fauna of their new tropical home. He had already found some wild orchids which he hung on the lower branches of the trees in their yard. The plants had buds and every day he checked to see if the flowers had opened. There were also several amaryllis plants blooming in the yard. The large white flowers with fine pink lines resembled bells. There were about six to eight stalks at each plant and every stalk had about five of the delicate blossoms. He was so amazed, plants that were carefully grown and cultivated in green houses in Europe grew wild where they now lived. He had also discovered an insect-eating plant, the so-called pitcher plant. It had pitchers at the end of long stalks which were filled with water. Insects were attracted to the pitchers, fell in and drowned. The bodies decomposed and the plant cells then absorbed the nutrients. Willi sketched the fascinating plant in his diary.

Toward the middle of November dark clouds began forming in the sky which was then followed by heavy downpours. After the rains the air felt a bit cooler, but it was still very steamy. Leny was busy with decorating the house. She was sewing new curtains and had already finished two rooms. She used the sewing machine of one of her friends, but planned on buying her own, so she could sew for herself and the baby. The temperature was getting hotter and hotter and the high humidity made both of them perspire profusely. Everyone else did too. Each morning Leny went to the store, the "toko". She ordered or picked out the items she needed which were then later delivered to the house. Sometimes she and Flori or another friend went to the nearby town, the "campong", where there were numerous stores run by Chinese, Japanese and Malays. All the transactions took place on the street and there was a constant hustle and bustle. The streets were unpaved, dust swirled around after every step and clung to clothes and shoes. After it rained, puddles formed everywhere, and their shoes were covered with mud when they arrived home again. Chickens and dogs roamed the streets and naked little children played games. Sometimes they followed the women offering to carry their bags, but the ladies only had their hand bags with them. Everything they bought was later delivered to the house. The store owners wrote all the ordered items down and at the end of the month a bill was sent.

Their social life was very active. Most functions were held at the nearby club, the Soos. There was also a swimming pool and tennis courts. They went to see films, went dancing, or partook of some other function. Something went on at the club every evening. There were also many formal balls where they danced to a live band. Willi was not much of a dancer, he preferred to sit and talk with friends. The men wore their white smoking suits, the ladies were dressed in their ball gowns. Waiters in white uniforms brought cool drinks and young boys stood near each table making sure that not a single fly landed on the white table cloths. Leny had to have more formal dresses made so she hired a local seamstress who was making a new gown for the new year's eve ball. She had found beautiful silk fabric in a small store in the village.

The Malays celebrated their new year on November 24th. The "kokki" baked a cake for the afternoon tea and surprised Willi and Leny with a delicious local dinner. She introduced them to yet another, never before tasted dish. The servants were very proud that their "tuan" and "njonja" had again enjoyed the meal so much. As always, the "djongos" waited on them, placing a small amount of each dish on their plates. While they ate he stood quietly behind them, waiting to see if they needed anything. When they were done eating he removed the plates. After every sip of water he refilled the glasses. Leny gave them the following day off and the two returned promptly at four in the afternoon to make the tea. When Leny told them that they were not going to be home for dinner they were overjoyed because they were able to celebrate with family and friends. Willi and Leny had made arrangements with two other couples to have dinner at a Chinese restaurant in the nearby village.

As the six enjoyed the meal, Willi said, "Here we are, six Swiss eating Chinese food in a Malay village in Borneo."

The weather was still very humid and hot and every afternoon thunderstorms rolled in and brought heavy downpours. The more rain they had the more there seemed to be insects in their house. The worst were the ants. If there was even the tiniest trace of food on a handkerchief and Willi placed it back in his pants, the next morning the entire pocket was eaten away, including the pants material. There were also cockroaches, lots of them and big ones which came in through the open windows. They were about two inches long and scurried along the walls. As soon as darkness set in the geckos came out and began their evening meal of roaches. Sometimes Willi tried to chase a roach, but it dashed behind some furniture.

"They were living at the edge of the jungle so they might as well get used to sharing their home with critters," Willi thought to himself. The hot-humid climate had many creatures, but so far they had not seen any snakes or other poisonous animals.

Hans Anders was still working in the jungle. The company plane was scheduled to pick him up on Christmas eve and he was going to spend the holidays with Willi and Leny. They were excited that it would soon be Christmas, yet trees, shrubs and flowers were in bloom. The acacias next to the house were full of yellow blossoms and butterflies took turns drinking the nectar. The lemon tree in the yard had white blossoms and ripe fruit at the same time. Every afternoon it rained and the heat and humidity turned the place into a steaming hot house. Every week Leny and the "kokki" carried all the bed linens, clothes, shoes and other items into the garden in the morning to be aired and dried in the sun. This somewhat prevented everything from getting mildew and rotting from the ever present high humidity. There were, of course, no air conditioners in the 1930's.

Their first Christmas in the tropics was a strange atmosphere for the two who had spent their entire lives in Switzerland in cold winters. Leny did not like the artificial Christmas trees being sold at the stores. They were imported from Japan and were made of green tinted straw. Instead, she went into the garden, the "djongos" following carrying a large basket, and collected as many flowers, twigs and fern fronds she could find, and then she decorated their living room with the fresh cut greenery. When Willi came home in the afternoon he surprised her with a beautiful blooming orchid plant which they placed on the dining room buffet. In the evening friends came by. They reminisced about Christmas at home, of cool snow flakes floating from the dark sky, of making snow men and having snow ball fights. Red, drippy noses and frozen ears were remembered. They talked about coming in from the cold into cozy, warm living rooms which smelled of freshly baked Christmas cookies, wax candles and pine needles. Here they were, in shorts and shirts, sweating and quenching their thirst with cold lemonade. They celebrated until late at night, enjoying many stories of Christmases past. Anders could not make it in time for Christmas. The plane had mechanical problems, so he arrived a day later. He brought a skin of a giant python which was about eight feet long. He also brought a hand-carved Dayak mask, a rarity, as these masks could only be found in the deep interior of Borneo's' jungle. Leny and Willi had many delicacies for him, they knew that spending months deep inside the jungle was difficult, food was sparse and mostly consisted of the same thing. While he stayed with them he had a soft, comfortable bed, a nice change for him who had spent the last several months sleeping on cots. In the evening he told them of his many adventures in the jungle. The next day they had a party and had a great time. Their friendships were deepening. Another family was scheduled to arrive soon, the Denners, whom Leny and Willi had already met when they lived in Holland.

One Sunday morning the Swiss men all went target practicing. They were able to arrange to use the guns and ammunition of the Dutch military. The men gathered in a clearing in the jungle, the hot tropical sun shining relentlessly down on their heads. Thousands of insects buzzed around them. Target practice was an old tradition in Switzerland and the men decided that they would practice every possible chance they had.

Willi and Leny celebrated their first wedding anniversary on January 21st, 1939. The "kokki" prepared a delicious dinner and for dessert Leny had baked a cake. She had decorated the dining table with small glass bowls into which she placed short candles. The bowls were filled with ice water so the candles would not melt. All around the bowls she placed flowers and leaves. After dinner they went on their daily, thirty minute walk, enjoying the cool evening air. Before turning in for the night they read the newspaper which had just arrived from Switzerland. It was two months old. The news from Europe was not good. The two talked for a while, each trying to reassure the other that there would not be a war, but deep in their hearts they knew that something bad was going to occur. They decided not to have negative thoughts, to believe in the good of humankind and that there would not be a war. Every Sunday Willi wrote a letter to his parents. He inquired about the situation and asked them to write to him what was actually going on. He wrote his parents that he felt very ashamed in front of the Malays who were listening when he and his colleagues discussed the situation developing in Europe. Here they would not hurt each other's hair, and in Europe, from where the so-called "civilized" people came, there was chaos and corruption. They were living in a world of peace, which was immediately felt when one arrived from Europe.

Leny had an easy pregnancy. By mid-February she had put on some weight, but still did not show very much. Every evening she and Willi went for a long walk. Everything was ready for the baby. Her friends advised that she hire an amah, but Leny decided that she wanted to take care of the baby herself.

Willi sent a photo of himself and his workers to his parents. Silatus was on the picture, sitting next to Willi. Twelve of his employees washed the material that came from the oil wells and prepared the foraminifers. Three of the workers were from Menado in North Celebes, one was from Sumatra, others came from Java. Also in the picture was Abdul Menar who was from Sumatra, and Sulandi. Will had an excellent team of workers and his men were very proud to have their picture taken with the white "tuan". Now his mother could see that his workers were not "wild men from Borneo", as she had asked in one of her letters.

They did not think that it was possible, but the weather turned even hotter. The moment Willi came home from work he went to the bedroom, took off his clothes, threw them on the floor and headed for the bathroom to take a cool shower. When he returned, the "djongos" had removed the dirty clothes to be washed and on the chair were a clean shirt, shorts and underwear.

On April 5th at 10:30 in the morning their daughter, Agnes Helene, was born. After making sure that both mother and baby were well Willi went to the office to tell all his friends the good news. He handed everyone a cigar. A few hours later the announcement appeared in the local newspaper. Everyone sent Leny flowers and best wishes. The first five days following the delivery only Willi was allowed to visit. The hospital was just a few minutes from their house. He spent every free moment with Leny and admired his little daughter. Ten days later mother and baby were allowed to go home. The flowers had already been brought over. The baby's room had been cleaned again by the "kokki", and Flori stopped by to make the final inspection and to make some last minute changes. Everything had to be perfect. The car was waiting outside and after one more glance around the house to make sure that everything was just perfect, Willi strode toward the car, his heart filled with joy and anticipation to have Leny home with their new baby, Agnes.

Willi's workers in Balikpapan1939. Willi seated second from left

JOURNEY INTO BORNEO'S INTERIOR

A week later, during the evening hours, Willi left on a journey to the oil fields near the lower Mahakam River to inspect the site. He climbed aboard a small boat waiting for him at the harbor. His native guide greeted him friendly and after Willi sat down, the boat began to move. The sun had just set and the ocean was calm. The small boat's ripples on the smooth surface glowed with the green luminescent bacteria seen often in tropical waters which had already fascinated him when they left Ceylon. The rising moon cast a silvery glow on the water's surface. The air was pleasantly cool. In the far distance lightning flickered on and off behind the clouds. The guide had taken the boat out on the ocean beyond the many coral reefs. On the distant shores the coconut palms lining the beaches cast their shadows against the dark sky. Occasionally, a red light lit up from one of the native huts. After they had traveled for several hours the boat turned into one of the mouths of the great jungle river. The delta of the Mahakam was very wide. Mangrove swamp forests lined the shores. They had been moving upstream for about three hours when Willi saw dim lights in the distance. As they came closer ghostlike outlines of factories, oil wells and oil tanks became visible. Day and night oil was being pumped from the earth into the pipelines which transported it to the refineries. They arrived around five in the early morning after having traveled for eleven hours. It was still dark since they were about one degree south of the equator, where the sun rises at six in the morning and sets at six at night.

At the harbor a driver handed Willi a note containing his lodging information. Willi had not slept all night long; the voyage through the still tropical night with a full moon and the green luminescence had so fascinated

28

him that he wanted to take it all in. Breakfast was waiting, and after eating a hearty meal he went on his tour. It was hot and humid and thousands of insects buzzed around him. The oil fields were generally free of malaria as the health department tried to control any breeding areas. Not a single item that could have contained some water lay around, not even a coconut shell. Petroleum was poured into the puddles to kill the larvae. Willi toured the area and enjoyed seeing some of his friends he had not seen in a while. These men spent most of their time working in the oil fields deep in the jungle and were often away from their wives and children for weeks. In the evening a light breeze came up and at six o'clock it suddenly turned dark. The chirping of thousands of crickets and other insects sounded from the surrounding jungle. Fireflies flew gleaming on and off in the dark night and congregated in a large tree. Suddenly, the flickering became synchronized. Willi looked up at the tree in amazement; it resembled a huge Christmas tree with thousands of little lights turning on and off in unison. What a strange appearance in the middle of the jungle. He thought to himself that it could be viewed as something mechanical, or, as the natives did, something ghost-like. He asked one of the men what they were called and was told that they were "api-api", fire. The songs of the frogs joined the concert of other nocturnal creatures. Occasionally, a snake slithered by and was barely visible on the gray asphalt in the dark. At the guest house, a primitive wooden hut on stilts, Willi had the choice of Dutch or native food. As always he opted for the latter, it was very spicy hot, but tasty and almost fat free. He did not like eating fatty food, it bothered his stomach. He sat in the lounge with his friends for a while, enjoying a cool beer. But he was very tired from being up all night and all day long, so he went to his room. He crawled under the mosquito net which hung around the cot and all night long the constant buzzing of thousands of insects sounded in the night. The tropical lullaby quickly made him sleepy. He glanced out of the window before drifting off to sleep and saw clouds appearing on the dark horizon, reflecting the red lights of the gas flares. He turned over and fell asleep. In the morning he awoke feeling rested and refreshed. He ate a good breakfast and enjoyed the luscious tropical fruit, especially the papayas. The roads between the refineries were paved and one could easily travel by jeep from one area to another. Alongside the roads stood the towers of the oil wells among the tall jungle trees. The pumps moved slowly up and down. A wild pig napped in a puddle, neither the car nor the oil wells seemed to disturb it. Later Willi traveled by boat to another oil field across the river; the great jungle rivers had no bridges. Near the delta the river flowed into many side arms where they encountered several native people. Often they were a man, woman and child on their long, wooden boat, a meal simmering on a coal fire as the boat slowly drifted down-river. The water of the river was of a brown color and the natives used it for drinking, bathing and washing. It was also used as a toilet. Willi observed a man relieving himself in the water and just down-stream a woman was washing herself and brushing her teeth. She rinsed and gargled her mouth abundantly with the brown river water.

At nine in the evening he started on his journey back. The small motor boat was waiting and soon they went down-river toward the delta. Stars twinkled above, some cumulus clouds hung over the horizon from which occasionally lightning rays lit up the heavens. The river was as smooth as a mirror. In the rays of the boat's lights the slanted eyes of the crocodiles lit up shining green in the pitch dark night. The reptiles lay motionless in the water waiting for prey. It splashed momentarily when a crocodile caught a fish and then it was still again. Willi glanced at the stars and saw the Southern Cross shining brightly in the southern heavens. The trip in the night on the jungle river was like a trip through a fairy land; millions of twinkling stars, a bright moon, while an eerie looking blue fog hung over the warm swampy forests, the songs of the jungle creatures sounding in the distance. They passed many native houseboats, the red embers of the cooking fires shining in the dark night. Around midnight the air turned cool and Willi dozed off. Suddenly, he was awakened by a jolt, the boat rocked back and forth, froth splattered on him and it started to rain. They had left the still waters of the river's delta and were once again on the ocean. The surf toyed with the small boat. After again traveling for about eleven hours they arrived in Balikpapan. Willi was not sea sick, but for some time felt as if he were still on the rocking boat. He was happy to be back with his wife and child. Breakfast was waiting for him and after showering and a change of clothes, he went to work.

SETTING UP HOUSE AT THE EDGE OF THE JUNGLE

The young couple settled into a routine. Leny took care of the baby and Willi went to work. Every week they anxiously awaited mail from home. Finally, the end of May, a letter arrived, it had taken a month to get there. Another Swiss couple arrived, Jakob and Emmi and their two children. The two couples immediately hit it off. Jakob was several years older than Willi, he was a topographer and had been working for the company for some years already. On June 3rd Willi turned twenty-eight and they enjoyed a delicious dinner the "kokki" had prepared. Afterward they strolled down to the club to see a film and join their other friends. Then they danced until the early morning hours. Before going home, Willi and Leny walked over the green lawn down to the beach. It was a beautiful tropical night, the tall palms rustled in the wind and the moon glowed silvery on the calm ocean. They stood for a long while, taking in the peaceful warm tropical night. When they arrived home, the "kokki", as always, was sleeping in front of the baby's bedroom door, two cats curled up next to her.

A couple of weeks later Willi, Jakob, Christian and Flori left early in the morning to go to the beach. Emmi and Leny stayed at home; Emmi was pregnant and Leny was still nursing the baby, she did not want to walk so far in the hot humid weather. The drive took more than an hour on a narrow dirt road. The shore was lined with large, beautiful palm trees. Among the trees were the dwellings on stilts of the natives. On the beach they found coral pieces, large shells and beautifully decorated colored snails which had washed ashore during high tide. They saw mud skippers and Willi watched in fascination as the fish with huge bulging eyes climbed up tree trunks and

31

branches of the Mangroves. A large dead shark had washed ashore and they were able to observe the predator from up close. The five strolled along the pristine beach, picking up shells and pretty pieces of coral when suddenly without any warning, the sky opened up, and rain poured down on them. In a few minutes they were drenched. They had brought some umbrellas, but they were useless. They were the cheap, Chinese umbrellas made of paper which were mostly used as parasols. The sky turned black and it looked as if the rain would last for some time, so they returned to the pick up truck and headed home where they changed into dry clothes, and an hour later they all met at Willi and Leny's house to enjoy a cup of hot tea and have a piece of cake Leny had baked.

Anders was back somewhere in the jungle doing his research work. Flori and Christian were getting ready to go on their vacation to Java and to Bali. Flori was going to stay in the mountains for two months. She needed a climate change because the hot, humid weather was causing her many medical problems. She was a tall, thin woman in her early thirties. She was a handsome woman, with large dark brown eyes, a straight nose and dark blond hair she wore cut short with bangs covering her forehead. She wanted so much to have a child, but kept having miscarriages. Christian was a big, heavy man with thinning light brown hair and big blue eyes. He was born in 1902, in north-east Switzerland. First he studied engineering and after getting his degree, decided to also study geology. He obtained his doctorate degree in Berlin in 1929. He then began to work for the oil company and after spending several months in The Hague, traveled to Java. He did research in West Java and later worked in Tjepu in mid-Java. He returned to Switzerland in 1935, and married Flori. He had met her before during his student years. They first lived in New Guinea and then were sent to Balikpapan in early 1938. Willi and Leny saw their friends almost every day and often Willi felt sorry for his heavy-set friend. He perspired so much that sweat always poured down his face. He was rarely seen without a large white towel draped around his neck which he periodically took down, wrung out, and then placed around his neck again. He was a gentle man who had a kind word for all. He always told jokes and funny stories. He also was a highly intelligent man.

The end of July Jakob and Emmi had a baby boy, their third child. A few days later, on August 1st, was the Swiss national holiday. All the Swiss gathered at Flori and Christian's house. They decorated the yard with Swiss flags and lanterns which were hung from tree branches and around the house. Everyone brought food. There were cakes and pies, sandwiches, salads and more. The party lasted until the early morning hours.

Around the middle of August Anders returned from the jungle. He brought with him some films he had taken deep in the interior of Borneo. Everyone was impressed, he had filmed rare animals and beautiful unusual looking plants. Willi and Hans were co-authoring a report, Anders on geology and Willi on paleontology. Finally, Anders had his gun and ammunition which Willi had brought from Switzerland almost a year earlier.

On the radio they heard that Switzerland had mobilized its armed forces. 'So', Willi thought,

'the Germans did not stop until the crisis began again. Lets hope that the German megalomania, and with it the entire regime, will soon fall.'

Leny was also concerned when she heard on the radio about the mobilization.

'Oh, this terrible scoundrel, what he has done. What will the future bring?' she thought. The German tyrant had actually started a war and its results could not be determined as of yet. They were being kept abreast about everything that was going on by both the radio and their local paper. Several German and Italian ships were in the harbor waiting for instructions. Also, everyone had to try on gas masks for safety measures. A few days earlier a German geologist and his wife arrived. They stopped by for a visit and both were extremely worried about their families. They feared the worst for Germany. Willi and Leny felt sorry for them; a German in a foreign country was in a precarious situation. The terrible war compromised all German citizens, whether justified or not.

Weeks went by, but no mail came. When they had first arrived in Balikpapan they had a letter from home every week. Willi and Leny wrote home regularly. They were very concerned and did not know how their families were doing. Both Willi and Leny were convinced that Germany would lose the war, the question was only, how long would it take. Every chance they had they went to their friend's house to listen to the news on the radio. Willi and Leny decided to buy their own radio so they could stay abreast of what was happening. Once a week they heard a Swiss radio broadcast late at night. At every gathering with friends they spoke of the war and much discussion and speculation went on.

Dr. Kant, a geologist from the main office in Holland, arrived. He invited Leny and Willi to a dinner at the home of the administrator. Willi and Dr. Kant were planning a trip into the jungle to the Barito river area. They would be leaving in a few days. During that time there were no topographical maps of Borneo. The company had an airplane which took aerial photographs of the geological regions. The photo-geologists then processed the photographs into maps, which the field geologists used as references. From time to time the amphibian plane was also used for excursions into the interior of Borneo, because trips such as these on the rivers would have taken about three weeks. Walking through the jungle would have been impossible. The area of the Barito river was where Anders had been working for many months. They were going to view a deep oil well which had produced rich oil sources from Eocene layers. It was turning light when they departed, the plane was waiting for them at the Manggar air strip. They flew westward over the dense jungle toward the Meratus mountains. They had to cross the mountain range to reach the area of the Barito river which flowed into the ocean near Bandjarmasin. The small plane had been in the air for about twenty minutes when they were suddenly in thick, black clouds. The navigator assured the two passengers that they would soon be out of the clouds; the Barito region had reported good weather conditions. They had to reach an altitude of about 6,000 feet to cross the mountain range. It turned cold and suddenly the small plane was jerked back and forth in the turbulence, and they were dragged upward by the strong wind. The navigator announced that they had reached an altitude of over 13,000 feet. Then, as suddenly as they had been in the middle of the storm, as suddenly they were out of it again. The sun was shining and the storm clouds were far behind them. Below in the blue haze was the jungle somewhere over east Borneo. The plane kept an easterly course heading toward the bay. Near Tanah Grogot, a settlement near the mouth of the Pasir river, they were once again over an area they recognized. The battle with the elements had used up much fuel and the pilot recommended they return to Balikpapan and try again the next day to reach their destination.

Their feelings were mixed when they climbed into the plane again the following morning. A flight under perfect weather conditions brought them to their destination. The plane landed on the water and a jeep drove them through the jungle and savanna to the deep oil well Tandjung. A short time earlier, a huge oil reserve had been discovered at the site. This had happened somewhat by accident. The field geologists had found an anticline, a fold, and its core was either Eocene, the second epoch of the Tertiary period, or even Precambrian, the earliest era of geological time from the formation of the earth to the first forms of life. Up to that time, oil in Borneo was found in much younger layers, and Tandjung became an exciting case. When a depth of about 3,600 feet was reached, the bore tool hit volcanic rock. The question was whether this might be the rudimentary mountain chain of Tandjung and thus could possibly be a failure. No sign of oil had been found as of yet. It also has to be said that unnecessary drilling was avoided because already in those days, exploratory drilling was very expensive in the jungles of Borneo. A core was obtained from the volcanic rock and sent to Balikpapan. The chief geologist was vacationing in the mountains of Java and his representative was uncertain as to what to do. The rock was very hard and drilling moved slowly. The chief geologist was contacted and asked whether drilling should continue or be stopped. He hesitated, stating that he had to give the situation more thought, and then the answer came by itself. After only about sixty feet of volcanic rock, the drill hit an enormous oil reserve. The gas pressure was so intense that it lifted the entire structure and a huge fountain of oil gushed into the air; the Tandjung oil field had been discovered.

Finally, the middle of October mail came from home. Willi and Leny were relieved to hear that everyone was well. Leny was busy sewing new curtains for the house, the old ones were falling apart from the high humidity and heavy winds. The extreme hot weather had brought more ants and it was hard controlling the terrible pests. They were everywhere; in the mornings even the shoes were covered with the tiny insects. Willi and Leny placed shallow dishes filled with oil or water under all the legs of the furniture. Leny was also concerned about the baby crib. She heard of a case where ants had eaten away at a baby within a short period of time during the night after the baby had spit up. The legs of the crib stood in dishes filled with oil, so no ants could reach her. Of all the critters they encountered in the tropics, Leny detested and feared the ants the most.

Each day they received news at the office about the war in Europe. Their new radio had arrived and they listened to the news every chance they had. Leny had suggested to the other Swiss women that they do something for the Swiss soldiers who were so heroically defending their homeland. They decided to knit socks and other needed items to keep the men warm during the cold winter months. One morning a week the women got together and knitted the socks. The consulate then made arrangements to have the items sent to Switzerland.

Once a year the company sent all their employees to the mountains of Java to recuperate from the hot and humid climate of Borneo. Willi and Leny were making arrangements to leave the beginning of November. They had made reservations at the hotel Bergmeer which was run by an Austrian couple. It was nestled on a hillside of the volcano Lawu and was surrounded by many small rivers, brooks and waterfalls. Both Leny and Willi were full of anticipation and looked forward to escape the heat for a while. The "djongos" asked if he could go to Java to visit his family while Leny and Willi were gone; he would return a week before they came home. Around that time Leny had picked up a fungus on her foot, probably at the swimming pool, and it became infected. Wounds were hard to heal in the hot and humid climate and Willi told her that it would probably not heal until they were in the cool and dry mountain air of Java. When Leny began to pack for their upcoming trip she was disappointed and shocked when she took their warm clothes out of storage. They were full of mildew stains and were falling apart.

VACATION IN PARADISE

Finally, the day of their long awaited vacation arrived. On November 28th they flew from Borneo to Java. It was a pleasant flight, the view from the air was spectacular. What a contrast between jungle covered Borneo and the cultivated area of Java and Madura with the immense rice fields and sugar plantations. They saw a narrow strait between Madura and Java below them, and on the water were many small fishing boats with large white sails. Leny was soon air sick; it was quite an effort for her to occasionally glance out of the window to see the beautiful scenery below. A car was waiting at the airport in Surabaya and drove them to Sarangan. It took about three and a half hours to get to the hotel. The moment they stepped out of the car they inhaled the cool mountain air, enjoying its invigorating freshness. They were at the foot of the volcano Lawu, at about 4,000 feet above sea level. The hotel was built overlooking a small lake, there were several bungalows which were surrounded by tropical trees and shrubs. In the distance they could hear the splashing of a nearby waterfall. It reminded Willi and Leny a bit of Switzerland.

They slept as they had not slept in many months. Warm blankets covered them cozily, and they breathed in the cool, fresh mountain air. There were no mosquitoes buzzing around their heads. Breakfast was served on the large terrace of the main house. They were famished, the coffee, fresh rolls and fruit tasted delicious. A local "babu", a nursemaid, was hired for Agnes; she did the baby's laundry and watched her while Willi and Leny went on hikes. The woman was very trustworthy, they could leave the child with her without having to worry about her welfare. The "babu" admired the baby, stating that she was "puti betul", real white. To the natives, the lighter the color of the skin, the better. Soon after breakfast Willi and Leny set off to explore the area. There were numerous Angel Trumpet plants; Willi saw one that had more than five hundred bell-shaped blossoms. They went to the nearby waterfalls on a small path that wound through a jungle of tall Angel Trumpet bushes. Ferns were abundant everywhere, some tree ferns grew to over twenty feet tall. On the steep hillsides they saw banana and wheat fields; it was too high up for rice cultivation. The weather was delightfully cool, a nice change not to be sweating all the time, and they were delighted not to be inundated all the time with ants. They could drink the water right from the tap, just like in Switzerland, without having to worry about catching some dangerous tropical disease.

Their bungalow had a living room, two bedrooms, a bathroom, and a beautiful porch facing the lake. Leny's feet were still giving her problems. It reminded her of when she was a little girl and always had sores on her ankles and knees. She thought of her mother who used to treat the wounds with herbal medicines and she wished that her mother was there. Willi was not one to sit still and he wanted Leny to accompany him on the hikes. He rented horses from a local boy; Leny just could not walk very well on her sore and open feet. The horses were very small and docile, and climbed the hills with ease. Up and down the hills and valleys to the huge waterfalls and through beautiful forests they went. The hillsides were all cultivated. Most of the work was done by women and children. They carried such heavy loads that if often seemed to Leny as if they would collapse any moment. Men, on the contrary, seemed to work very little, or not at all.

On Sunday, they were just getting ready to leave on another hike, there was a knock on their door. There stood Dr. Kant and his wife who were spending the week-end at the hotel. After Balikpapan they were in Tjepu for several months, and they were planning on leaving for America in a few months' time. The two couples caught up on the latest news and spent a nice visit together. The Kant's were renting a house in Tjepu and invited Willi and Leny to come for a visit. It would only be a one day trip, but Leny decided to stay at the hotel while Willi visited them; she did not want to leave the baby with someone else for an entire day. The next morning a company car picked up Willi to drive him to Tjepu. Leny spent a quiet day at the hotel. While the baby was sleeping Leny was reading on the porch. After some time she heard a sound, looked over, and there was the young boy who always accompanied them on their hikes. In his hands he held an orchid plant with about ten blossoms. The flowers were beautiful, the center was purple, the outer edges of the petals were of a light yellow color. He handed her the plant with a big smile on his face. Leny thanked him and told him to wait a moment. She took some money out of her purse and gave it to him. She knew that the mountain people were very poor and that his family could probably buy enough food to last them for some time. He was such a pleasant young boy, always tagging along, pointing out anything of interest. Leny admired the beautiful flowers and wished that her family could see them. If only she could give them to her mother; how beautiful they would look in the comfortable living room. She was thinking of her loved ones at home, and for a while she was lost in thought, wondering how they were doing in war-torn Europe. Willi returned just in time to have dinner. Before retiring for the night, they went on a long stroll, admiring the area. There was a full moon, its light illuminated the abundance of roses, lilies and other tropical flowers in the lush gardens around the lake. Leny was able to walk much better, her feet were almost completely healed. A few days later Willi left on a two-day hike to the top of the volcano Lawu. The peak was covered in fog, and as Leny glanced up to the peak she hoped that it would clear so that he could enjoy the view from atop. Leny had caught a bad cold a few days earlier, she was quite sick with a fever and sore throat. She worried that the baby would catch it so the wife of the owner of the hotel took care of Agnes for a couple of days. Poor Leny lay in bed, it was hard for her being sick and not having proper care. It made her realize how alone they actually were in such a foreign land. She though of her mother again, who had always been there for them when she or her siblings were sick; she missed her mother a lot. In a few days she was over the cold and felt much better. Agnes was doing well; her cheeks turned rosy from the fresh, clean mountain air.

Willi had enjoyed his trip to the top of the Lawu and returned excited about all the new things he had seen. It was the middle of December 1939, and Willi wrote his parents a letter while they were sitting on the porch, enjoying the brisk, cool evening air. In Switzerland Willi had been an avid mountain climber, he had scaled some of the high peaks of the Alps in search of interesting rocks and crystals. (His letter arrived in Switzerland on June 2nd, 1940). The excursion to the top of the volcano Lawu was quite a different experience than mountain climbing was in Switzerland. Here all the supplies, including the food, were carried by coolies. For steeper areas small horses were used, and a trip to a mountain top was more like a nice walk. The Lawu was an inactive volcano. There was a gorge where hot steam and sulfur were ejected with an incredible force. In some areas the ground was so hot that they could not stand there. The noise of the steam eruptions was so loud that they could not even hear their own voices. Everything smelled of sulfur. On the top of the Lawu there were numerous Hindu temple ruins; even in those days the volcanoes were still considered to be holy mountains. Their Javanese guides saw spirits everywhere, and many areas could not be walked on so not to disturb the spirits of the gods. It was always best to respect the beliefs of the local people, and Willi heeded their warnings. They saw shrines where the people made offerings to their gods and brought bananas, coconuts, rice, and even the head of a young stag was among these items. They spent the night in a hut. The following morning they made their descent on foot back to Sarangan. Trees hung full of orchid plants and the humid ground was covered with lush ferns. The view from atop the Lawu was incredibly beautiful. Willi had enjoyed the trip and the mountain sun had turned his skin into a dark tan.

According to the calendar it should have been Christmas soon, but nothing reminded them of that in Java. Everything was green, flowers in the garden were in bloom, and every day fresh roses decorated their living room table. They could swim in the small lake by the hotel, and it reminded them of a nice summer day in Switzerland. Their vacation was coming to an end and on the 20th they had to return to Balikpapan.

Lawu mountain guides with horses, Java 1939

40

UNIQUE DISCOVERIES

After their vacation in the mountains they spent a few days in Surabaya where Willi attended several meetings. The city was hot, they could not sleep at night and longed to be back in the cool mountains. A few days later they left Surabaya, below them Java slowly disappeared from view. The plane flew over the island Madura with its rice fields, palm trees, villages and rivers, which from the air appeared like a colorful woven rug. On the northern horizon was the Java Sea. Just a short while later the small plane was over the ocean with its dark blue water. They flew into storm clouds and the plane began to rock, but fortunately, the turbulence did not last very long. They refueled in Bandjarmasin, then crossed the Barito river area, the mountains and the immense jungles and swamps, heading toward Balikpapan. Friends picked them up at the airport and drove them home. The "kokki" and "djongos" were overjoyed to see their little "noni" and Willi and Leny were glad to be back in their own home again. Christian told them that films could no longer be sent to Europe because of the danger of espionage, and an export prohibition had gone into effect while they were gone. Willi hoped that the two films he had sent just before leaving for Java had made it home in time and had not been confiscated.

They spent a quiet Christmas at home. The temperature was hot and humid, but they had become accustomed to it. Leny again decorated their home with fresh flowers and plants. She even baked some cookies. New Year's eve was spent at the club where more than five hundred people had gathered. At midnight the sirens of all the ships in the harbor went off. Everyone had a glass of champagne to toast in 1940. What would the new year bring for Europe, they often thought, and had a difficult time trying to imagine how things were on the other side of the Indian Ocean. Here they were living in a country of peace and in a land of plenty. Importing groceries from Europe had become more difficult, so they simply adjusted to using goods imported from Australia and America. Lamb, veal, pork and rabbit were now available at very reasonable prices, imported from Australia. Rice, sugar and vegetables were plentiful, as this was grown locally. They did not need any heating oil and gasoline "they made themselves."

On January 2nd they were informed that they would be spending two more years in Balikpapan, and then return to Switzerland for an extended vacation the end of 1942.

Willi was very busy. During that time, Balikpapan was one of the few places where full-time work was still being done. His staff had increased to fourteen native workers, four European assistants, and two young geologists who were being trained by him. One was from Holland, the other from America. The company had requested that every geologist be trained by him on paleontology before being sent into the field. Also, as a result of Dr. Kant's visit, who was sent to observe the work being done in Balikpapan, Willi received a pay raise. Kant had written an extensive report to the main office in which he commended Willi's achievements and hard work.

The days and weeks went by. The Swiss men still went target practicing in the clearing of the nearby jungle whenever they had an opportunity. Around the middle of February, on a hot Sunday afternoon, they had a competition between company employees and the Dutch military. The group, which consisted of mostly Swiss men won, and the Dutch military officer commented at the end that the competition had actually been between the Swiss and Dutch. The next day there was a short article in the paper, and the writer recommended that everyone watch these competitions because "direct descendants of William Tell always hit the bull's eye".

By the end of March 1940, it had been five weeks since a letter had arrived from home. Faithfully, though, they wrote home each week. They began to number the letters because it was apparent that some were getting lost. Each day Leny anxiously awaited the mailman, but he rarely brought her a letter from home. Agnes had her first birthday and they had a small party. Anders was still in the jungle, but he was not doing well at all. He had to be hospitalized in Amuntai because he had another bad case of malaria, and on top of that, had also contracted dysentery. He was scheduled to go to Switzerland in about a year.

On the news they heard that the Germans had invaded Denmark and

Norway had declared war with Germany. They still all hoped that the German plague in Europe would soon come to an end. A letter finally arrived from Leny's family. Her sister, Liny, wrote about possible evacuation plans. She asked if they should send Willi's books to Bern where Tabitha lived. The books were with Willi's parents. He wrote them back that he was going to leave the decision up to his parents, but did stress the fact that it was extremely important to safeguard his books. He had received several from his grandfather that were over two hundred years old. He also had books on geology written in the nineteenth century which an old geologist he knew when he was a student had given him.

Everyone was getting more and more concerned about the situation in Europe. They formed a Swiss Association and had a fund raiser. The proceeds would then be sent to Bern. They donated money because there was not much else they could do to assist their country from where they lived. Also, they were safe, they had enough food, and life was completely normal.

Willi again went on a trip deep into the jungle and saw many new and interesting things. His friend Jakob went along, and they drifted for hours on wide jungle rivers surrounded by dense swamp forests, rarely seeing signs of humans. During high tide the river deltas flooded large areas and during low tide the roots of the trees became exposed. There were masses of crocodiles in and along the rivers. From the boat they could see many fish and crabs. The natives obtained most of their food from the rivers. At night the river banks turned into an orchestra played by thousands of insects; mosquitoes buzzed around their heads, thirsty to suck their blood. One of the most beautiful sights were the thousands of fireflies which floated through the dark night resembling threads of fire being woven in the darkness. When the moon rose and the blue haze spread over the rivers and jungle Willi felt as if they had been transported into a mysterious world. It was so full of magic that the two men did not even realize that when they spoke they whispered. The beauty of the moment entered their souls where the image remained forever in their memory.

During May it began to occasionally rain again. Everyone looked forward to the storm clouds that brought a bit of cooling off. Leny did not want to complain about the heat. She kept thinking of her family in Europe and what they had to endure. Hot weather did not warrant complaining. She longed for mail, and at times the waiting became unbearable. She worried because Switzerland was threatened by the Germans. No matter what, they continued to write home regularly.

Several of the Dutch employees had to go back to Holland as they were needed there. Willi was still very busy at work, training another assistant. They were beginning to tire of the social life and preferred to spend quiet evenings alone or with a few close friends. On May 14th, 1940, Willi sent a postcard home. It had gone through censorship. Part of the text was covered up with black ink when his family received it. He had written:

Dear parents, all of us, as I am sure you too, are suffering from the appalling actions of the Germans. (That part had been blackened out). So far, things are normal here. Do not worry about us. From now on, please only write us on postcards, without pictures. Agnes is well and happy and we are in good health. Best regards to all, Willi, Leny, Agnes.

The end of July mail was being routed to Europe via Australia and America. Agnes was growing and walking. Every day Leny took her to the swimming pool at the club. The weeks flew by; and even though no mail arrived, Willi and Leny wrote home every week. September arrived and there had not been a letter for three months. Leny was so glad to have the baby who distracted her from having frightening thoughts and worries about their families in Europe. Then something occurred that depressed the young couple. Their friends, the Schmidhof's, had received a telegram in which he was informed of his termination without a word of explanation. It was a terrible shock for all. Christian and Flori packed their belongings and moved to Java where he was going to look for work. It was hard for Willi and Leny to lose their friends during these difficult times. And then a short while later Leny had to hire a new "kokki". Suddenly the old cook had turned moody, refusing to do her work. Leny had no other choice but to let her go. It turned out that the couple was having marital problems and the "djongos" had divorced her. He begged Leny to let him stay, and, of course, neither Leny nor Willi wanted him to leave. He was very devoted and loyal. Leny found a younger woman who was an excellent cook and had a pleasant personality. She was a hard worker and kept everything spotless.

Leny made an appointment to see the doctor. She already felt that she was pregnant, but wanted to make certain. The doctor confirmed the pregnancy, the baby was due the end of January. At first, Leny hesitated to write home, but finally wrote her family the end of September to tell them the happy news. She knew that her mother would worry about her and assured her family that she would be in the best of hands.

Around the middle of October, on the spur of the moment, they decided to go to Java for a vacation. Another year had gone by and they were both ready for a change of climate. At first they had planned on waiting until after the birth of the baby, but then the doctor also felt that it would be good for Leny to spend some time in the mountains and gave her permission to travel. Their friends, the Schmidhof's, were still in Java. Several weeks after Christian received the termination notice, it was reversed. They had decided to remain in Java for a while and to return to Balikpapan the following January or February. Both were having medical problems. Also, Flori was finally pregnant, and the two were looking forward to having a baby.

They departed the end of October. This vacation they were going to Batu in central east Java. The area was surrounded by volcanoes and the climate was excellent. It was warm during the day, the nights were pleasantly cool. The air was dry and there always was a pleasant breeze. It was very dry; no rain had fallen in more than seven months.

They met several times with Christian and Flori. The two men went on long trips and hikes, while Leny and Flori enjoyed the quiet and peaceful surroundings of the hotel. The men visited the famous Borobudur temple. The natives brought offerings of flowers and incense to their gods at the temples. Willi and Christian also went to an ancient temple city on the Dieng plateau. Goats and small horses grazed among the old temple ruins, wild fuchsia and ferns grew from cracks in the walls of the old structures. Then, on November 11th, they drove from Ngawi to Trinil, the famous archaeological site of the discovery of first man, Pithecanthropus erectus Dubois, the Java Man. The moment they arrived, villagers, both children and adults, brought fossilized bones, deer antlers, antelope bones and more. What a feeling it was for Willi to hold the remains of contemporaries of primitive man. For only a few cents he bought molars and fossilized bones of stegodons and ruminants, several antlers and also numerous silex artifacts.

Leny and Flori went for walks near the hotel. The climate was good for Agnes, she was never sick, and soon had rosy cheeks from the healthy mountain air. Their vacation went by much too fast, and the middle of November they had to return to Balikpapan. When they arrived home they had a letter and a postcard. The letter had been opened by the censors. A note was attached, with instructions that it was not allowed to use thin paper, letters were not to be too long, handwriting had to be clear and legible, and only one side of a sheet of paper could be written on. A couple of weeks later another letter arrived, it had taken eleven weeks to reach them.

Christmas 1940 was already their third Christmas away from home. Willi was off for two days, but no matter what they did, it just did not seem like

Christmas. There were no church bells, and even though they had a little tree, it was not a pine tree, and the fragrance of Christmas was missing. Instead, the air smelled of humid swamps and exotic flowers. At night hundreds of mosquitoes descended on them, and ants found the tiniest openings to enter the house and eat away at clothes and books.

Their next door neighbor brought a young Gibbon ape from one of his trips to the jungle. It soon became Agnes' new playmate and came over every morning to play with her. The two romped in the grass, the Gibbon grabbed her legs, Agnes ran off, the ape in pursuit, and then the two strolled off hand in hand. Willi took out his camera to film the two tiny play mates and to show their families in Switzerland what kind of exotic pals their little granddaughter had in Borneo. Before long the owner of the Gibbon was transferred and the little primate came to live permanently in their household. Whenever it managed to get in the house it terrorized Leny. It jumped on top of the china cabinets, swung from the lamps or curtains, threw dishes from furniture, and managed to get into everything. He was, therefore, banned from the house and mostly roamed around the yard and kitchen area, trying to find something he could get into. He did manage to sneak into the house several times causing havoc, swinging from lamps and curtains, the "djongos" in hot pursuit until he was outside again.

Work kept Willi very busy. His foraminifers collection grew. He often thought of his old geology professor who would be surprised to see such an impressive collection. He also had a visitor at the lab, an American paleontologist who worked for the United States government and who lived in California. Willi enjoyed the visit and the two colleagues had many long and interesting discussions.

On January 25th, 1941, their second daughter, Ruth Elizabeth, was born. Leny awoke in the middle of the night and told Willi that she was having contractions. Willi timed the contractions and at ten minutes to four in the early morning hours he called the doctor. A car was sent to the house and a few minutes after four Leny was already in the hospital. Forty-five minutes later the baby was born. Willi took the day off. Agnes was staying with Jakob and Emmi while Leny was in the hospital. In a few hours Leny's room was filled with flowers; there were carnations, gladiolus, chrysanthemums, orchids and many cards. Every day Willi picked up Agnes at the Winter's and they visited her new baby sister. After her ten-day stay in the hospital, Leny and the baby were able to go home. A "babu" was hired to look after Agnes, who, at two years old, had to be watched constantly. Soon after the baby's birth,

46

Christian returned to Balikpapan to resume his work for the company. Flori remained in Surabaya for some time. She had to have surgery and needed the time to recuperate before returning to the hot, humid climate of Borneo. Unfortunately, she also lost the baby and they were devastated. Flori was already in her thirties; she seemed to be unable to carry a baby to term.

The end of March was approaching. It was still very hot and little rain fell. When it finally did rain, it brought some relief to humans, animals and plants alike. Willi was so busy that he seldom had time to think about the heat. The weeks and months flew by. He had been informed that another paleontologist would be arriving soon; to his delight it was Chang, the Chinese paleontologist he had befriended when they were still in The Hague. He was looking forward to seeing his old friend again.

On April 24th Willi set off for another trip into the interior of Borneo. Of great interest to him were the Dayak, the aborigines of Borneo, who used poisonous darts in their blow pipes. After traveling for some time up a jungle river he arrived near a Dayak settlement. His guide called out a greeting and soon the very shy people surrounded him. The settlement was quite large, small naked children ran around amidst pigs, chickens and dogs. Under a tree, an old Dayak sat on the ground, surrounded by his pipes. Willi approached and the old man invited him to sit down next to him. He proudly showed Willi his weapons. At one time the blow pipes were used during warfare, but in recent times were mostly used for hunting. The pipes were made of iron wood. Openings were drilled by inserting a glowing metal wire which was then sanded with a coarse leaf attached to a piece of rattan. A good blow pipe, the old man told Willi, had to be pliable so it could be used at any angle. A spear was attached to the tip. The arrows were about eight to sixteen inches long and were made of bamboo. The tips were made of metal, shark teeth, or the arrow was sharpened to a point. Behind the point was a notch allowing the arrow to break off upon entering flesh. At the end of the arrow was a piece of wood shaped like a cone with a flat base. Upon blowing into the pipe, air pressure collected in the cone. The poison of the arrow, called "upas", was derived from tree sap, mainly of the species Antiaris toxicaria. The color of the sap was light brown. The old Dayak agreed to show Willi how the poison was prepared. He placed the fresh tree sap in the sun to evaporate. He had several containers which had been in the sun for some time already. The mass was then boiled over a coal fire. The old man used bamboo containers as well as metal pans. He boiled the mass until it turned into a thick, brown paste which was placed on the arrows. Willi knew that the effect of the poison was very intense. A dog would die in less than five minutes, a deer or a wild pig in about ten minutes, and a rhinoceros in about one to two hours. Also birds were hunted with blow pipes. Willi had read in old books that a human would die with severe cramps within about ten minutes after being hit by a blow pipe arrow. The old Dayak explained that the meat of the dead animals was edible because the poison entered the blood stream and not the stomach. A hunted animal immediately had its throat artery cut to release the poisoned blood. Several spices, including "lombok", red pepper, were added to the mixture which to Willi seemed to be of no importance in the potency of the poison. The arrows were kept in elaborately decorated bamboo baskets. A gourd container hung on the basket in which the cones were stored. The old Dayak sold Willi a complete blow pipe set with container for very little money and a couple of packs of cigarettes. They talked a while longer and then Willi had to continue on his trip. The old man invited him to visit again the next time he was in the area.

The end of May the rainy season began. Willi and Jakob went pig hunting. The animals foraged in the tapioca fields next to the jungle where they caused tremendous damage and the natives were always glad when someone hunted them. One day the two left in the morning with their two native guides. They had hiked for some time when they came upon a herd of wild pigs near a small creek. Willi's first bullet brought an animal down, it was a young, about half year old pig. The animal was immediately eviscerated, tied to poles, and carried back to the car. Since the two natives who accompanied Willi and Jakob were Moslems, the honor was theirs to carry the pig. Moslems could not come in touch with such an "unclean animal", they were told. When they arrived home, they butchered the meat, divided it into portions and gave their friends some. That same evening, Willi and Leny had pork roast for dinner, and even Agnes, a finicky eater, ate a piece. The meat was delicious and a nice change. Their friends told them that they wanted more, so they went hunting about twice a month. On one of the hunts in July, Anders, who was back in Balikpapan, joined them. This time they decided to go during the night using head flashlights. As they walked through the jungle, Willi suddenly stopped dead in his tracks. A beautiful black and yellow panther was just ahead of him. Its eyes shone orange in the reflection of his head lamp. Willi watched the graceful animal for some time until it silently disappeared into the thick underbrush. Finally, after quite some time they came upon a large herd of pigs. Willi had never seen so many at one time. They shot three pigs, an old one and two young ones. The three men had a heavy load to carry back to the car; each had an animal on his back. It was pitch dark and they got lost in the jungle. After about four hours they finally arrived at the car. They were tired, soaked, and covered with leeches. Some were four inches long and inflicted painful wounds when they attached themselves to the skin to suck the blood with their beak-like mouth pieces. The natives called them "lintah". It took quite some time to remove the bloodsuckers off their arms and legs by burning them off with lit cigars. The three pigs were loaded on the truck and the men started on the trip back to Balikpapan where they arrived after midnight. Each took a pig. Willi immediately eviscerated and skinned the animal, so he could put the meat on ice before it turned bad.

The months went by and the plan was that they would go on their leave to Switzerland the following October. Mail trickled in, the letters now took six months to reach them.

On Sundays they frequently took the children to the beach before going to the swimming pool at the club. One day they were walking along the water's edge, picking up shells. Agnes was running ahead and Willi carried the baby on his shoulders when they came upon a large white heron. Willi approached the bird cautiously and saw that it could not fly, it had been injured. He handed the baby to Leny and gently picked up the big white bird. They took it home and tended to its wounds. It remained quiet for a couple of days, but took fish and raw meat. In a few days it was walking but unable to fly. It became very tame and followed them everywhere. It stayed in the yard where it could roam free and they had the bird for a long time.

The end of October they began again making plans for their Java vacation, another year had gone by. Leny was planning on leaving a month before Willi. Agnes was having a tropical fever about every three to four weeks. The doctor assured her that it was not dangerous, but the fever drained the child of all energy. They planned on spending their vacation in the mountains near Surabaya and then to spend a week in Bali. The "kokki" was coming with them and was leaving a week before as she had to travel by boat.

PREDICTIONS OF WAR

Earlier that year a comet lit up the sky. Every night Willi and Leny went outside to gaze at the fascinating phenomenon in the dark sky. One day Willi's assistant, Sulandi, stopped by for a visit. He said that Leny and the children should leave for Java right away. There was an ancient prediction from Djojobojo about a war that would begin when the comet Lintang Kamukos appeared in the skies. The comet's arrival, he said, was the last warning. Yellow warriors will invade the island world, and the warriors themselves will then be caught in a cage. Foreign seafarers will disturb the yellow warriors in the cage until peace will once again be with them. The war will last for three years, three months and three weeks, and will end with a lunar eclipse. Five seafarers will drive the yellow warriors away and Indonesia will be a free country. Both Leny and Willi listened intently to Sulandi's serious foretelling, but neither of them believed in superstition or predictions. They continued to watch the comet in the sky for some time.

Another old school mate of Willi's arrived in Balikpapan; Otto and his wife Rosa. Leny and Willi were delighted to see their old friends. When Willi began his studies of geology, Otto was just completing his doctorate degree. He had worked for the company for some time already and they had been living in South America. Otto was a brilliant man. He was short of stature. He had thick, straight hair and a small, pointed nose. He adored women, and lusted after every young female he saw. He came from a wealthy old family, but no matter how much money he had, he did not want to part with it. They seldom purchased anything nice because Otto just did not want to part with any money and his poor wife had only a small budget from which she could buy household goods. Rosa was also short, she was about

50

the same size as Otto. She had an ample bosom, her dresses and blouses always hung loose about her body. Her hair was curly and stuck to her forehead which was always damp from perspiring. Her big blue eyes sparkled and she always had a smile on her face. They had no children, but there were always several cats and dogs in their household.

Leny and the children left for Java several weeks before Willi's vacation began. The "kokki" had already left and was to be at the bungalow when they arrived. Talk about anticipated problems in oil places began to increase, so Rosa decided to also leave for Java. She and Leny rented a house together until the men joined them. They were flown to Java on the company plane and a car drove them to the house in the mountains. There was a large living room, three bedrooms, a kitchen, bathroom, and a room in the back for the "kokki". They arrived in the evening hours and Leny was getting dressed for dinner. The baby was in the crib while Agnes sat on the floor playing. Suddenly, Leny spotted a large, black scorpion near the door. She grabbed both children and called for help. By that time about half a dozen more scorpions entered the room through a large crack in the door. Several people nearby heard Leny's call and came running with brooms and sticks. They caught the scorpions and Leny insisted that every crack be immediately sealed. She was used to having all kinds of tropical critters around, but was not about to put up with scorpions which, if one stung a small child, could be deadly. After this initial unpleasant experience she saw no more scorpions around the property. The company sent some workers to check the entire house and to seal any possible hiding places or cracks.

On November 24th, 1941 Leny's mother wrote a letter which they received months later. She wished them happy holidays and hoped that they would all spend the following Christmas together. Things were becoming harder and harder and food was being rationed even more. There was now a third mandatory meatless day which made it especially hard for the men who worked from sunup to sundown. They received two eggs every two weeks and could not even think of baking cookies for Christmas. She wrote that maybe if they were lucky they could scrape together enough flour to bake a cake. The business was keeping them busy. Every family member was taking first aid courses and they were all in the blood donor program. Leny's brother and his wife had taken in a foster child from Poland. She wrote that there were over twenty children in their hometown from Germany, Czechoslovakia, Romania and Poland. Many of them were Jewish children whose parents felt safer to have them in the country where they could enjoy the fresh air, be safe from the war and out of harm's way.

DECLARATION OF WAR

Willi flew to Java the first week in December to join Leny and the girls. In the meantime they had moved to a house in Prigen Tretes in east Java. On December 8th, 1941, the day after Willi arrived, he and Leny sat on the cozy porch enjoying a cool drink. The girls were asleep. Soft music came from the radio, the news would be on in a few minutes. It had just turned dark outside, some birds were still singing somewhere high up in a tree and a pleasant breeze blew cool mountain air. The music stopped and the announcement came:

"Japan has attacked Pearl Harbor without declaring war. Following the attack, Japan officially declared war with the United States of America and with Great Britain."

Willi and Leny looked at each other, shock and fear in their faces. What was going to happen to them now?

Four days later a telegram was delivered to the house. Willi was instructed to immediately return to Balikpapan without his family. Still in shock over the uncertainty, Leny packed some of his clothes, and early the following morning she accompanied him to the airport of Surabaya. Everyone was running around, people were nervous and excited, screaming and crying, and there was much confusion. The airport was heavily guarded by military wearing steel helmets. Willi was immediately let through the barricades when he showed the telegram, but Leny had to stay outside. It was one of the hardest moments of their lives. Balikpapan was an oil field which would probably soon be occupied by the Japanese. After all, the oil the Japanese needed came from Netherlands East Indies. They hugged and clung to each other for some time, but Willi had to go and Leny went back to the waiting car. It was still early in the morning when the DC-3 rolled onto the runway and the passengers climbed aboard. There were twelve, one a nurse who had been given permission to return to Balikpapan to join her physician husband. The rest of the passengers were all men. The plane was filled with land mines and grenades to defend the important oil place. It started its engines and was ready for take-off. It rolled, but did not seem to gain speed, probably because it had too much cargo. It was unable to gain the necessary speed for lift-off. Willi felt ill at ease. He tightened his seat belt, cleared his throat and tried to relax. The plane was approaching a wide ditch at the end of the runway. Suddenly there was a jolt, a coffee pot and sandwiches flew through the air past Willi. A man was thrown forward; he did not have his seat belt secured. For a few seconds everything was totally quiet, then people began to scream. The DC-3 was lying in the drainage canal, the propellers were bent and the emergency exit blocked. The co-pilot came out of the cockpit, his nose was bleeding and he had an injured arm. He was talking on the radio when the plane went into the ditch. His face hit the equipment and he fractured his nose. Finally, it seemed like an eternity to Willi, a lid was unscrewed and they were able to climb out of the wrecked plane. Fire trucks and ambulances were lined up, expecting the DC-3 with its highly explosive cargo to explode. Fortunately, the only injuries were two fractured arms and a broken nose. The land mines and grenades did not explode. Everyone climbed out, was accounted for and quickly escorted away from the wrecked plane and into the airport building.

The passengers were given a choice to travel to Borneo by plane or by boat. Willi decided to fly, it seemed unlikely to him that the same thing would happen a second time. Most of the other passengers decided to go by boat. After some delay, he boarded another DC-3 and flew to Bandjarmasin where he had to spend the night. They departed early the following morning and landed in Balikpapan a few hours later. Willi was home again, but the house was empty. At night the air alarm sounded, but nothing happened. A few days later eight hundred land mines exploded; a coolie had stepped on a mine which set off the entire mine field. Nobody knew what had to be done if bombs were dropped. There were no shelters and the only thing to do was to seek protection in one of the ditches. They were poorly informed and were not aware of the threat of a Japanese invasion on Borneo until they noticed that no more Japanese ships came to the harbor to get oil.

British North Borneo was attacked, then Tarakan. There were now five Swiss in Balikpapan. They did not know what to do. A few days later a fleet of American battle ships were seen at the harbor. They had been holding maneuvers near the Philippines when the Japanese attacked Pearl Harbor and had been immediately deployed to the south. The fleet consisted of a battleship, three cruisers, seven torpedo boat destroyers and a carrier. Everyone was excited, there was a party at the club; they were all convinced that the Americans would protect them from the Japanese. But that was not to happen. The Americans had no live ammunition, they had been totally surprised by the Japanese attack. Days of hopelessness followed. They felt that they were trapped and that there was no way out.

Their Dutch colleagues were mobilized. The natives did not know what to do either and rumors spread to make the Dutch look bad. One of the rumors was that the Dutch cut off the heads of native children to sacrifice to the gods at new factories. The heads were being transported in a red truck in the middle of the night. Of course, this was untrue, but the rumor had its desired effect and caused even more chaos.

One day a Japanese fighter plane dropped the first bomb in the bay, but it did not hit any target. Each day, one or two Japanese planes dropped bombs, but as far as Willi could determine, nothing was hit. The Netherlands East Indies army had two canons to defend the harbor and oil installations. The canons were shot at the Japanese planes. The one near the factories released about three shots and then stopped for good; it had an irreparable loading defect. The second canon had a similar fate; it was hit and destroyed during the next air attack. Gone was the air defense and the war had barely begun. Now the Dutch army was convinced that the Japanese would drop parachutists on the area to occupy the oil installations. On December 19th a defense system was begun at practically no cost. Pointed bamboo poles were stuck in the ground which were supposed to impale the Japanese if they tried to parachute into the area. 750,000 sticks were needed. Otto was in charge of supervising the field crews who cut the bamboo poles. About two thousand were stuck in the ground a day. It would require about a year to place them all in the ground and that would then only cover company grounds; as if the Japanese intended to only land there! There was little news on the radio. They knew that something was going to happen, everyone was tense and nervous. The Dutch were mobilized, every man was given a uniform and a gun. Many had never held a gun in their hands, but they had to learn how to shoot and how to handle a gun. Without hesitating, the Swiss offered to teach their Dutch colleagues how to aim and shoot. They had all participated in target shooting practices against some of the best marksmen of the Swiss army, many of them with high marks.

During that time there were also some Dutch who belonged to the NSP, the National Social Party, i.e. the Nazi's. Willi himself once saw a Dutch officer and a company bookkeeper give each other the Nazi salute. The company director could no longer trust his own people, so he asked the five Swiss scientists to take over guarding the tank installations. They were given guns and ammunition and were told that they had full authority to shoot anyone who approached the installations, with no questions asked. The men worked all day long at the office, then, at six at night when it turned dark, they went to the oil installations and guarded the site until six in the morning. Then they went home, took a shower, ate breakfast and went to work at the office. They did not know what would happen to them when Borneo's large oil harbor was attacked by the Japanese. They all knew that this would occur sooner or later. After all, Japan relied on Borneo's oil. A way had to be found to prevent the Japanese from getting the oil. The natives whispered rumors and told Willi that they should flee the area. The question was, where were they to go? They were surrounded by dense jungles, practically uninhabited. There was talk of sending them into the jungle with the Chinese and native workers for about three weeks until Holland had won the war with Japan. They were convinced that the Americans would come and drive the Japanese away.

At that time, all the Swiss wives and children were in Java. One day Flori went to the Swiss consulate in Surabaya and told them that her husband and other Swiss men were still in Balikpapan. She demanded to know what was going to happen with the men. The Swiss consul told her that he was not going to interfere with company business. Flori stood her ground and responded that she was not going to leave his office until she had been reassured that something was going to be done to get the men out.

During that time, Willi and his Swiss friends heard that the Japanese had given the Dutch an ultimatum if the oil installations were to be destroyed. He later found out what happened. The Japanese advised the Dutch Knil commander, Lt. Col. C. van den Hoogenband that all Dutch citizens would be killed if the oil installations of Balikpapan were to be set on fire. Captain Colijn was to be the messenger and deliver this ultimatum. The message was written in Japanese, translated into Dutch and given to Colijn. It read:

"If the garrison of Balikpapan destroys the installation thereof as well as those of the surrounding areas, the officers in command shall kill every Dutch soldier and Dutch citizen with no exceptions. Captain Ciren and Captain

Reruhof (both names were misspelled by the Japanese) are being sent to advise and deliver specific instructions."

Colijn and Reinderhoff left Tarakan on January 16th.

On January 20th the installations were set on fire by the Dutch. The Japanese landed in Balikpapan during the night of January 23rd.

On January 8th, with sorrow in his heart, Willi wrote a letter to his parents.

Now the war has come close and I know that you are worried about us. I can assure you, Leny and the children are safe in Java where they have been for about two months now and you do not have to worry about me. I will be careful. The beginning of December I spent a few days in Java, but when the war started I was called back to Balikpapan. Leny has rented a house in the mountains and they are well. The mountain climate is very good for the children and I am glad that they were able to get away from the hot and humid climate of Balikpapan. Leny's address is: Huize Kawi, Punten, Java, N.O.I. Punten is near the town of Malang in east Java. Best wishes to all.

ESCAPE

On January 15th, 1942, Willi received a telephone call from the director, informing him that all the Swiss were to depart immediately for the nearby air strip per request of the Swiss government. It was ten minutes before noon. The air strip was over forty miles away. The other men were contacted and told where to go. Willi and Christian rushed home. Lunch was already on the dining table. Willi told the servants that they had to leave immediately, gave them some money, grabbed a few clothes and he and Christian jumped in the car. The two men had been sharing the house since their wives were gone. The road was bumpy and curvy; at times they had to swerve not to hit a wild animal roaming the area. As they approached the air strip they saw that the plane was already there. They drove the car next to the banks of a nearby river, left the ignition on, and climbed out. Placing their two small suitcases on the ground, they pushed the car into the river to prevent the Japanese from getting it. Cars were very sought after by the Japanese. Then Willi and Christian took off running toward the plane. Soon they were all there, Otto, Jakob and Hans, Christian and Willi and the plane took off. It flew to a secret air strip deeper inside the jungle, Samarinda 2. It was near the upper Mahakam river between Long Iram and Muara Pahu and had been used by the company to transport its employees. A simple rice table was served for dinner. The men were hungry, they had not eaten all day. A primitive hut next to the strip had some cots, the beds for the tired men. Willi could not sleep, he kept waking up staring out of the window into the black jungle. He heard the buzzing and croaking of the night animals, but his ears tried to pick up the sound of planes. All night long he felt extremely uncomfortable. What was out there? Toward morning he fell asleep, but was abruptly awakened when the air alarms went off; forty enemy planes had been sighted over Balikpapan. Six Dutch fighter planes took off, but they returned about two hours later without ever seeing the enemy's bombers. One of the pilots told them that the situation in the air was hopeless and they did not have enough fighter planes. A short while later additional military enforcement arrived, the tiny air strip was bustling with activity. They were told that they were continuing their evacuation to Java shortly. First, the DC-3 had to be fueled and this had to be done by hand. The military were not available to assist the civilians so the Swiss men lined up behind the small pump. They pumped until they could no longer move their arms and then the next one began pumping. None of them realized how much fuel such an airplane took; especially, since the pump had to be activated by hand. Finally, everyone constantly glancing skyward, they were ready for take-off. The plane flew over immense jungle areas which looked like cauliflower from the air. Occasionally, they saw a small native village near a river. Willi was extremely uncomfortable, what if they encountered a Japanese fighter plane? His thoughts were with his family, his only wish was to land safely and to be close to his wife and children again. The plane followed the wide Barito river which ran into the Java sea near Bandjarmasin where they landed at 1:30 in the afternoon. More passengers had to be taken on, mostly women and children. In the evening the plane took off again. Shortly after they left, they saw the remains of a passenger ship which had been destroyed by Japanese torpedoes. It was the ship with which the passengers had wanted to go to Balikpapan on December 13th who were on the same plane as Willi was when it crashed into a ditch in Surabaya. The people thought that it would be safer to travel by sea; all aboard the ship perished.

The plane was packed full. There were forty-one passengers, most of them evacuees from Bandjarmasin. The plane had already been converted into a transport machine, all the seats had been removed and the refugees sat huddled together on the floor. Willi worried that there were more Japanese planes out there. Were they going to make it without being shot down? Would he ever see his family again? He had left all their belongings behind, their entire household which they had brought with them three years earlier. All his artifacts he had collected. Leny had been able to take some linens with her in the old chest as well as some extra clothes for the children. The most important thing, though, so far they were still alive. He decided to think positive and envisioned seeing his wife and children the following day.

They landed safely at the Surabaya airport where everything was in disarray. Everyone coming off the plane had to go through a very strict customs inspection as they were coming from a war zone. They had to strip naked in front of the Dutch customs officials and were searched mainly for possession of gold, nobody knew why. Night had fallen when they were finally allowed to leave the airport. The men took off in different directions, promising each other to try and stay in touch. The wives and children were scattered at different locations in Java. Willi stood at the airport exit, unshaven, with wrinkled clothes, holding his small suitcase with a couple of shirts, slacks and some underwear. He was exhausted, thirsty and hungry, but immediately ordered a taxi to take him to his family the first thing in the morning. He spent the rest of the night sitting on a chair inside the airport. Leny, who was in Punten, did not know that he was coming. The next morning the taxi carrying Willi pulled up in front of the house. Leny ran outside and threw her arms around her husband. They hugged and kissed for a long time. Now, at least, they were all together again, even though they were in a foreign country in which the Japanese persecuted everyone, regardless of nationality.

WAR IN PARADISE

On January 19th Willi took a taxi to the oil place Tjepu, about sixty-five miles west of Surabaya. He had been instructed by the company to continue the research he had been working on in Borneo. Leny and the children remained in the mountains. It was impossible to accomplish much work because air alarms went off constantly. No bombs were dropped, but every time the alarms went off, they had to run to shelters.

Willi's old assistant and friend, Sulandi, had also returned to his home in Java. Every now and then he and Willi met. Willi often helped him out and gave him some money. Like everyone else, he was also having a hard time surviving. Sulandi always spoke of Djojobojo and the war which began when the comet appeared. So far, according to him, the prediction had come true. The Australians bombing the Japanese, the invaders of Borneo, were the foreign seafarers disturbing the yellow warriors, as had been predicted.

Some time later Willi heard that the Japanese discovered the secret air strip Samarinda 2 on Borneo on January 24th and completely destroyed it with bombs. This was only nine days after he and his Swiss colleagues were able to flee from there. Samarinda, on the Mahakam delta, was occupied by the Japanese on February 2nd. Five Dutch men who had remained were killed. Four were government employees who the Japanese first tortured in a terrible manner and then decapitated. The fifth victim was shot to death. Willi knew all five men.

Toward the end of January Willi, Leny and the other Swiss families had an opportunity to leave Java on a Swedish ship headed for South Africa. The Swiss consular representative organized everything. Of course, they had to pay for the trip themselves. Japan had already granted neutral citizens permission to leave the occupied island. The Swedish ship, the "Christholm", had come from the United States carrying Japanese diplomats back to Japan and picked up American diplomats to take them back to America. The ship was anchored at a harbor in Java. The Swiss government then began a campaign to prevent any Swiss from leaving the occupied island world far from their homeland. The justification the Swiss government used was, "the boat is full". Switzerland did not want its citizens back as the small country was already taking in many war refugees from Europe.

On February 17th, 1942, a squadron of twenty-seven Japanese planes flew over Tjepu, but no defensive action whatsoever was taken by the Dutch. About an hour later Willi heard that Malang and Surabaya had been bombed. The Dutch panicked and hope of any kind of defense of Java was waning. Since the Japanese had no oil of their own, mainly the oil places of Borneo, Java and Sumatra were in danger of being attacked. Willi was almost able to predict when the Japanese were going to attack Tjepu. The Dutch military worked intensely at building a defense line. They were digging ditches around all the oil installations. In case of an attack, the ditches would be filled with oil and set on fire. Hundreds of coolies worked on the project. It was never completed. Another defense strategy was to destroy all the houses of nearby native villages and create a cleared zone along the river about a thousand feet long so that the Japanese parachutists could be seen if they were to attempt to land. Everything was cut down. Trees and huts were taken down. The soldiers guarding the city were clad in steel helmets, but as soon as the air alarms sounded, they all ran to the bomb shelters where they were safe.

During that time Willi had to live in Tjepu while Leny and the children remained in the mountains. He shared a house with Dr. Alfred Lang. Only a few days after Willi moved into the house, Dr. Lang had to go to Kopeng where he organized the evacuation of women and children of company employees. He was an older geologist who had spent many years in Netherlands East Indies. He was born in 1893, in a small town not too far from Willi's own home town. He attended school in Basel where he also studied geology. After graduating he became an assistant professor at the university and in 1925, began working for the BPM in The Hague. Shortly thereafter he was sent to Venezuela and in 1927 went to Netherlands East Indies where he worked until 1934. He then returned to Holland, but in 1939, once again returned to Netherlands East Indies to continue his work on geology, this time on the island of Buton. In 1941, after the war broke out, he moved to Tjepu on Java.

On February 27th all the Swiss geologists, topographers and chemists were ordered to immediately leave the oil place Tjepu. The company gave each man emergency money, quite a substantial amount, advised that they join their families in the mountains and to wait it out to see what would happen. The men went directly to the mountains where the wives and children lived. On the way they met hundreds of Dutch soldiers who were in the process of destroying their vehicles and ridding themselves of their weapons. Willi had not yet seen a single Japanese soldier.

The Dutch men said, "Why should I fight for this stupid country." They had been given weapons, German Mauser pistols with attachable butts. The British had taken them from Rommel's army in Africa and shipped them to Netherlands East Indies. Each man who had been given such a weapon had also been given bullets; two to be exact!

On March 1st Java was attacked. At that time Willi and Leny still had a radio. The broadcasts always sounded more or less the same:

"Our troops have successfully retreated to newly prepared positions." During the night of February 28th to March 1st, 1942, three Japanese infantry regiments landed in east Java, a total of 20,000 men."

Shortly after Willi left Tjepu they moved into a house in Tawangmangu. It was on a hill close to a native village at the foot of the volcano Lawu. A few days later more Dutch soldiers arrived from Tjepu. They came by vehicles or on horseback, as many of the vehicles had already been destroyed. The men greeted their families, immediately removed their uniforms and changed into civilian clothes. Then they burned their uniforms. A few of the men decided to keep their weapons and uniforms so they could participate in the victory celebrations after the war in a couple of months. An old acquaintance Willi had know in Borneo handed him a package one day and asked him to keep it until the war was over. It contained the man's green army straw hat, his uniform, the Mauser pistol, and the two bullets. Willi wondered what he, a neutral citizen, was going to do with a weapon that was strictly forbidden and which could have placed them all in grave danger. On the way home they passed a deep ravine with a flowing river. He threw the entire package into it. Later he explained his action to his Dutch acquaintance. The man was glad that Willi had disposed of the weapon, especially since he was now also convinced that the war would not last only three months as was officially anticipated by the Dutch.

More and more Swiss families were arriving in Tawangmangu, the town at the foot of the volcano Lawu. The natives called the mountain Gunung Lawu. It was about 9,795 feet high, and was an inactive volcano. On Java there are twenty-seven active volcanoes, thirteen in west Java, five in middle Java and nine in east Java. There were many more inactive volcanoes. Tobacco, coffee, tea, sugar, rice, tapioca, coconuts, kapok, vegetables and fruit were the main agricultural products of the island. This is where they were living when the Japanese occupied Java. The frenzy of the war continued. A sad story was the Dutch military's order to destroy everything and the order turned into an absurd destruction frenzy. Sacks of rice were thrown into the rivers, coconut oil was poured out and gasoline poured over food at the markets. Mineral water, wine and liquor were also destroyed. The alcohol was thrown out so that the Japanese would not get hold of it, get drunk and then get out of hand. Willi never understood why the food was destroyed.

On March 8 the war in Java was over. It was the same everywhere; there were no officers, there was no food, no leadership and, therefore, there were no battles. The Dutch officers ran away, there were not enough weapons to fight the enemy. The city guards fled and looting began everywhere. Willi found out that at 7:45 in the morning of March 9th, 1942, the capitulation was broadcast over the radio by the Japanese.

On March 17th they saw the first soldier, a Korean serving in the Japanese army. He spoke Malay quite well. The Korean came to their house, accompanied by a representative of the Sultan of Surakarta. They were conducting a census count of all the residents in the area. The Korean checked all the homes. When he came to the house, he did not enter nor did he conduct a search, but he asked Willi if he had any weapons or a radio. The radio was confiscated. Other than that he was quite a decent fellow and did not bother anyone.

More and more of their old friends arrived from all over the archipelago. The Swiss decided that they would all try to live close together to help each other out and to try to live in an evacuation colony rather than be spread out. All around areas propped up where they settled, usually one or two of the men organized and assisted the families. From the arriving Swiss, Willi heard numerous stories about the battles that were going on in Java. One such story was about Dutch officers in Batavia who waited with white sheets and towels for a day and a half for the enemy so they could surrender. They waited at all the entrances to the city. Batavia was taken by one hundred fifty Japanese, Bandjarmasin on Borneo was taken by thirty Japanese soldiers on bicycles. Most of the Japanese were ill with malaria, but the Dutch still ran away and did not put up a fight. In Balikpapan the Japanese came from an area where nobody expected them to come from, namely from the Grogot area. The bamboo spikes stood erect in the fields, not a single Japanese had been impaled as they did not come from the sky. Two men of the company were missing, they were last seen in Bandung. In Djokja about three hundred fifty Dutch soldiers surrendered holding a white flag. Willi heard that apparently one of the Japanese officers questioned the Dutch soldiers why they did not want to fight. About seven hundred Dutch city guards in Tjepu were without an officer, so after three days they went to Solo. Willi and Leny became desperate, they had no food, they were surrounded and they were on their own. The people from Solo did not find out until the following day that the city had been occupied.

Often the Swiss gathered at one of their homes and more and more began to arrive. The stories they heard terrified them. The Japanese soldiers were extremely cruel at the front. They had attacked an oil place, the island of Tarakan on the east coast of Borneo, where no one had expected that they would attack. The battle was quickly over and early in the morning at five the Japanese hoisted the white flag with the red sun. Everything happened extremely fast. There had been no time to inform the Dutch military of the capitulation and the Dutch coast artillery sunk a Japanese torpedo boat. There were two hundred fifteen men in this artillery who were soldiers of the regular Netherlands East Indies army. All were captured. The Japanese army commander assured the Dutch military commander that the soldiers would not be punished because they had sunk a Japanese ship after the capitulation. The Japanese army moved southward and the Dutch prisoners of war were handed over to the Japanese marine. A week later they were taken on a ship, were shackled and were then thrown overboard in the same area where the Japanese ship had been sunk. All two hundred fifteen Dutch soldiers drowned.

The Governor General of Netherlands East Indies instructed all government officials to remain at their posts to make certain that civilian life would be as normal as possible. Many of the officials were murdered by assault troops made up mostly of Koreans under the command of a Japanese lieutenant. This unfortunate fate happened to one of the government officials of the city Blora near Tjepu on Java. He, his wife and two young sons were taken to the center of the town where he was ordered to dig his own grave. The soldiers then killed him with their bayonets in front of his wife and two children and threw his body into the grave he had just dug. They frequently murdered people by stabbing them with the bayonets or decapitating them to save the bullets. The wife was taken to a soldier bordello for three weeks. Both the wife and her two children somehow managed to survive the war.

Another tragic incident occurred near Willi and Leny's house in Tawangmangu. A large mob of natives, armed with knives and sticks, chased two Australian prisoners of war who had escaped. The Japanese spread rumors that the Australians were poisoning the drinking water supplies. The two fleeing men ran toward Willi's house. Unfortunately, a Korean in civilian clothes was already standing there, his pistol drawn. He commanded the two to halt or he would kill them. The Australians did not understand the Korean who was speaking Malay, so Willi called to them in English. The Korean told Willi to explain to the Australians that they would be unable to survive as white people in the densely populated area. He put the pistol up to the two men's heads and commanded they get in his car which then drove off. Willi was extremely upset, if only the Korean had not been standing there; he might have been able to help the two to hide or escape. He found out later that both were killed with bayonets in the prison as their friends watched. Anyone who tried to escape from a prison camp was killed in this manner. They were always stabbed to death with bayonets in front of their friends to show the rest of the prisoners what would happen to them if they were to try to escape.

Another frightful situation happened within the first few days of the Japanese occupation of Java. The natives went on robbery rampages. In the beginning they were provoked to do so by the Japanese soldiers. It began in that the Japanese entered stores by force, took merchandise and handed out cigarettes and other items to the people standing nearby. Soon looting began everywhere. The homes of the Europeans were completely emptied out, even the locks on the doors were removed and electrical wiring was torn out of the walls. Willi saw a man at the train station in Surakarta remove all the tickets from the dispenser and then tear them to shreds. Anything that had previously been forbidden was being done. The Japanese had a firm goal in mind with these transgressions; after three days of rioting they gathered groups of people in different areas. In Surakarta thirty natives were taken to the center of the town, lined up and then mowed down with machine guns. The corpses were left to decay in the humid climate. This was the way the Japanese intimidated the native population, with the stench of decaying corpses. They announced, "This is how Japan deals with thieves." They also punished thieves in rural areas who had stolen small amounts of food. If a man was caught stealing rice, sugar or onions, his left-hand middle finger was cut off. A second offense cost the middle finger of the right hand. For thefts of larger items, one or both hands were severed. Willi observed such an incident himself. A shackled man was carried to the center of the town on a stretcher made of bamboo. He was taken to the Japanese governor's residence which at the same time also was a tribunal. The prisoner had apparently taken about sixty pounds of garlic and was to be sentenced according to Japanese fashion. Both his hands were cut off with a sword. After that Willi often saw the man near the market, his stumps wrapped in leather pouches, sitting on the ground begging. Such cruel methods of punishment for minor thefts horrified Willi and Leny and all their friends. After some time the looting stopped and things returned somewhat to normal. The natives as well as Europeans were spared further pilfering.

VOLCANOES, TEMPLES AND GODS

The culture and history of Java was very interesting. Willi and Leny often hiked to the nearby volcanoes. They saw Hindu temples and more and more began to study the history of Java. They spoke with the local people and read about Java in some of the books friends had loaned them. Of specific interest to Willi was the history of the Madjapahit era.

The Javanese time calculation started during the seventh Sjaka century. This was during the era of Adji Saka, around 78 AD. According to legend, Adji Saka was a powerful prince of god-like descent who arrived from India and settled in Java. He gathered the archaic people for worship and brought the alphabet to Java. Adji means prince and Saka is a Sanskrit word used by the Hindus to describe nomads. There was another legend that the Sjaka prince was the Scythian prince Kanisjka. Some of the more famous kings were Mpu Sindok, the first king of the Mataram house who settled in east Java and reigned from 928 to 950. Airlannga reigned from 1010 to 1049 and divided the kingdom between his two sons, Kediri and Djanggala. The most powerful prince of Kediri during the 11th century was Kertaradjasa who took over the throne of Madjapahit in 1216. He died in 1231. Ken Angrok killed the king of Djanggala and the dynasty of Singasari began (1222 to 1293 AD). He first conquered Djanggala and then Kediri. The supremacy went to the kingdom of Tumapel. Ken Angrok took on the royal name of Radjasa. Under one of his descendants, Rangga Wuni, began the definite union of east Java. The capital Tumapel spread out and was renamed Singasari. In 1250, Tribhuwanottunggadewi, or Dewi, took over the throne and the kingdom flourished under her reign. Kertanagara reigned from 1268 to 1292. He was killed by Kediri's under king, which ended the reign of Tumapel-Singasari.

Kertanagara's son-in-law, Raden Widjaja, fled but later returned. He founded the new city Madjapahit in 1294 and became the sole sovereign of Java. King Hayam Wuruk became one of the most famous kings of Java and reigned from 1350 to 1389. Shortly thereafter the dynasty deteriorated, the lands were lost and hunger broke out. Madjapahit was declining rapidly and in 1520 the dynasty disappeared. This was probably the time the Moslems conquered the area and Islam began to spread across the island. The Portuguese came to Java in 1511 from Malacca, but were soon driven away. The first Dutch ship arrived in Bantam in 1596. A new empire developed in middle Java under the Sultan Agung. During the 17th and 18th centuries, the British, Dutch and Portuguese came to Java. The Dutch colonized the archipelago in 1618 and Java became part of the Netherlands East Indies.

Willi and Leny settled into their life at the foot of the volcano that held so much history. They soon befriended the people from the nearby village. Often they went on hikes, exploring interesting temples and were able to partake and learn about local customs and practices. The natives frequently invited them to their village to attend festivities and celebrations.

Around the middle of March, they left on an excursion to one of the many nearby temple sites, specifically the temple Tjandi Sukuh. First they had to walk through the village Pantjot. At the temple remains Willi discovered an old sacrificial altar stone. He was so fascinated by the site that several years later he wrote and published the following article:

"Sacrificial flower offerings at an altar stone in Java"
by Dr. W. A. Mohler
Bulletin of the Swiss Society of Anthropology and Ethnology, p. 91-95.

During a one-year stay in mid-Java (February 1942 to February 1943) I had the opportunity to study in detail the people and surroundings of the area of Solo (Surakarta), particularly from the regions of the western slopes of the volcano Lawu. The mountain people in this region still utilize certain ancient cultural rituals which are known to westerners only from prehistoric times. One of the most interesting objects I encountered was a sacrificial altar stone in the village Pantjot near Tawangmangu (3,600 feet above sea level) near the mountain-pass road connecting Solo with Madiun. This town was also called village Hindu which still had remains of Hindu structures. The name, village Hindu, referred to the old religion of the village population who still practiced ancient Javanese and Hindu rites. It is of interest that all these old shrines, especially the altar stone, are still being worshipped by the mountain people. In this mountain region the Islam influence is quite insignificant and the people eat pork and consume alcohol (arak), mostly during religious ceremonies. This sacred shrine, which includes the altar stone, is under a large "waringin" tree (Ficus Religiosus). The tree has numerous aerial roots and has a diameter of about thirty feet. The roots cover the bulk of the former Hindu temple. Some of the temple stones can still be seen quite well between the roots. The base of the wall is approximately thirty feet long and encloses the temple which is quite well preserved. This is an indication that the altar stone had been inside the former temple and was situated at a west-eastern angle. The altar stone is an andesite stone with crude sides. The surface is slightly concave and has been artificially polished. On the surface there are hollowed-out cups. Most are round and about one to two inches deep, the larger ones deeper than the smaller ones. I could not determine any particular order of the cups. The crude and primitive work is indicative of the fact that this sacrificial stone is not of the Hindu era, but is of archaic Javanese origin and is a so-called terrace relic used for animism rites. It can thus be derived that the old Hindu temple was erected at the sacrificial site. This can also be observed from time to time in other areas of the region. Presently there are four remnants of Hindu sculptures on the altar stone which cover some of the cups. These sculptures come from the Hindu temple and are probably there by coincidence. The altar stone stands under a roof of a small sacrificial hut made of bamboo. I have frequently observed such huts at other Javanese worship sites. The whole relic is surrounded by a bamboo enclosure and the "waringin" tree.

I had the opportunity to attend several sacrificial offerings at this altar stone which I will describe in detail: Small red blossoms and petals of red roses are placed in a cup filled with water. The cup is then placed on the altar stone. To the left of the altar stone are hot coals on a brick on top of a smaller stone. The priest who is performing the sacrificial offering takes some incense (resin) and slowly pulverizes it over the hot coals. Simultaneously, he summons the gods. When the blue, sweet smelling incense permeates the area, he takes the cup in his hands and fills the openings with the mixture of water and blossoms. At the same time the fragments of the Hindu sculptures are also sprinkled. The remainder of the sacred water is then poured into the larger cups which are at the front left side of the stone. During the entire process the priest murmurs prayers. It also needs to be said that according to Javanese belief, the aroma of flowers and incense is the nourishment of the gods. The incense is used to entice the gods and alert them that one wishes to speak with them. There are two main rituals a year at which the entire population participates, then also food is offered such as rice, bananas and roasted chickens. The items are then placed on a table inside the small hut. I spoke with several people from the village Pantjot about the rituals at this altar stone to obtain a clear picture. Each narrator had his own version, but the following can be established: The temple is considered to be a source of fortune. It is worshipped by the Javanese, as well as the Chinese, Indian and Arabic people living in the area. In order to be granted good fortune, offerings of flowers are made to the gods at this particular stone. No further deeper significance seems to be known to the Javanese of the area. Whether or not the red flowers and petals of the sacrificial water represent blood offerings seems to be an assumption, but it is noteworthy that exclusively only red colored flowers are used. The people of the village Pantjot believe that the hollow openings in the stone are the foot prints of the Hindu god Kotjonegoro.

To reach the temple site of Tjandi Sukuh Willi and Leny first had to walk through the village Pantjot which was just below their house. The small road wound down to a river and then up through the hills. There they came upon another small offering site called Kembang Sore, Evening Flower. It was one of the most beautiful areas they had ever seen. The vegetation was lush and the view breathtakingly beautiful. The two stood for a moment, looking out at the surrounding volcanoes in the background and listening to the songs of the birds in nearby trees. Flowers and incense had been placed at the site, and the air had the sweet aroma of the mixture of incense and mountain flowers. They stood pensively arm in arm, taking in the beauty of the area. For a brief moment they were able to forget that they were caught in the middle of a terrible war. After a while their hike continued on a small path through fields of tapioca, beans, garlic and onions. They reached the temple area in about two hours. Tjandi Sukuh was the larger temple and was on three terraces. In earlier times, steps leading from the valley up to the temples were used which were several miles long. They were still visible, but had not been taken care of for a long time and were totally overgrown with vegetation.

Willi and Leny approached the temple. At its western side was a large stone gate through which they could enter. A relief carved in stone depicted a blacksmith's forge, with weapons and utensils as they were still being used in present times. Near the temple site was an iron ore and Willi immediately realized that there must have been a weapon forge at the site at one time. The entrance into the temple was decorated with numerous reliefs, but a Javanese had to explain their meaning to the naïve westerners. A frightful looking mask at the entrance warded off evil spirits from entering the holy area. On the ground was a large relief which somewhat resembled a coat of arms, in Willi's opinion. A Javanese guide, who accompanied the two, explained the meaning to them. The relief depicted a vagina and a penis about sixteen inches long; the relic sanctified the phallic cult. They were told that many weddings were held in the temple Sukuh. The bride had to pass a chastity test. When she entered the temple she had to walk by the phallic symbol. If she was still a virgin she was happily greeted by all the participants; if she was no longer a virgin, her "sarong" slid from her body and shame fell upon her.

On each side of the temple gates were many strange carvings whose meanings Willi and Leny were unable to figure out. The guide, an expert on Hindu-Javanese symbols, pointed out a scene depicting a date. It showed a giant devouring a human being. Birds were sitting in a tree, under the tree was a dog looking on as the human was being eaten. Certain words, according to Javanese interpretation, depict numbers. A human means one, to devour means three, a giant means five and a gate means nine. This added up to the Javanese year 1359, which was 1437 AD. 1359 was probably the year the temple was completed.

The main monument of the temple was a pyramid, at its foot was a huge turtle carved of stone. The turtle was the symbol of the earth; an island in the ocean as was Java. There were reliefs of Garuda, the "sunbird", on which the god Wishnu rode, the snakes in its claws representing the enemy. They also saw numerous small demon-like figures devouring humans. Many of the figures reminded them of the images that appear in the Javanese shadow

The temple Sukuh near Tawangmangu, Java 1942

The "wajang" is a play performed with flat figures mostly carved out of leather. The figures project their shadows onto white fabric screens.

There are seven different types of "wajang" performances: 1. "Wajang Purva." Old Javanese symbols indicate that this "wajang" was already performed during the 11th century AD. It was believed that the "wajang" originated in Java and symbolizes religious ceremonies to honor the gods. A shadow play is called "lakon", which means drama in the English language. Each play follows strict rules and most of the time the same type figures are used. The plays are either in the form of poetry or prose, or from the actual ancient guide books. The stories can be divided into two categories, a) ancient Javanese or Malay-Polynesian myths, and b) Indian sagas of the Sanskrit literature. 2. "Wajang Gedog." This "wajang" was developed during the reign of the king of Madjapahit. The music accompanying the play is called the "Gamelan Pelog." The hero in this play is Raden Pandji, the prince of Djanggala. 3. Wajang Kelitik or Karutjil. The main characteristic of this play differing from the previous two is that in this performance actual dolls are used and not their shadows. It was developed later and is thus much newer than the other two forms. The figures appearing in these plays depict the eras of the Padjadjaran and Madjapahit reigns. Siyung Wanara and Damar Wulan are famous for their amorous and heroic adventures. Damar Wulan was once a stable-hand who became king of Madjapahit. 4. "Wajang Golek." This "wajang" performance also uses wooden dolls and the plays depict stories from the Amir-Hamza era. 5. "Topeng." In this play Pandji plays the lead role. The plays are performed by people wearing masks and often, traveling actors called "Wong Barbarang," perform on streets as people gather around to watch. Another form of "Topeng" is performed where the actors wear animal masks, mostly of tigers, horses, crocodiles or birds. 6. "Wajang Wong." These plays originated during the 18th century under Mangu Negara I. Here the actors do not wear masks, and use their own dialogs. 7. "Wajang Beber." This play differs from all the others in that there are no figures, dolls or actors. It is a musical performance in which thin plates made of tree bark are used. It is not known when this originated. On the side of each plate are two thin sticks which are placed into wooden containers. The plates are twirled which produces a fine sound. The "Wajang Beber" is rarely performed any more.

After climbing further up on the mountain, Willi and Leny encountered the much smaller temple Tjeta. It also was built on terraces. On one of the terraces was a large triangular stone slab. In the middle of the slab were three toads surrounding a crab, a horseshoe crab (Limulus) and an eel. In each of the three corners were lizards. All around the temple were numerous reliefs of turtles. Only the native Javanese, whose fathers passed on the meanings of the symbols, understood them. Few foreigners were ever told the true meanings. As far as was known, the temples were constructed during the 15th century AD. The temples are of Hindu-Javanese culture which, even with the spreading of the Islam, were able to be preserved in the isolated area.

Below the peak of the volcano Lawu Willi discovered a pair of upright andesite slabs with reliefs of a sun pointing precisely to the west where the sun sets. The two temples Sukuh and Tjeta were located in this line. The mountain guides who accompanied them stopped at the monument and spoke with each other in their native dialect. Willi sat down and made a sketch of the interesting symbol.

It was a time when Willi and Leny saw many interesting things which they probably never would have had an opportunity to see during normal times when they would have been working.

The nearby village Pantjot with its huge "waringin" tree and the sacred altar stone fascinated Willi. During March 1942, he sketched the village as they saw it through the living room window of the house they were living in. In front of each village house were andesite millstones which the women used to grind rice into a fine powder used for baking.

Willi was able to buy two millstones from the village Pantjot. A short while later he was able to buy an ancient artifact used for animism rites at the Gunung Kidus in Djokjakarta. He had learned from one of the natives that if the figures were upright they represented male ancestors, lying figures those of female ancestors.

Some time later he traveled to a small village called Nglepah just below Tawangmangu. In each native house there were one or two hand looms. Women did all the weaving, making the indigo-blue fabric worn by the people of the region around Solo. He noted that in contrast to the area of Djokjakarta, where the fabrics were more colorful, the fabric from the Solo region was always indigo blue. This was because the Sultan of Mangu Negara of Solo owned the entire indigo culture monopoly. Willi was able to buy a complete hand loom in Nglepah. He sketched the entire loom. The weaving sword, called "liro" in Javanese, was made of palm wood. It was placed in the warp during weaving so the shuttle with the weft could be cast through the threads. He found out that the weaving sword was a sacred object; the natives believed that it could kill a person by simply raising it toward someone. It was very important to the Javanese that an inexperienced person never handle a liro because an accident could have easily happened. He was told by one of the Javanese friends that thieves were more afraid of a weaving sword than of a cocked gun.

Willi began collecting other items of interest, especially old Javanese kris, the daggers with wavy blades. The end of April he bought two old Madjapahit kris in Tawangmangu. It was a pair, representing male and female, called Kudi Trantang Pusaka. The word "trantang" means with holes. The kris are passed from one generation to another and were rarely sold. Willi felt fortunate to be able to obtain two such rare and old pieces.

The beginning of May they were invited to attend a child wedding at the village Pantjot. Children married at the age of about thirteen to fourteen, but remained in the homes of their parents for about another year. Weddings were big celebrations. On the wedding day, the young groom rode on a horse, accompanied by the wedding entourage. An umbrella, "pajong", was held over him to shield him from the bright sun. Ahead of the groom a man wearing a tiger mask surrounded by peacock feathers lead the group, together with dancing "wajang orang" figures and musicians. The feast began on the eve before the wedding day at the house of the bride. It lasted for a week. Then everyone went to the home of the groom where the festivities continued for another week.

THE SAMURAI SWORD

On May 14th, Willi and Jakob, who now also lived nearby, decided to travel to Solo. The year was 2602 (1942) according to a Japanese order. They were no longer allowed to refer to the western time calculations. The Japanese military governor Fukinama resided in Solo. Tawangmangu had become an official evacuation site for Swiss and other neutral citizens. Many Dutch men had already been arrested and were in concentration camps. Most families had children. Food was beginning to run out; flour, oats and oil were no longer available. Everyone had lost much weight and the children, especially, were suffering. The two men decided to visit the Nippon commander in Solo to see if they could make arrangements to receive food supplies. They had their Swiss passports with them, which had been translated into Japanese. Upon arrival they were admitted and recognized as representatives for all the Swiss of the area. They requested a meeting with the colonel. After waiting for some time they were taken to the high ranked Japanese officer. He was dressed in his officer's uniform, wore black boots, and a shiny Samurai sword hung from his belt. He quickly told Willi and Jakob that the Nippon wanted to help all the civilians. An interpreter by the name of Misato translated the Malay, which Willi and Jakob spoke, into Japanese. Willi soon realized that Colonel Fukinama was the officer who had conquered Balikpapan. Fukinama chatted with them, telling them that one of the Swiss men had remained in Balikpapan and that he was doing well. He even offered to take a letter from his wife, who lived with the rest of the Swiss in the mountains, and have it delivered to her husband in Borneo. Willi and Jakob immediately felt that the colonel tried to impress them and wanted them to believe that he was a noble Samurai warrior. He agreed to assign them food and have it sent to the evacuation site in the mountains.

About ten days later Willi and Leny were startled by a loud knock on their door. A soldier was standing outside, handing Willi a note, summoning him to appear before the military colonel Fukinama. Willi wondered what this meant and what the colonel wanted. He knew that they always had to be prepared for the worst. He had no other choice but to again undertake the trip to Solo. After he arrived he was immediately escorted to the colonel's office. Fukinama did not hesitate for a moment and came to the point right away what he wanted from Willi. He made it very clear that he provided the Swiss with food for their families, now he wanted a favor in return. One of his captains was soon to be promoted and needed a Samurai sword for the promotion, but Fukinama did not know how to obtain one. He told Willi that he heard that on the other side of the mountain lived an old Dutch man who spoke Japanese who apparently owned a Samurai sword he had received from friends when he lived in Japan years earlier. Fukinama told Willi that he wanted that sword and that Willi was to get it for him. It sounded easy enough, except for the fact that it was strictly forbidden to possess any types of weapons, swords included, which, if Willi could obtain this desired sword, he would have to transport through an area filled with soldiers. He told the colonel that he would try to obey the order and get him the sword.

After he returned home he immediately went to look up his good friend Pandirdjo of the village Pantjot. He told him that he had to cross the mountain to go to Sarangan. Pandirdjo let him use one of his small horses and told Willi to place a kris in his belt where it would be visible for anyone to see. In case a thief tried to rob him as he crossed the mountain, the dagger would protect him. As soon as a Javanese saw the sacred dagger he would leave him alone. During that time there were many gangs and thieves who attacked and robbed anyone at any time. If someone were to try to harm him, Pandirdjo said, the kris would release itself from the belt and pierce the would-be attacker with its mystical powers.

Willi left early in the morning the following day on his journey over the mountain. He followed narrow paths, traveling on the back of the little mountain horse, his feet touching the ground, the kris stuck in his belt. It was quiet on the narrow mountain road and the trip was fascinating and interesting. Nothing happened and he arrived safely on the other side of the mountain in Sarangan. Christian and Flori lived there, Christian was in charge of the Swiss that lived there. He knew where the old Dutch man lived and they went to look him up. The old man had been left alone by the Japanese up to that time and had not yet been incarcerated as were most of the Dutch. Willi told him why he had come. The man was glad to be rid of his souvenir, he knew that sooner or later the Japanese would have taken the sword from him anyway. Willi handed him an envelope filled with money which Fukinama had provided to pay for the sword. Willi wrapped it in an old sugar sack, climbed on the back of the little horse and rode over the mountain again. He arrived home just as the sun was going down. He never saw any thieves and the trip was again quiet and peaceful. The following day he took the sword to Fukinama. The colonel was very pleased, except that he did not like the rust on the blade. Willi immediately returned home to his family.

A few days later, as he was writing in his diary, he heard a woman scream. Three Dutch women lived in the house next door to theirs. At that time, many of the Japanese soldiers were vacationing in the area nearby and they consumed tremendous amounts of alcohol. Two of the women were always dressed nicely, they painted their lips and nails and wore make-up. The Japanese considered women who wore make-up to be prostitutes; only Geisha girls in Japan painted their faces. One of the women had been standing on her porch when an inebriated Japanese officer walked by. He spotted the well-dressed woman, entered the house and tried to take the frightened woman into the bedroom. One of the other women began to scream for help, so Willi ran over to see what was happening. When he entered the house the officer was harassing the woman. He had taken his pistol out of its holster and placed it on the dining room table. Willi began to intervene. The Japanese spoke very little Malay and would not leave the woman alone. He held her by the arm and tried to drag her into the bedroom. Willi's mind was racing. What could he do to end this annoying and frightening attack on his neighbor? The soldier became more and more belligerent, picked up his gun, pointed it at Willi and told him to leave. Slowly and very clearly Willi said in Malay, "I personally know colonel Fukinama."

The soldier was taken aback when he heard his commander's name, placed his gun on the table and stumbled out of the house. The women, thank God, were safe, but what was Willi to do with a Japanese gun? If they had found the gun they would probably have killed everyone, Willi, his family, as well as all of their friends nearby. He wrapped it in a piece of fabric and the next day went to Solo again. He had seldom been so nervous while traveling on a bus. The Japanese routinely searched Europeans who were traveling on buses or on trains. Fortunately, Willi was spared any encounters with the detested soldiers and he arrived at his destination. After waiting for some time he was taken to Fukinama. Willi handed him the pistol, explaining exactly what had happened. Fukinama considered the situation to be extremely serious and assured Willi that such an incident would never happen again. Later, the assistant told Willi that the officer in question was ordered to the front. Willi and the others were glad to be rid of the annoying Japanese.

Their hatred toward the very cruel and unpleasant soldiers increased daily and more and more they encountered the dreaded enemy. Most of the time when the Swiss families went somewhere they went in groups. They had to wear a Swiss identification pin written in Japanese. They became so frustrated by constantly living in fear of the military, who, even though they were extremely cruel and shot people if they felt like it, on the other hand often acted friendly, polite and bowed. Soon the Swiss men began to play a dangerous game. They all spoke a Swiss dialect which only the Swiss could understand. Whenever they met a Japanese, they bowed back, and at the same time, with a smile on their faces, called them every profanity they could think of. There they were, in front of an armed Japanese officer, their hands clapped in front of them, heads bowing, while they called him every cuss name they could think of in Swiss. The soldiers usually smiled and bowed back. Had one of them understood what they were saying, they would have been killed on the spot. This became a joke to them, it released their tension and often made them laugh. Whenever they were able to get together they had a competition to see who had been able to call a Japanese the nastiest words. They all tried desperately to keep their humor during the terrifying times.

Shortly after Willi and Jakob met with the Japanese colonel to arrange for food deliveries they found out more about Fukinama's activities in Balikpapan which totally disgusted them. Toward the end of February 1942 he took seventy-eight European hostages and ordered they all be killed. Willi and Leny knew all the victims. This is what they were told: After the oil place Tarakan had been taken over by the Japanese, the two Dutch captains had to go to Balikpapan with an ultimatum as related earlier. If the Dutch were to set Balikpapan on fire, all Dutch citizens would be killed. A unit under a friend of Willi's, a Dutch geologist, set all the oil tanks on fire. When the Japanese landed during the night of January 23rd, all the Europeans who had not been able to flee were arrested. The group consisted of two Dutch government officials, a physician who was the Red Cross representative, eight hospital patients, a minister, three priests, several engineers of the company, some other persons, and the company physician who had delivered

Agnes and Ruth. The doctor had been ordered to perform liver surgery on one of the Japanese officers before they killed him. All were thrown in prison for a month. Exactly a month after the Japanese landed, on February 24th, 1942, they fulfilled the ultimatum. All the prisoners were taken to the beach near Klandasan, were ordered into the shallow water and then shot or stabbed to death. The natives had to watch the massacre.

Life continued more or less peaceful in the mountains. Willi spent much time studying native customs. On May 27th their "djongos", Mas Pawiro, told him that he felt sorry for the kris the "tuan" had, since they had not been fed for a long time. According to the Javanese, kris have souls, and, therefore, need to be fed from time to time. They ate like the gods did, incense and the sweet scent of flower petals, "sari". The blade of the kris had to be protected by a sarong, a sheath, preferably made of wood, sometimes of silver. The souls of kris were called "empu", and were the souls of the smiths who had made the blades. Mas Pawiro offered to feed all of Willi's kris on his behalf. The sheath was removed from the blade and placed in the smoke of sweet smelling incense. It was then rubbed with lemon juice, flowers and "warangan", arsenic, which was left on the blade overnight. Kris, Mas Pawiro said, had to be fed two to three times a month. Willi sat on the floor next to his "djongos" and observed Mas Pawiro carefully. He picked up one of the old kris, looked at it sadly, and said that it was almost dead, "stenga mati". He shook his head saying that it had not eaten in a long time, probably for a whole year. With proper nutrition, though, it would be possible that it would recover. Good days to feed kris are Tuesdays, "selasa", Thursdays, "kamis", and Fridays, "djumahat". Willi took notes. He already had quite a collection of old kris and other weapons. Many of his old Javanese friends and also the "djongos" were able to determine the name of a kris by looking at the blade and immediately know who the smith had been.

Willi had already collected more than ten old kris; some were several hundred years old and were from the Madjapahit era. He also had a sword which was an old pirate weapon from the Sula islands. There were many fascinating stories associated with these ancient weapons which Willi wrote down. His friend, an expert on kris, told him the following story: If an "empu" determined that a kris was not good, he stated out loud, "This is not a good kris," then crushed the metal with his hands whereby water flowed from the blade and only a small amount of iron remained.

There was still an "empu", a maker of kris, in Kendung, between Tjepu and Ngawi. Kris were always handed down to the oldest son. Younger sons could receive a kris from an older brother only by consent of the father. Javanese will not buy outside kris because of possible curses and bad luck which might accompany such an heirloom.

THE PRINCE PIG

On Willi's 31st birthday, June 3rd, 1942, early in the morning, he and Jakob went to Pringgodani on the slopes of the volcano to check the traps they had set the day before to catch wild pigs. Food was beginning to dwindle and more meat was needed. It was not going to be an easy task as they were forbidden to have any kind of weapons. The two had made a contraption with a hook, in hopes that they would catch a pig. They made the hook from metal scraps they had found and hid it inside a banana. They concluded that if the pig ate the banana the hook would be swallowed and the pig would get tangled in the wire. They had even attached a small bell at the end of the wire, so the ringing would alert them that they had caught a pig! The two men climbed the mountain side full of excitement and anticipation. The bait was gone. The hook had been too small, the pig had eaten the banana, probably carefully avoiding the hook, and then just walked off. The two friends were not giving up, so they set the hooks again and built another trap. They were desperate for some meat and were willing to try anything. This time they were going to catch dinner with a sling. The night before they had carefully devised their plans and Willi made a sketch of the contraption.

Around the slopes of the volcano Lawu there were many wild pigs. It was virtually impossible to hunt these wild animals without rifles, which, of course, had been taken from them. One day the two built another trap and dug a large hole in the soft volcanic tuff about six feet long and wide enough to hold a good sized pig. The trap was covered with twigs and they carefully placed bananas in the middle. As soon as a pig tried to get to the treat it would definitely fall into their trap, they thought. In the evenings the two men went home exhausted. Each morning they returned full of expectations, armed with long bamboo sticks in case they had to give the animal its final death blow. When they arrived at the trap, the bananas were again gone, but the trap was empty. They had more bananas with them and again placed them in the middle on the twigs. This time they decided to stay for a while. They found a hiding place far enough away, but where they still could see the trap. After a while rustling was heard in the undergrowth, but no pig came. A tiny mouse carefully approached the bananas, then another, and another. Soon an entire mouse family was eating the bananas which disappeared at a fast rate. Again, they had failed, but they were not giving up. The next morning they returned to the site with a long rope; this was going to be the sling trap they had so carefully planned. A small tree was bent toward the ground, the rope was attached, anchored into the trap, and a loop was at the end of the rope. Again they used bananas as bait. They built the trap next to a game path they had discovered some time earlier, and they were sure that they would be successful this time. They decided to wait for a while and sat down on a fallen tree trunk. A group of black mountain monkeys swung from tree top to tree top. There were so many monkeys jumping in the canopies of the trees that it sounded as if a storm wind were blowing through the jungle. After some time the two men decided to leave and began to descend the mountain.

They had walked for several minutes when Jakob said to Willi, "Did we remember to put the bananas on the trap?"

Willi was not absolutely certain either, so Jakob went back to check it while Willi waited.

All of a sudden he heard Jakob call, "Hey, come quickly and help me."

Willi jumped to his feet and ran up the hill. He reached the trap and there hung Jakob, upside down, his leg caught in the noose. Their trap had worked! Jakob had forgotten where it was and stepped on it. Willi pulled the little tree down and released his friend from his precarious position. They baited the trap again, secured it, and left. When they returned the next morning there was no pig hanging in the tree. For weeks they faithfully climbed the mountain, devised more traps, but never caught a pig.

Time went by. Willi was able to buy several more kris in a small town called Klaten. His friend told him that it was a good kris to fight battles, or, if a person encountered a tiger, fire would spew from its point. The other kris, a Sapointen from Mataram supposedly brought success and fortune to business people. Soon thereafter, all the kris had to be cleaned again and

Willi made more observations, carefully writing everything in his small notebook. According to the "adat", the laws, cleansing should only be done by older, more mature men, forty to fifty years of age. Mas Pawiro told Willi that he knew how to clean kris, but felt that he was too young for some of them. He was about thirty-one years old, the same age as Willi. If someone attempted to clean a strong kris when he was too young, he could turn blind. The soul of the kris will be insulted and blind the person out of revenge. Willi had many very strong kris and it was better to have an older person do the cleaning.

Willi began writing down his notes in Swiss dialect, which was much more difficult than German and also much harder to read. They had been warned to be very careful about writing things down; the Japanese had a habit of going through homes looking for diaries or notes, and then punishing the people whose names they read. Willi and several of his friends traveled to Surabaya on June 21st. Fortunately, they encountered no problems along the way. All the bridges destroyed by bombs had been rebuilt. They met their old friend Denner and another Swiss. The two men had only recently been able to leave Balikpapan. It had taken them seventeen days from Tarakan, traveling on a small prau, a Malay boat with a large triangular sail and a canoe-like outrigger. They told many stories. Three company employees had been killed. Fifty people died during the Tarakan battle. The Japanese attacked at night using knives and hand grenades. The Dutch soldiers shot blindly which gave away their location and they were attacked. The "ones with the sun" only lost about fifty to sixty men. On April 27th the first tank of Tarakan oil had been blown up. All women and children were evacuated from Tarakan in May, but later the Dutch sent for their families. The women and children were put in concentration camps, their homes were plundered. In Bandjarmasin, Peter met Dr. Weiss of the Basel mission. So far, all the missionaries were doing well, and were receiving money to continue their work. Peter was returning with Willi and Jakob to join his wife. While in Surabaya they also met with the Swiss consular representative who was still trying to help get them out of the war zone and back to Switzerland. On their way home they stopped in Malang. Things seemed to be normal, but it was very noticeable that all the Europeans had disappeared from the cities. The Swiss men stayed at the hotel Splendid, and, except for four women, were the only European guests. Several Japanese army and navy officers were also staying at the hotel, making the Swiss feel very uncomfortable. They went back to Surabaya the next day and then traveled on to Solo. There they met a Swiss who came to Indonesia in 1917 and who had never returned to his homeland. His name was Stauber. During his youth he worked in the bank of Willi's home town and they had many mutual acquaintances. Stauber ran a rubber plantation near Pekalongan and had very little contact with other Swiss. When Willi addressed him in Swiss dialect, the old man was so happy that he could barely talk. The encounter reminded Willi of a popular Swiss song: *"When I was far from you, oh Helvetia (Switzerland), often I was overcome by deep sorrow, but many a time it turned to joy, when I saw a son of yours".*

After having been gone for several days, Willi was glad to be back with Leny and the girls. He did not like leaving them. Life continued in a more or less peaceful manner, there was not much to do. Foremost on their minds was their concern to have enough food. A week after his return, he and Jakob went back to the Pringgodani mountain for yet another attempt at catching a wild pig. More hooks had been made to build another trap. On the sunny tree-less slopes they saw many ground orchids and the Javanese Edelweiss, Anaphalis javanica. They worked for hours building another trap and returned tired and hungry in the evening. When the sun was rising the next morning they climbed the mountain slopes once more. On their way they saw a beautiful fat pig, but without a gun it was impossible to get it. They were so hungry for meat that their stomachs growled just looking at the animal. Again, not a single pig was attached to a hook! One banana had been eaten, but the hook was on the ground several feet away. Mosquitoes descended on them and sucked their blood. Dark brown squirrels with thin tails and three stripes over the heads, backs and tails jumped from tree to tree. In the thick underbrush they came upon fresh foot prints of a large panther. A short while later they heard its roar, it was very close. For days in a row they climbed the mountain at dawn to check on the traps. Mice always ate the bait. Once they saw an abandoned nest of a wild sow. The nests were usually about nine feet in diameter and were made of twigs. Hunters always approached the nests with great care because if the piglets were still inside, the sow would be nearby, attacking anything that came near. Wild pigs were considered to be dangerous animals and the two men were always cautious. For a while they watched some black monkeys and then went home, disappointed that again they had been unsuccessful in catching a pig.

Several weeks later a Javanese who heard of Willi's interest in kris stopped by with a nice but very rusty Madjapahit Tjala Kulpuntut kris. Mas Pawiro checked it for Willi and told him that it possessed great magical powers. If it were taken into the jungle and a tiger was near, it would release itself from its sheath and kill the tiger. Willi bought it and later placed it on his desk near the window. The next day Mas Pawiro told him that the kris was indeed very strong; he had seen it light up the dark room and saw a small upright green flame near the window. He was certain that the light came from the kris.

A few days later all the Swiss were invited to a "slamatan" in the village Pantjot. About fifteen attended, it was a feast given in their honor by the natives. Everyone gathered below the "waringin" tree. There were baskets filled with food, rice, baked chickens, vegetables and more. The food was carried to the altar. A container made of brass was filled with water into which flowers and petals were placed. Incense was burning to bring forth the gods and then the people asked the gods for good fortune. A banana leaf was filled with sweet smelling flowers, "wangi," and placed on the altar. Native men were seated next to the altar, one of them talked to the gods. Every now and then the other men answered in unison, saying yes, "nge." Following the ceremony food was brought from the sacrificial hut and all were invited to eat the consecrated food. The remainder of the meal was divided into portions for each villager to take home. After the meal was over, a "wajang orang" performance took place under the "waringin" tree. One of the actors wore a tiger mask surrounded by peacock feathers, it was the "borongan" who danced ahead of the arriving group. The mask was the same one used during wedding ceremonies.

A few days later, Willi and Leny traveled to Solo. They sent a telegram to their family in Switzerland and then walked around the town. They bought another kris in a store filled with artifacts. It was a Rentjong Atjeh. The sheath had decorations of gold. They also bought vegetable seeds. As soon as they returned home, Willi began to prepare the vegetable garden. He planted lettuce, parsley and cabbage. The "djongos" helped him, and showed him how to build terraces. A few days later some of the seeds had already germinated. The weather was ideal; in the day time it was warm and sunny, at night there was usually a light rainfall. They received notice from the Swiss consul on that day, telling them that he had arrived safely in Tokyo. They were upset, now there no longer was an official Swiss diplomat and they felt that they had been abandoned by the one person who could have helped. The man was now far away from the occupied islands, while the Swiss families were more or less left to fend for themselves.

August 1st was the Swiss national holiday, the official Japanese date was 2602. All the families from Tawangmangu and Sarangan gathered in the morning to go to Tjemoro Sewu, halfway up the Lawu, to celebrate their national holiday. They had butchered a pig which they had bought in the village and roasted over an open fire for about three hours. Everyone brought a surprise, they had cookies, strawberry punch, cakes, herb brandy, roasted chicken and more. Everyone had scraped and saved small amounts of flour and other ingredients to prepare the special treats. They ate and drank a lot and played games. Swiss flags were hung on trees at the edge of the jungle, but, of course, they also had to hang the flag with the rising sun. They had to get special permission for the celebration because gatherings of groups were strictly forbidden by the Japanese. There were a total of twenty-six Swiss, including the children, who celebrated their national holiday on the tropical volcano of east Java in the middle of a war. It was a nice day, and for all of them probably the nicest first of August they had celebrated in Netherlands East Indies. The mountain air was very pleasant, after all, they were at an elevation of over 5,000 feet above sea level. They had built a large fire, as was usually done in the Swiss mountains on this day and the flames kept them warm. The mountains reminded them of their homeland far away. For a brief moment they tried to forget that they were living in the middle of a war on a foreign island far from their beloved native soil.

Willi frequently walked to the nearby village to visit his native friend Pandirdjo. He was about thirty years old and was considered to be invulnerable by the villagers. After a stabbing during his youth when three people were killed, he was arrested and sent to Sumatra as a so-called "chain-bear." This happened some time ago during the Dutch government. Prisoners became the servants of Dutch military officers. During the day they had to perform their duties and at night were shackled with chains; hence the name chain-bears. After completing his prison term, Pandirdjo returned to his village, he had seen the world, was well mannered, and he had earned the respect of the villagers. He lived in a large bamboo house with his family. Willi and Leny were often invited to share a meal with him. Occasionally, Willi lent him some silver coins if he had not yet been able to sell his beans or his garlic. In return, he often let Willi ride one of his small mountain horses and Willi was glad when he could ask him for advice. The man knew all about the many temples and relics nearby, and he was an expert on Javanese kris. One particular day the two men again sat cross-legged on the floor of the hut and talked. Willi told him about the many wild pigs, "tjeleng," he and Jakob had seen in Pringgodani, and their attempts at setting traps to catch one. Pandirdjo looked at Willi with a shocked expression on his face when he heard that they were trying to catch wild pigs in Pringgodani, and he told Willi that one may not hunt in Pringgodani, the pigs were all enchanted people, and if a pig were killed by someone then that person would have to die. He also said that one of the pigs was actually a prince. The prince pig was small and was black and white. The man was very serious and Willi respected his concerns. Actually, Willi and Jakob had noticed that the natives never hunted pigs in that particular area which was probably why there were so many. They had seen herds of twenty to thirty wild pigs at a time. The jungle ground often appeared to have been plowed. Pandirdjo suggested that Willi contact a local hunter. The man he mentioned hunted with spears and dogs, and knew exactly where there were no enchanted pigs. They talked a while longer and then Pandirdjo took Willi to see the hunter Wongso. After telling him all about hunting, Wongso promised that he would bring him a pig real soon. He also explained his hunting technique. The dogs chased the pig and cornered it, and then the animal was killed with a spear. If the pig did not die right away, then Wongso made use of his sacred weapon. It was the handle of a bronze mirror with Sanskrit lettering. He had found it many years ago in the ruins of a Hindu temple. Only a few days later, Wongso and his three helpers arrived at Willi's house, a dead pig hanging from poles the men carried on their shoulders. Coffee was served, cigarettes were handed out and the dealing began. The sow weighed about sixty pounds eviscerated. Now they had to determine the price. The natives always bartered, the whole deal took time, they smoked, drank coffee and talked. An agreement was often not reached for as long as several hours. After bartering and talking for about three hours, they finally agreed on a price; five and a half Guilders in silver coins. Then Wongso said that he still needed to take the left ear and the left front foot to be sacrificed to the gods on the mountain where they hunted so the next hunt would also be successful. Of course, Willi agreed, the necessary parts were cut off and the four Javanese left. Apparently, the hunters had been content with the transaction; two days later they appeared again with another pig. What a welcome change it was to have fresh meat. The Swiss men now decided since they had plenty of meat, they were going to make sausages. None of them knew exactly how this was done nor how much salt had to be added to the meat. They traveled to Surakarta to buy intestines and a small meat grinder. A funnel was attached to the grinder. They spent hours grinding the meat. The skins were placed over the funnel and the meat was pushed directly inside. Finally they had forty nice sausages. Now they were ready to smoke them. The sausages were attached to wires, Willi climbed on the roof and hung them inside the chimney. They burned wood day and night. After four days they pulled the sausages out to check if they were done. Willi was surprised, the sausages were three times as thick as they had been when they were made. He punctured one of them and the whole thing collapsed; all were ruined. They soon figured out what they had done wrong; not enough salt had been used and the meat had gone bad. They dug a large hole in the back yard and buried the whole mess. Everyone stood around the grave, burying the sausages was as somber as a funeral. Only a few days later Wongso and his helpers brought another pig. The men did the entire process over again; they ground the meat until their arms almost fell off. The next batch was finally ready, this time they had added enough salt. The meat was spiced with coriander, cumin and garlic, and they became experts at making delicious smoked sausages. Often, the Swiss families gathered at one of the homes, or a visitor arrived from the other side of the mountain, and then they served home baked bread, smoked sausages and strawberry brandy. More pigs arrived. Willi marinated his portion with a mixture of salt, pepper, nutmeg, bay leaves, onions and garlic, and cooked the meat for about ten minutes. The "kokki" made "denden," the meat was cut into strips and then placed in the sun. When it was dry it was hung up until the meat was completely dry, and it could then be preserved for some time. She often served "denden" with a rice table.

On August 4th Willi's notes in his diary were again written in the Swiss dialect. A Japanese had visited him. He was an officer and had just arrived from Balikpapan. He even spoke English. He was well informed about conditions in Balikpapan, and knew the names of all the employees who used to work there. He wore the uniform of a marine and was an engineer. He offered Willi a job to work for them. Willi told him that he was a paleontologist. This was fine, the man said, he could pursue his career as paleontologist if he came to work for them. Willi, who felt very ill at ease, and who was not certain what to make of the visit, told the officer that he would not leave his family. The Japanese bowed curtly and left the house.

Mas Pawiro must have felt that Willi was a good kris owner; he sold him two that had belonged to his grandmother who had died and Mas Pawiro had inherited them. His grandmother's funeral cost him one hundred Guilders, a lot of money for someone who earned about six to ten Guilders a month. He had borrowed the money from the village bank, but it had to be paid off within two weeks. As dictated by the "adat", and he was the male heir, he had inherited the two kris.

DEATH OF A SALVATION ARMY OFFICER

Time passed slowly. Willi worked in his vegetable garden, made sausages, and tried to keep busy. Leny had her hands full with their two small children. They went on long walks, and Willi taught the girls about the interesting flora and fauna even though they were still very young. Their life was quite peaceful in the mountains. Then in mid-August the Swiss families received a form to be filled out for their speedy evacuation to Switzerland. They wanted to leave the occupied area and return to their homeland. Later that same evening, Pandirdjo stopped by for a visit. He brought a kris he wanted to sell to Willi. It was a Senglat Marjatjaran and was supposed to protect its owner from robbers. He told Willi that if a thief enters a house, the kris begins to knock. Willi knew that during the looting earlier that year, kris were never touched, and often were the only items left in a house after the place had been totally ransacked.

Willi and his friend Peter Denner decided to go on a hike to Pablengan Djurangdjeru to see the mineral wells and gas eruptions. It was a well known bathing place and one of the wells was even considered to be sacred. It was called "ajer latung." They took water and soil samples. Later on the two men walked to Matiseh to a pawn shop. Willi bought two more kris and two wajang figures. All the pawn shops were filled with treasures and many ethnographic artifacts. They spent hours in the store, admiring the many interesting items. People needed the money and sold their treasures to buy food to survive the terrible war. Willi and Leny had to spend their money carefully; they too only had the emergency money the company had given them at the onset of the war and the money they had saved, but they were not employed and had no income.

Toward the end of August a group of friends set out to climb to the top of the volcano Lawu. Willi found out much interesting information about the mountain from his native friends. According to legend, the volcano was once called Wukir Maendro. An illegitimate son of the king of Madjapahit and one of his under-wives, Djaka Kebuk, had no right to the throne. He fled to the top of the mountain where he intended to spend the rest of his life, taking his wife along. One of his brothers searched for him, eventually finding him living on top of the volcano. The brother elevated him to Sunan Lawu. Sunan Lawu built structures, temples and walls surrounding the terraces. Daily Sunan Lawu prayed on the peak of the Arga Tiling and he went there to die. After his death, his wife who was renamed Retna Dumilah lived on the highest peak of the mountain until she too died. The Gunung Lawu has three peaks, the Arga Dumilah, the Arga Tiling, and the Arga Blunka; all are over nine thousand feet above sea level. Just below the Arga Dumilah was another sacrificial stone called Selo Pundutan. The natives called it "the stone of wishes," and believed it possessed mystical powers.

The small group was accompanied by three mountain guides. They were all on horseback. Before taking off, the guides advised the group that nothing of green color was ever allowed on the mountain. No green hat, no clothing of green color, not even a green pencil; they considered the Lawu to be a holy mountain. The people lived by strict rules and beliefs, and Willi felt strongly that when one lived in a foreign country one should try to live by the customs and rules, whether one believed in them or not. A young Swedish Salvation Army officer, who had also fled to the mountains when the Japanese invaded the island, joined the group. He had on green pants and the guides pointed this out to him. He was told that he would insult the gods of the Lawu and would then have to die. The Swede replied that he was a Christian and did not believe in the superstition, he would take the risk. The guides became extremely agitated, they were convinced that an accident would happen. Finally, the group left. At six in the morning they had already reached Tjemara Sewu, where they had celebrated their national holiday. An hour later they were at Kawa Tamansari. The path became steeper, they had to leave the horses behind and continue on foot. There were many interesting stone and terrace relics. The view from the top was beautiful. Below them they saw the temple Tjandi Sukuh they had visited not too long ago. The vegetation on top of the volcano consisted mostly of grassy bushes. Another Hindu temple was near the peak, the Sokro Srengini. Near the tourist hut was another temple, the Arga Dumilah. The guides carried the food which was cooked over an open coal fire. Everyone enjoyed a delicious meal on top of the beautiful mountain, looking down at the surrounding areas and rice paddies. They were tired from the hike and the mountain air, and soon retired for the night. Willi and Leny went outside one more time. The night air was cool, all they saw was the black sky speckled with millions of bright stars. They stood for some time taking in the peace and quiet on top of the mystical and beautiful volcano. The trip had been fascinating and interesting and nothing had happened. They arose early the next morning. After a hot cup of coffee and rice cakes for breakfast they began their descent and returned to Tawangmangu in the early afternoon.

The following day the young Salvation Army officer was dead. The Europeans said that he died of a heart attack; the natives were convinced that the white man had insulted the gods of the Lawu and had to die because he had carried something green onto the sacred mountain. The belief came about that green was the color of the prophet Mohammed. The Hindu king had to flee to the mountains when the Moslems arrived. It was also forbidden to mention Allah's name on the Lawu because the people from the Madjapahit dynasty had to flee the Islam. They settled on the Lawu and built the many temples.

Willi and Leny also often went to the nearby small mountain towns higher up. The "desas," as the villages were called, were very clean, and the people were friendly. They never ran into any Japanese, the paths leading to the small villages were very narrow and only passable on foot or on horseback. In the lower regions they saw the people working the rice fields, in areas above twenty-seven hundred feet they grew garlic, beans and onions. The mountain people were very frugal and hard working.

THE SACRED ZODIAC CUP

They also traveled to Djokjakarta and Kaliurang on the slopes of another volcano, the Gunung Merapi where they planned to visit one of their favorite stores, the antique business of Den Held who was known for his exclusive pieces. They found the wife alone in the store; her husband had been arrested by the Japanese. She showed them a zodiac cup from the Tengger mountain region which she offered to sell them for twenty-five Guilders. A Japanese officer wanted to buy the piece, offering her the same amount but in Japanese occupational currency. He would probably return for it, and under no circumstances did she want the rare piece to end up in Japan. There were only very few of the zodiac sacrificial cups still in existence. The mold from which it had been cast no longer existed. Leny and Willi knew that they were looking at an exceptionally rare artifact. They debated for a long time whether or not they could afford to buy it. After all, they were in the middle of a war, they were not employed, and had no idea how long the Japanese occupation would last. After giving it careful thought, they decided to buy it. At home, Willi looked up the information on this rare piece in his encyclopedia. It described a zodiac cup as a container made of bronze or copper from the era of the Madjapahit dynasty, the Hindu empire which reigned from 1293 to 1520 AD. During that time, the cups were used in the Tengger mountains. The Javanese name "perasen" was derived from the Indian word "rasi" which means zodiac. The containers have a flat base, the sides extend straight upward, extending outward at the top. On the inside of the base there is an eight-pointed embossed star or a four-petaled flower. The distinctive marks are the twelve signs of the zodiac which appear embossed on the lower side on the outside of the cup. Some of the signs are different than what westerners are accustomed to.

On their cup they appear as follows: *1. Aries: a goat with curved horns and goat's beard; 2. Taurus: a Brahma bull with a huge hump; 3. Gemini: two horseshoe crabs (Limulus). This is the symbol for twins in Java because they are always found in pairs; 4. Cancer: a crab; 5. Leo: a legendary animal standing on its hind legs with large fangs and huge eyes; lions do not exist in India or in Indonesia; 6. Virgo: a seated woman; 7. Libra: a scale with beam balance with two pans; 8. Scorpio: a scorpion; 9. Sagittarius: drawn bow and arrow; 10. Capricorn: a prawn with long antennae; 11. Aquarius: a water urn with a wide middle part; 12. Pisces: a fish with the head of an elephant.*

Some zodiac cups are dated. The dates refer to the Sjaka date calculation of ancient Scythia (the ancient nomadic people from the region north of the Black Sea who lived from the 9th to 2nd century BC). This time calculation was brought to Java by the Hindus and began in the year 78 AD. The zodiac cup depicts the symbol of a legendary figure located above the Gemini sign (the pair of horseshoe crabs). It is dated from 1321 to 1430 AD. Over the zodiac signs there are figures of human and animal legend symbols; they resemble the Javanese "wajang" figures. Above the sign of the Sagittarius is a bird, and above the bird a half-star which represents the sun. Above each sign is the symbol of its god. Zodiac cups are still used at weddings, funerals and fertility ceremonies in the Tengger region. They are filled with holy water and flower petals. The priest "dukun" uses this holy water to sanctify the sick, newly weds, the dead and during offerings. Simultaneously, he moves an incense holder back and forth. The priest chants prayers during the ceremonies, which start with either a Hindu "mantra" or Arabic "dowa" incantation. In all the small towns of the Tengger mountains, remains of the Madjapahit dynasty were still around. The priests lived in seclusion and their rites resembled those of Brahma priests. Each priest had an old zodiac cup. According to belief, the dead pass through the purgatory on the volcano Bromo and later arrive at the heavenly mountain Smeru, the residence of Brahma.

THE SORROW OF A PSYCHIC MOTHER

The weeks went by and September arrived. The Swiss often received messages about their acquaintances and friends who had to stay behind in Borneo. Willi and Leny were concerned as to what had happened to Willi's two assistants, Silatus and Deloten. When the war began they were called into the army and had probably not been able to leave Borneo. A strange thing happened to Willi at the vacation resort Kaliurang at the foot of the volcano Merapi. The parents of Silatus lived there, and Willi had promise him before he left Borneo that he would visit them. He went to their house to tell them that their son sent his best regards. Unfortunately, eight months had gone by since he had last seen him.

When Willi met the parents, the mother said to him, "Our son no longer lives." She was a short woman with native features. She sadly continued to tell Willi, "He died at the edge of a tapioca field in the arms of his colleague Deloten. He was burning up with fever and was having a severe malaria attack. His head rolled from side to side and his lips were parched from thirst."

Of course, Willi tried to console the family. No one had been able to receive official news about their son. One of the daughters took Willi aside and whispered that her mother was a psychic; on the day her son had died she had experienced every detail of his last moments in Borneo hundreds of miles away. Willi was full of doubt when he left, but promised to return as soon as he was able to find out anything reliable about their son.

The middle of September Willi was already harvesting tomatoes and radishes. His garden had grown, he had planted beans, potatoes, onions, cabbage and more. Wongso and his hunters brought pigs routinely, and the men and women made sausages, cured bacon, cut the meat for roasts and chops. Also, on September 12th fifty bags of flour arrived from the Japanese administration for the Swiss families. Everyone was overjoyed, they could bake bread again because the flour had run out. On that same day a letter arrived from the Swiss consular representative in Batavia. It stated:

Regarding repatriating Swiss citizens, we have received notice from the Swiss Embassy in Tokyo requesting that the Swiss colony be informed of its content. I am honored to forward the content of this letter as follows: Considering the present conditions, the return to Switzerland from the Far East of Swiss citizens is to be avoided. Even though a voyage could be arranged, a safe return would be questionable due to blockades and contra-blockades. Also, the returning Swiss will feel embarrassed upon encountering great disappointment in their homeland, since they will not find work or anything to do. The fact that the Political Department is presently unable to realize the return of Swiss citizens does in no way mean that our government does not have concerns for its Swiss citizens in the Far East, and that we do not have understanding for the problems they encounter. On the contrary, the Political Department is willing to help and to assist its citizens according to necessity. The government prefers to assist the compatriots in the area where they were previously employed, where, after all, the Swiss will be better able to look after their personal interests. In order to successfully accomplish this, it is necessary that the compatriots not depart from their prior employment area, and to wait until they can again commence with their work. As long as it is not absolutely necessary to live in groups, as had been considered in some areas, the Political Department does not recommend this measure. It recommends to its citizens to try to continue to live a normal life, and is certain that only a quiet, dignified conduct can pave the road for the future. Signed: Swiss Consulate in Batavia.

They were stunned. Once again they felt that their country had abandoned them. But, life continued. Willi smoked more pork and hung the meat in the chimney. Every day he worked in the vegetable garden. The terraces were easy to water. So far, he had planted one hundred seventy cabbage plants, two hundred fifty heads of lettuce, one hundred twenty tomato plants, about two hundred each strawberry plants, peas, spinach, onions, rhubarb, peppers and radishes. The vegetables had to feed more than twenty people.

The end of September Willi and Peter returned to the limestone cave near Karangloh to do some excavating. When they reached a depth of about twelve to fifteen inches, they found a compact layer of fragments and shards. The cave was quite large and high up on the mountain. Willi had been planning on digging at the site since May when he had already found some shards. He was especially interested in finding silex artifacts. They found two pieces and an old andesite rice grinder. It turned late so they went home. They returned a couple of days later to take some measurements. The two men had been working for some time when an old native came to see them. He watched silently for some time and then warned them to be careful; their measuring tools could be viewed by a Japanese as radio equipment they were hiding in the cave. One never knew and there were many spies around. Willi and Peter thanked the old man for his concern and for warning them, heeded his advice, and continued on to Matiseh. The risk was too great in case a Japanese spy did come to the remote area and saw them. Europeans were being arrested more and more, some were incarcerated and tortured.

On October 8th Willi's notes in his diary were again written in Swiss. They had just received the first one hundred percent trustworthy news via jungle runners from Borneo. Unfortunately, the death of Willi's kind and good assistant, Silatus, was now confirmed. He had died of malaria in the jungle of Borneo, and Deloten was imprisoned in Bandjarmasin. The Swiss also received official confirmation of the tragic news that all the Red Cross employees, including the medical personnel from Balikpapan, had been executed by the Japanese. After most people had left, the Red Cross employees were ordered to stay, even though the Japanese had threatened to kill everyone. Willi and the others had already heard rumors about the massacre, but it was the first time that it had been officially confirmed. As Willi had promised, he returned to Kaliurang to bring the sad news of the death of Silatus to his family. Willi knew that the father had a heart condition, so before going to the family's house, he went to see the physician to ask for advice. He told Willi not to worry and to go ahead and go there since the family was convinced that the mother's predictions about her son's death were true. When Willi entered the house, the father collapsed; he had a mild heart attack from which he fortunately recuperated fully in a few hours.

The mother said to Willi, "I know it because I experienced every detail of my son's death."

Some weeks later Willi and Jakob again left for Solo to get more flour, lard and oil. Via the Swiss consular representative they received one hundred twenty cans of lard and sixteen cans of oil which were divided among the Swiss families living in the mountains of Java. Later that evening Wongso brought two more pigs. Willi and Jakob had just arrived from Solo, they were tired and worn out, but they had to cure the meat right away and worked until late into the night.

INCENSE AND FLOWERS FOR THE DAGGERS

October 11th was one of the three yearly big Javanese celebrations, the "garebeg puwasa" to observe the end of the fasting month. The entire population participated in the festivities, gamelan music was heard everywhere. Mas Pawiro told Willi that he needed to pay tribute to his many pusaka (heirlooms), and that he should offer them incense and sari. It was interesting to Willi that not only the kris, tumbaks, knives, etc. of Javanese origin were given offerings, but also his Swiss army knife, his geologist hammer, and his butcher knives; all metal knives and tools were brought offerings. Mas Pawiro said that he would again do it on Willi's behalf. He placed all the kris in a row according to their rank. Pusaka described not only kris, but any heirloom, and each piece was treated with great reverence. A pusaka is a fetish, and it was believed that the souls of persons who lived in times past lived on in the pusaka. First, Mas Pawiro burned incense to call forth the spirits. He then informed them that he wished to make an offering on Willi's behalf. Each blade was held over the smoke of the incense, starting with the oldest. He knew the names of each blacksmith and each was greeted individually. Following the incense, a floral offering consisting of flower petals was made on which perfumed water was sprinkled. He then placed the petals on the blades. According to belief, a regular person could not see how the kris ate. The Javanese prepared for the ceremonies by fasting for three days and three nights. They did not sleep, eat or drink, and were then able to see the souls of kris as persons. Mas Pawiro saw and recognized them, and could see how they inhaled the aroma of the incense and the flowers. From time to time the kris had to undergo a cleansing so that the striations in the dark patinated blades would be visible. This was done yearly during the Javanese new year celebration. The blade was placed in a mixture of coconut milk and the fruit of the plant Morinda citrifolia. This mixture was called "kudu" or "menkudu." The kris were then rubbed with a mixture of arson sulfide, called "warangan," and lemon juice which brought out the dark and light designs on the blade called "pamor." The regular iron turned black after it had been treated with the mixture, whereas the meteor iron remained light colored. After the cleansing of the kris a special celebration was held. Later that same evening Mas Pandirdjo came for a visit with his wife to wish Willi and Leny a happy new year. He brought about twenty bananas, two rice cakes and a butchered chicken. They had on their best clothes, his wife wore five gold pins on her blouse and a golden pin in her hair.

THE DIENG PLATEAU

About a week later Willi and Peter went to Wonosobo. It was going to be quite a journey, they traveled via Djokja, Magelang, Parakan to Wonosobo. They stopped at a Swiss hotel, the Montagne, in Magelang. The owner offered them a glass of real Swiss Kirsch, the brandy made of cherries. The taste brought back fond memories of their homeland, and they sipped the rare treat to savor every drop. They met another Swiss who was a vanilla grower. After leaving Wonosobo they traveled on a horse drawn cart to go to the Dieng plateau. It took only three hours to reach Kedjadjar, thanks to the two little horses pulling the cart. Willi met the same guide he had two years earlier when he and Christian visited the plateau. They gave him a lift to the top. It took another two and a half hours to reach the Pasan Graham cabin. The entire plateau was farmland; daisies were being harvested, as well as leek, barley, wheat and oats. The farmers used horse manure to fertilize their crops, and the small mountain horses were mainly kept for this natural fertilizer. Willi was curious who had imported the wheat and other vegetables to the area. Every time he asked a native, they always replied, "Tuan William". It must have been a European. Even though most of the Europeans had been arrested and put in concentration camps, they were curious to find out more about this "Tuan William". What a surprise they had. "Tuan William" lived in a nice village house, he was dressed as a Javanese "tani," a farmer, but wore shoes. He spoke only Malay, and invited the two to sit with him by the fire; at an elevation of about 6,000 feet above sea level it was quite cool.

They told him that they were Swiss and he replied, "Saja punja papa ada djuga orang Zwitzerland." His father was from Switzerland. "Tuan William" was sixty-five years old. His father had emigrated to Holland at the age of twenty-one in the year 1870 and was then sent to Java as a soldier. He retired when he was about forty years old and was sent to the Dieng Plateau as an overseer. He married a Javanese woman and his children were raised in the village. He died in 1923, at the age of seventy-four. His son, William, became a farmer. He grew mostly tobacco, and over the years had imported many vegetables. Willi and Peter met several of his children, they all spoke Dutch and had learned a profession. One of his sons was an architect who had designed most of the new houses in Tawangmangu.

They spent the night in a small guest house, and the following day studied and admired the temples and stone reliefs of the ancient temple city; there was not a single stone that did not have some design on it.

The Dieng Plateau is part of the Prahu massif, and in pre-historic times there must have been a tremendous destructive eruption, covering the entire area with molten lava. Temples were built on the plateau during the Hindu era, with temple cities to honor and worship the Hindu deity Siva and there were dwellings for the priests. They represent the most ancient relics found in Java; the oldest inscription found was dated Sjaka 731. Stairs led up to the terrace relics at one time, but only few remained. There were numerous solfatara, volcanic seas, cold and hot wells, caves and grottos. The name Dieng was probably derived from the word "di'hijang," golden mountain. It was considered to be the holiest place in all of Java. They shuddered when they looked at the boiling and hissing volcanic mass of the solfatara. Many bathers used the wells for medicinal purposes. Late in the afternoon they started on their descent back to the valley to Wonosobo. On their way home they spent a day in Kopeng on the slopes of the Merbabu. They met Dr. Lang and other Swiss families. From Kopeng they went to Salatiga, Bojolali, Solo and then back to Tawangmangu. It took them two days to get home.

THE BUDDHIST TEMPLE BOROBUDUR

Only a few weeks later Willi embarked on yet another trip, this time accompanied by Leny. They were going to the famous Buddhist temple Borobudur east of Djokjakarta. It was the center of Buddhism on Java. The Borobudur was built in 800 AD. The structure consists of nine levels, four galleries, a plateau, three terraces and a main stupa. There are over a thousand reliefs depicting scenes from the life of Buddha, battle scenes, ceremonies, and more. There are over four hundred niches, all containing a statue of Buddha. The three upper levels contain seventy-two small stupas with statues of the sitting Buddha. The temple depicts the image of the Buddhist's view of life. The base of the structure is about three hundred sixty feet and ascends to about one hundred feet. At one time there were over five hundred Buddha figures at the site. Borobudur was well maintained by the Dutch until 1941. When the Japanese invaded, the maintenance stopped. Japanese Buddhists still went to the well known holy place, but there were more serious concerns than to maintain an old temple. The two traveled on horseback, the small road taking them through rice paddies and coconut plantations, through villages and past smaller temples which were probably associated with Borobudur. Especially the small temple Mendut left a deep impression on them. They stepped through a gate and entered the dimly lit temple. There was the immense statue of the sitting Buddha. The room was filled with the sweet smelling aroma of flower offerings which had been placed at his feet. His knees and toes shone brightly of the aromatic "boreh" salve. The salve was an offering and was made of coconut oil mixed with the yellow powder of the ginger root. It was also used for medicinal purposes, body care, and to ward off evil spirits. The exotic aroma could be smelled in all the temples, and it permeated the air at all the celebrations and ceremonies. Pensive men and women worshipped their Buddha and brought offerings. Upon entering the temple, the sandals were removed, the people entered silently, remained in front of the statue deep in prayer and then departed silently again. It had been another fascinating and impressive experience.

LEAVING THE MOUNTAINS

On November 2nd Willi undertook another trip to Wonosobo to see a friend who was quite ill with a tropical disease. Everywhere on the way people were busy preparing for a celebration and all the villages were decorated with Japanese flags, lanterns and banners; it was for the birthday of the empress of Japan. The lanterns were electrically illuminated and big victory banners hung from every building. The bus fares were reduced to half price during the days of celebration.

Back home Willi continued to work in his garden and make sausages. Wongso brought him a deer. The meat was divided between three families, each ended up with about twenty pounds of fresh meat. It was a nice change to eat venison after mostly only eating pork.

The middle of November Willi again went to Kaliurang. Den Held was still in a prison camp, his wife was alone. He bought a silver kris handle with ornate designs. He met several old acquaintances, everyone was getting concerned. The situation seemed to get worse, and more and more they heard of terrible acts against the Dutch and other Europeans by the Japanese. Willi was anxious to get back to his family. On the way home he somehow became infected with meat poisoning after eating "tjap tjai," a vegetable and meat dish, and he was very ill.

The end of November Willi's notations in his diary became very brief. He only wrote of the pigs Wongso brought, how many sausages were made, curing the meat, and making meat loaves. Then, on December 5th came the order that every household had to darken all the windows at night. December 8th his notation in his diary was that "they" celebrated the day in great fashion. Leny and Willi remembered the sad day a year ago when the Pacific war broke out.

Back in Switzerland Willi's parents received the following letter:
Lumina AG Shell Products, December 9, 1942.
Mrs. E. Mohler, Gelterkinden.
We hereby inquire whether you have received any information from Dr. Mohler. If this is not the case, we would like to attempt once again to find out where Dr. Mohler may be at the present time. Please let us know his last known address. We would appreciate hearing from you as soon as possible.
The telegram Willi and Leny had sent had not been received by their families.

Then, on December 13th, Willi received a letter from the Swiss consulate in Batavia, informing him that he had to pay his 1939 Swiss military taxes. The letter also stated that the notice had been delayed due to the war in Europe and poor postal services. They no longer received a salary because the Japanese had taken over their company. The emergency money had to be used very sparingly, they had to survive, and tried to live off one Dutch guilder per person per day from which they also had to pay rent and food. They were stunned that under those conditions their government actually requested they pay military taxes. The consul had moved to Tokyo shortly after the war where he was safe. More and more they felt that their own country had abandoned them, but there were more important things to worry about than to be concerned about paying military taxes; they had to survive. The Swiss were not too pleased with the consuls. The last one had been given a nickname, "peut-etre oui, peut-etre non," maybe yes, maybe no. It had come about in that a Swiss woman traveled from south Sumatra to Batavia when the war broke out. She and her husband worked on a plantation and they had two young sons. They needed advice as to what to do. Should they stay in Sumatra, or try to flee. The woman had made the long, complicated and very dangerous journey so she could seek help and at least advice from the consul.

She described their desperate situation to him and asked, "Mr. Consul, should we remain in Sumatra, or should we try to come to Java?"

The consul thought for a moment and replied, "Maybe yes, maybe no."

The woman looked at him and said, "Well, now I know what we should do. You have been a great help, Mr. Consul." She returned to Sumatra, the couple packed a few necessities and traveled to Java. They had made the right decision without any assistance from the consul. Many Swiss plantation workers were killed in Sumatra by the Japanese and by local extremists. After all, they had a white skin just like the Dutch did.

Near their home lived a Dutch woman who had two small boys. Mrs. Vrede became very ill with cancer of the breast and was in such poor health that she asked Willi and Leny to take her boys to spend time with another family in Sarangan. Her husband was somewhere in a concentration camp and she did not want her boys to see her so ill. During that time Willi had a bad infection on his left foot from a recurring eczema. It was urgent that they take the two boys to friends in Sarangan, so he and Leny left around the middle of December. The family was well know to the young children, and Willi and Leny felt also that it would be better for them to stay away for a while until the mother's health improved. The boys were happy to see their old friends and quickly settled in. Willi almost did not make the trip back. A few days after returning home he could no longer walk and had to spend the day sitting in the living room with a poultice on his foot. Medication had long run out and all the doctors had been arrested. He spent the days making Christmas decorations and toys for the girls and he could not leave the house. Friends stopped by and had devastating news. All the Dutch women and children in the area had been arrested and were taken to Solo to a school building. On Christmas day he found out more details. From Solo the women were taken to Ambarawa to a concentration camp. A few days earlier many of their Dutch friends came by bringing with them boxes and bags. They begged Willi and Leny to safeguard their valuables until the war was over. Each item was wrapped and marked with the person's name. Willi and Leny hid the packages in an old trunk. Nearby lived two women, a German and a Dutch, both were married and had children, whose behavior shocked the entire community. They were given permission by the Japanese to go to all the homes of the people who had just been arrested, and help themselves to all the furniture and personal belongings that had to be left behind. The Japanese even provided them with two trucks to transport all the stolen goods to their homes. Both women had been having affairs with Japanese officers while their husbands were being tortured somewhere in a Japanese concentration camp.

Willi was still limping, the eczema had not yet healed. Several days after Christmas Peter stopped by, he had been able to find one tablet of Cibazol. One such tablet was more valuable than gemstones or gold. Willi carefully scraped thin layers from the tablet with his pocket knife onto the infected area. The wounds began to heal, and after only a few days he was able to stand on his foot again.

Just before New Year they had quite a scare; a high ranking Japanese officer and his adjutant suddenly appeared at their front door. The man was a well known Japanese paleontology professor and knew several of Willi's old geology professors from Basel. It turned out that Willi had briefly met the man in 1936 or 1937, when he was still a geology student and the professor had visited the university. Willi had little recollection of the man; he looked so different in his uniform. All he remembered was that during that time there had been a Japanese professor visiting the geological institute in Basel. The man asked Willi to work for them in Borneo, but Willi stated that he would absolutely not leave Java. He then offered Willi jobs in Sumatra or Java, or at the geological museum in Bandung in west Java. Willi just could not quite figure out the Japanese; they always smiled, but he never knew if they were sincere or not. He stood his ground and told the Japanese that he would not leave his family.

Back in Switzerland, On December 30th, 1942, Willi's parents received the following letter:

Swiss Political Department, Division of Foreign Affairs, B.51.318. Neth. Ind. EA

Mr. Mohler, Gelterkinden.

Dear Sir, we have just been notified telegraphically by the Swiss Consulate in Tokyo, and are honored to inform you that Dr. W. Mohler and his family are in Tjepu, Java, and send you their best wishes for the new year.

Please submit payment of Swiss Francs 4.80 to cover the cost of the consulate in Tokyo to send you this notice. Please accept, dear Sir, the assurance of our respect. Chief of the Department of Foreign Affairs. An invoice is enclosed.

On new year's eve they cooked the traditional Swiss roasted flour soup and onion pot pie, for dessert they had slices of fresh pineapple. For dinner they ate potato salad made from their own potatoes and home-made pork sausages. At night, it was around eight o'clock, there was a loud knock on their door. A Japanese officer who had just returned from Balikpapan handed Willi a note from a company employee. The note contained the names of all the people who had been massacred. Several of the wives and children were still living in the colony, they had not yet been incarcerated. With sadness in their hearts, Willi and Leny had the painful task to bring the sorrowful news to the surviving family members.

Leny celebrated her thirty-third birthday with family and friends. Willi gave her a beautiful bouquet of flowers. He and the girls decorated the dining room table with pretty blossoms and leaves and they enjoyed a fine rice dish.

A few weeks later Ruth celebrated her 2nd birthday. She was a very active little girl, always tagging behind Willi in hopes of discovering an interesting worm or caterpillar.

On January 29th, 1943, another Japanese came to visit Willi. It was the director of the geological services in Bandung. Willi knew that the visit was obviously a follow-up to the professor's visit in December. He was again asked to work for the Japanese, in Bandung, where he was to do research work at the museum. It was a difficult situation for Willi. All the Swiss had previously agreed that none of them would go to an oil place; these would be the first targets of the Americans and Australians. None of this could, of course, ever be mentioned to a Japanese. Willi knew one thing for certain, he was not going to go back to Balikpapan. He also knew that the Japanese could send him anywhere they wanted to. He made it clear that under no circumstances would he leave his family or Java. Finally, he told the director that before making any decision he wanted to see the place. They agreed that he would go to Bandung on February 3rd. As soon as the Japanese left Willi went to see his Swiss friends. They sat for a long time and talked. Finally, a solution was found. If the Japanese were offering Willi a position at the geological services in Bandung he should accept the offer. All the company documents were at the museum and if Willi were to work there he could find out what happened to all the valuable papers and documentation. They would have preferred to stay in the peaceful mountains in Tawangmangu where they saw relatively few Japanese. Willi also felt that it would be safer to accept the offer to work in Bandung than to be at the mercy of the Japanese who could have sent him anywhere. After all, the Japanese had made it very clear what they thought of the Swiss and called them the neutral enemy, "musu netral." They could do with them what they wanted. After spending much time talking it over, they decided that it seemed to be the only thing to do, especially, if Willi worked in Bandung the whole family could stay together.

On February 1st, 1943, they traveled to Bandung. It was a long journey by train and took all day and all night. They talked about the day five years ago when Willi was supposed to start work and had the day off because the Dutch princess was born. They remembered how excited they had been to be going to exotic places. Never did they dream that they would end up on an island occupied by the Japanese. When the train pulled into the station in Bandung they took a taxi to the house of friends they had not seen in some time. They were invited to stay with them and were happy to be able to wash the dust off their bodies and have a good night's sleep. The following morning Willi went to the museum to meet with the Japanese director of the geological department. He was offered four hundred guilders a month, in Japanese occupational currency, and was to begin his new job on the 15th. He was briefly shown around the museum. In one of the rooms he was able to exchange some words with a well known scientist; a mammal and hominid specialist. The Japanese in the room curtly ordered Willi away from the older man, but he managed to tell him that he would see him soon. They remained in Bandung for another day and found a house to rent from a Dutch family. The children had stayed in Tawangmangu with Rosa who at the time was living with them because Otto had not yet been able to join her. As there was very little time they began packing right away. During the year they had spent in the mountains they had collected many treasures and had over twenty trunks. Hunter Wongso stopped by one more time, bringing a fat pig. Willi made smoked sausages to take with them. All their friends, both Europeans and natives, stopped by to wish them farewell. Pandirdjo was sad to see his friends go with whom he had spent so many interesting hours. Willi and Leny, too, were sad; their life had been peaceful and quiet, and they did not really know what they would encounter in Bandung.

AT THE MERCY OF THE INVADERS

They left the peaceful mountain town on February 12. People from Gun Sei Bu loaned them a truck and car for their move. Rosa went along, Otto was still in Palembang. It was a long, complicated and tiring drive and they arrived the following morning. The house they were renting was fully furnished. On February 15th, early in the morning, Willi rode his bicycle to the Mijnbouw museum, which had been renamed Kokyo Jimusho by the Japanese. He was eager to start his new job in the geological department and continue his research on paleontology. An officer escorted him to his office and left. Willi familiarized himself and organized his new workplace. After some time there was a barely audible knock on the door and Heinrich, the hominid authority, cautiously approached, glancing down the corridor to make sure that nobody saw him. They spoke for a while and after some time Heinrich showed Willi his original Java man material as well as an incredible collection of Javanese stone-age tools. Willi was in awe when he saw and touched the fossils of one of the world's oldest human remains. He and Heinrich soon became close friends. The Japanese had arrested and incarcerated him. Every morning he and several other European scientists were driven from the prison camp to the museum, they worked all day, and at night were taken back to the concentration camp. Soon after Willi began his new job, Leny made a stack of sandwiches for all the imprisoned men which Willi took to the museum every day and placed in a drawer in his desk. At around nine in the mornings, one after another of the prisoners quietly entered his office, making sure that they were not seen by the Japanese. The hungry men devoured the food. All were very thin, they only received one small meal a day consisting of a handful of rice with a tiny amount of some leafy greens. The Japanese always commented that the more enemy that died the less they would have

110

to shoot or decapitate. Leny tried to make the sandwiches as healthy as possible, piling meat, tomatoes, cheese and butter between the slices. Unfortunately, after only a few days, the Japanese discovered the snacks and forbid Willi to ever bring food into the museum again.

Life in Bandung was completely different from the peaceful and more or less tranquil year they had spent in Tawangmangu. Things were more hectic and nervous, and they constantly heard the most incredible and distressing rumors, never knowing what was true, and what was not. There were no radios or newspapers.

At the museum Willi was completely left on his own as to the work he did and it was up to him to decide what he wanted to do. He stayed busy exploring the museum and discovered drawers filled with fossils, old books and documents. He was very interested in the mineral material the government geologists had collected in central Borneo. Also of special interest was the collection of a Swiss geologist who had worked for the government during the 1920's.

THE JAVA-MAN SKULL IN THE STEGODON SKELETON

A completely new scientific frontier opened up for him with the material of Java man, Pithecanthropus erectus, on which Heinrich worked. He was of German nationality, but in protest against Hitler some years earlier did not renew his passport and was thus a man without a nationality. The Dutch tolerated him because he was not a Nazi, but many of his colleagues still considered him to be a "mof," an insulting word describing a German. Since May 10th, 1940, he worked on his discoveries in the basement of the museum. He wrote a publication that same year, in German, but the Dutch held it back. When the Japanese invaded the area he had to wear a uniform and was given a gun, and was forced to become a soldier. Never in his life had he held a gun in his hands. He had no nationality, the Japanese arrested him, and he became a prisoner of war.

His wife and daughter still lived in the city, they had not yet been arrested. Willi and Leny routinely visited the two and tried to help them as much as they could. They were not allowed to see Heinrich or be in touch with him. Willi began bringing his friend messages from his family, and to do so, they used code names for the wife and daughter. To be on the safe side, they called them by the names of foraminifers so the Japanese would think that they were discussing fossils. The wife was called Alveolina and the daughter Glubulina. Willi and Heinrich were only allowed to speak German together in the presence of a Japanese. They were constantly being spied upon, and neither of them knew if the Japanese officer, who was always in the room with them, understood German. They watched him closely, and on several occasions told each other jokes and funny stories, carefully watching the man to see if he reacted. After some time they saw that the man never blinked an eye, there was not the tiniest hint of a smile, and they were sure that he could not understand what they were saying. Still, their conversations were often whispered or coded, because they could absolutely not risk that a Japanese could hear what they were saying. Heinrich told Willi that he wanted to prevent the Japanese from taking material of primitive man which had not yet been publicized. One day he removed the valuable material from its hiding place and gave it to Willi who smuggled it out of the museum, took it home, and buried it in the back yard. In the middle of the night he went outside, dug a deep hole, placed the tin can containing the fossils inside, and planted a small tree on top. It was a very risky thing to do, for if the Japanese had discovered his actions, he would probably have been executed. The most valuable piece, the Neanderthal skull from Ngawi, Homo Javanthropus soloensis, had already been taken by the Japanese right after the invasion and sent by special messenger to the Japanese emperor. Heinrich also told Willi that the Japanese were looking for the skull of a child, the oldest one found in Java, and had seen a short article he had written. He showed Willi where the valuable piece was hidden; it was inside the skull of a Stegodon, which was part of the skeleton of a large Proboscidean (mammoth) exhibited in the museum. Nobody would think to look for the skull there.

The Japanese knew that the two men were good friends. They kept asking Willi if he knew where the piece was, they wanted to present it to emperor Tenno Heiko too. One day one of the Japanese officers was again interrogating Willi and some of the other European scientists. The men were all lined up. Willi was standing with his arms crossed in front of him. He said he knew of no hidden skull. The Japanese officer in full uniform, with black boots and screaming loudly, was swinging his sword back and forth in a threatening manner. Suddenly he brought it down with full force on Willi's arms. He cringed from pain the blow caused, but stood straight, looking at the man with disgust. Later he went to the museum director and complained about the incident. The old officer told Willi with a cold look on his face that the Japanese treated their own in the same manner and that nobody ever complained. For days Willi's arms remained swollen and sore.

The museum director, Dr. Okada, was an older man, about sixty-five years old. He was the one who had visited Willi in Tawangmangu. In the 1920's he had written a publication about foraminifers and he was quite a well known international scientist. He suffered tremendously from the heat and always wore shorts. He was such a strange appearance, he had skinny legs with varicose veins, and he wore holders so the socks would not roll down his skinny legs. Willi often had a hard time keeping a straight face when he screamed an order at someone; the little man just did not look like a mean soldier. He was a genius, though, and truly a strange individual. He had an assistant who was a micro-paleontologist, Dr. Atako. The man doused his body with a strong perfume, and Willi and the others immediately knew when he was nearby or approaching because the strong cloud of perfume always preceded him or lingered in the air after he had left. Then there was professor Takadane who was a mineralogy professor who had studied in Berlin and who knew Willi's old professor from the University of Basel. He was quite a nice person, but Willi and his friends had to be extremely cautious what they said to each other for he knew German. Occasionally, the professor strolled into Willi's office and asked him what he thought of the war.

Willi always responded, "I only hope that it will soon be over." Had he said something derogatory against the Japanese, he would have been arrested.

The Japanese army was very disciplined. One day Willi saw a Japanese soldier snatch the purse of an old woman as she walked across the street. A Japanese officer had seen the incident too, screamed at the soldier, took the purse, and handed it back to the old woman. Then he shot the soldier dead.

On March 6th, 1943, Willi met a Japanese prince. He was a paleontologist working in Borneo at the Tandjung oil well. When the Japanese announced that the prince was coming to visit the museum, Willi and the others were told that they had to bow when being introduced to the high official, for not only was he a very high ranked marine officer, but he was also from a very noble family. Willi dryly responded that he had never been forced to bow for anyone, but he would do his best. A few hours later the door to Willi's office suddenly opened.

A marine officer entered, took off his hat, extended his hand, and said to Willi, "How do you do, Dr. Mohler." The two men shook hands and had quite a long conversation about various oil wells. It turned out to be the famous prince, a very pleasant and polite professional who acted more like a scientist than a prince and soldier.

Another Japanese paleontologist who had worked in Mexico before the war, began working at the museum. His name was Homishoto.

One day he came to Willi's office, shook his hand, and said, "Oh, we have already lost the war."

Willi was not sure how to respond; should he smile, should he frown, or should he look sad and shake his head. The professor told Willi that there had been a battle in the Coral Sea during which the Japanese had practically lost their entire fleet. Willi had heard rumors about the battle. As a matter of fact, shortly after the battle had taken place everyone was ordered to hang up a Japanese flag; by that time all the Europeans had to have a Japanese flag in their homes. They were forced to celebrate the victory of the fleet in the Coral Sea. In actuality, it had been the opposite, the Japanese had lost the entire fleet. Willi only found this out much later. Homishoto told him all about the battle, but Willi never uttered a response other than a very neutral one; he did not trust nor believe any Japanese and it might have been a trap.

Generally, he had very little contact with the Japanese, and was more or less left alone in the museum other than being constantly watched. He kept himself busy with various projects. He had an excellent relationship with the natives who were also employed there. He gave them English lessons and taught them about foraminifers and fossils. There was a good library where they often spent time looking up various items of interest.

One day Okada told Willi that the police had brought over boxes filled with cards on foraminifers. After taking a quick look, Willi immediately saw that the boxes contained the famous foraminifers index of Dr. Hans Thalmann who had worked for an oil company in Sumatra. He had compiled an index of foraminifers from all over the world, but it had never been published. The collection was unique. There were many boxes which had been found somewhere in west Java on a tea plantation. Apparently before that, they had been stored at police headquarters. It was the material they had been looking for and which had been lost for some time; it was one of the reasons Willi had taken the job working at the museum in hopes of maybe finding out what had happened to the valuable data. He was excited, but did not show it. Instead, he pointed out to the director of the museum that Thalmann was a Swiss citizen, and the material could not be confiscated because it was the property of the Swiss government. Soon after he arrived home he left again to inform the Swiss consular representative of his discovery. He also wrote a letter documenting that the entire card index of Thalmann was stored at the museum in Bandung. The Japanese agreed that all the books as well as any other material containing the name Thalmann would be sealed and considered to be the property of Switzerland. Anything else without that name, including many books, were confiscated. Later Willi was reprimanded by the Japanese for reporting to the Swiss government that the index was stored at the museum in Bandung. Fortunately, nothing further happened, probably because the Japanese were having political difficulties at the time. No further action was taken that Willi had interfered. For the time being, the boxes remained at the museum.

Willi spent as much time as possible talking with Heinrich about his discoveries. Once he told Willi how he had prepared the fossils he had found. He made plaster impressions of the bones and mixed the plaster with brick powder which made it lose its white coloring and thus more resemble old fossils. The plaster impressions were then boiled in paraffin which hardened the casts.

During that time, Willi met another old friend in Bandung, the Swiss geologist, Dr. Werner Preiss. He was born in Basel in 1903, where he attended school. His passion were the mountains and nature, and he decided to study geology. After completion of his studies he worked for some time in Switzerland, and then joined the BPM in 1933. He worked in The Hague for several months, and was sent to Netherlands East Indies that same year, to Tjepu in east Java. From 1935 until 1937, he worked as a field geologist in the still unexplored jungles of west New Guinea. He had a severe case of malaria and was sent back to Java to recuperate. In 1939, he left the company. He was a free spirit, and did not like the many strict rules of conduct the Europeans demanded from their employees.

He was not able to return to Switzerland, so he settled in Java and Bali, and, in his own words, "The most beautiful time of my life began." He pursued his ethnographic and artistic interests, and traversed the paradise-like countryside of east Java. Then he moved to Bali, the island of the gods, where he settled for some time, and lived with a native woman. He collected textiles, Hindu-Javanese artifacts, rare weapons, and he became an expert on Java and its people. Werner moved to Bandung when the war broke out and began working at the museum. He explored and excavated an area in Dago near Bandung where he discovered bronze artifacts and weapons made of obsidian. Willi joined him often and on March 14th the two men again set out to do some excavating in Dago, the newly discovered site of obsidian microliths (small flints made of glassy black volcanic rock and flint tools of the Mesolithic, Stone Age, period) as well as ceramic shards of that same period. They also found siliciferous coral limestone, the raw material used for stone hatchets. They were mainly interested in finding casting molds used to make spears, bracelets, swords and daggers. One day they returned to continue looking for more artifacts. In the meantime it had rained quite heavily which was always a good time to see what had been exposed by the rain. In an hour and a half they found over two hundred shard occlusions and microliths, of which twenty-two pieces were in excellent condition. One of the pieces had red coloring on the inside. Then Willi found a fragment of a cone shaped, hand drilled piece of andesite. After walking around some more, he suddenly spotted something in the dirt. He bent down and carefully began to dig. He could not believe his eyes, he had found a casting mold used to make bronze arm rings. Part of it was missing, but it was an exciting find. Many years later Werner wrote and published an article in a Swiss scientific journal.

The article also described the obsidian microliths found at the site. Below is a brief excerpt of the article, "Molds for Bracelets."

My friend, Dr. W. Mohler, was able to prove that in Dago also rings of bronze, probably arm rings, had been cast. He found the only mold so far discovered. It was slightly damaged, and only half of a mold. Unfortunately, the piece was lost after the war. Fortunately, though, Dr. Mohler had made a detailed sketch of the mold.

Going to Dago became a routine outing and often the entire family went along, looking for more microliths. One day Willi found a fragment of a spinning whorl on the northern side of the hill. The girls enjoyed looking for stones and rocks, they could run to their hearts' content, and again, for a brief moment, Willi and Leny were able to forget that they were caught in the middle of a terrible war. As they watched their two little girls running, their blond hair shining in the bright sun, they wondered what the future would bring for their precious little children. Many times Werner stopped by their house in the evenings, he was not married and enjoyed the company. One day he told them that he thought that it might be Easter, but that he was not certain. Neither one of them knew, they were, after all, in Asia; there was a war, and they did not know what was happening in the rest of the world. They were not allowed to listen to radios, there were no newspapers, they were completely isolated and shut off from the rest of the world.

Willi rarely wrote in his diary any more. The Swiss were now routinely threatened and over and over were told by the Japanese that friends of the enemy were also Japan's enemies. The work at the museum continued. The Japanese also continued questioning Willi about the skull, accusing him of knowing where it was hidden. He remained steadfast and insisted that he knew nothing. On a day in May while Willi was looking at foraminifers under the microscope, the door to his office suddenly opened. The old museum director entered, his skinny legs bare, the purple veins standing out in contrast to his light skin.

He came right to the point, apologized to Willi for having been suspicious and accusing him of knowing where the skull was hidden, and said, "We have found the skull, but the difficulty is, we have found two of them."

The unexpected discovery was shown to a general who was visiting the museum at that time. Willi was summoned to be present and to make a presentation about the skull, where it had been found, how old it was, and the significance of its discovery. He was taken to a large conference room with a table in the middle. The two skulls were carefully placed on the table, six high ranking Japanese officers stood erect with serious expressions on their faces as Willi spoke.

At the end of his presentation he said, "One is the original, the other one is a copy." The general gesticulated with his arms and hands, and motioned to Willi that he wanted to find the original. He picked up each skull, held them in his hands, he smelled them, tapped on them with his fingers, turned them around, peered at them through his thick lenses, and then he said, "This is the original, and that is an imitation." It was very quiet in the room, all eyes were on Willi who replied, "Mr. General, you have discovered it."

The general started to laugh, slapped Willi on his back and proudly announced to everyone in the room, "Me paleontologist." The Japanese officers all began to laugh, the tension was broken, and they shook the general's hand, bowed, and talked very fast. The two pieces in question were carefully wrapped in cotton and placed in a safe. Willi, of course, knew that both pieces were copies; one had a hole in its base for mounting, the other was a true copy. Both casts were made by Willi's friend in the manner he had described. Nothing more was heard about the skull. Only Willi and Heinrich knew where it was, safely inside the Stegodon skull in the skeleton room of the museum.

DISCOVERING AN OLD LIBRARY

June arrived. Things became more and more difficult, nobody knew what was happening. The Japanese had forbidden the Europeans to listen to radios, and many who somehow managed to hear bits and pieces from a forbidden radio were caught and tortured. Stories of atrocities were heard more often. Everyone feared the Japanese secret police, the Kempetai, and it was best to stay out of their way. The Swiss were now constantly watched, but they still managed to visit each other and help where they could. One evening Werner stopped by again, his usually happy face had a very grim look. They went to the living room and sat down.

Willi, who knew his friend well, sensed that something was terribly wrong and he asked, "Have you been able to get some information as to what is going on?"

Werner looked at both Willi and Leny and said, "We have to be very careful, we are no longer protected under the Swiss neutrality law. I just found out that Fritz has been arrested by the Japs. They accused him of siding with the enemy, and have sentenced him to die. They are not sure what to do with him because of his Swiss status, so for the time being they have held off killing him. They have, though, tortured him, and pierced both his ear drums. He was thrown in jail, and his old "djongos" just managed to bring me the news. We have to do something to get him out and get him to a doctor. I will try to find out exactly where he is." Willi and Leny were horrified. They had already heard stories of people having their ear drums pierced. The Japanese interrogated the people for so long that some of them confessed to listening to a radio even though they had not, just so the torture would stop. It did not, though. While being interrogated, the Japanese inserted thin bamboo sticks or even sharpened pencils in the ears. With a hard blow the sticks were

119

shoved deep inside, piercing the ear drums. Most of the victims were then thrown in jail. Werner stayed for a long time and they talked into the wee hours of the morning. They were becoming more and more desperate because there just seemed to be no way out and no end in sight of the terrible war. Fortunately, after several days, the Japanese let Fritz go. He was another Swiss scientist who had worked on the island of Sumatra.

One day around mid-June they once again ventured into the city, taking the only transportation they had, their bicycles. It was time to go to the market to buy vegetables and fish. Agnes was on the back of Willi's bike, Ruthie sat in a basket in the front of Leny's bicycle. Slowly they pedaled through the busy streets; the Japanese soldiers looked at them, but left them alone. They wore their pins with the Swiss flag and Japanese writing stating that they were from neutral Switzerland. As they turned a street corner they saw an old building, and at the entrance, in big letters, still in Dutch, read the word "bibliotheek," library. What a surprise. They decided to check it out. It was well stocked and had remained more or less as it had been during the Dutch government. Slowly they walked up and down the aisles, reading the book titles. Only an old native woman sat at a desk, her head bent over as she read a book. Their steps echoed as they slowly walked up and down the abandoned aisles filled with rows and rows of books. Willi could not believe his eyes when he saw several books by one of his favorite Swiss authors, Gottfried Keller. He took the two volumes along with several others and checked them out. With the vegetables and dried fish they had bought at the market, and a large package of books, they rode home. Willi took the leather bound book in his hands, opened it up, and there, on the inside cover was the name of one of his old geology professors from Basel. What an incredible coincidence. To find a book by one of his best liked authors in an old library on an island at the other end of the world from his homeland was quite incredible in itself, but then to find his old professor's name on the inside was almost unbelievable. How had it gotten there? Willi wondered. He was anxious to once again read the favorite words of this well known author he had studied in school and whose stories he almost knew by heart. Willi's favorite prverb of Gottried Keller was: *"Absorb, oh eyes, all that you can, of this earth's golden abundance."*

Gottfied Keller was born in Switzerland in 1819. He wrote many novellas about the transitional times in Switzerland from the old government to more liberal times during the nineteenth century. His stories were very readable and beautiful. Here they were, living in terror of the occupational force of

120

the Japanese where everything was forbidden. They were not allowed to speak English or Dutch, carrying arms was punishable by death or incarceration, and if they helped the Dutch prisoners of war they would be decapitated, shot or stabbed to death with bayonets. They always thought of their homeland, a free country. Gottfried Keller's books were all about freedom and the struggles the people had to endure to achieve this freedom. Willi opened the first page, Agnes on his lap, Ruthie was curled up in Leny's lap, and he began to read from the novella "The flag of the seven upright." The story was about seven Swiss citizens who had formed a target shooting club. He read:

Master Hediger's quarters were immaculate. He himself resembled more an American squatter than a tailor. His strong facial features were covered with a full beard, his large bald head was bent as he read the newspaper, and with a serious and critical expression on his face he studied an article in "The Swiss Republican." The walls of his room were decorated with portraits of Columbus, Zwingly, Houston, Washington and Robespierre. Next to the worldly heroes his walls were decorated with portraits of several Swiss notables. Alongside his bookcase stood a well cared-for shiny shotgun with a bag of ammunition which at all times contained thirty sharp rounds. This was his hunting rifle with which he did not shoot at hares or partridges, but at aristocrats and Jesuits, who, in his opinion, were breakers of the constitution, and thus were traitors. He must have been protected by a protective star that he had not yet spilled any blood. More than once he took his shotgun and rushed to the town center. It was, after all, a time of revolts....

The children had fallen asleep, but Willi continued reading out loud to Leny several more hours. The next evening he began another story, Keller's epigram. Night had set in, the windows were darkened and the children had curled up on the couch next to Willi. Leny sat across from him as he began to read the story about a young scientist who was sitting in his room, studying and working with his instruments. His thoughts began to wander and he pondered that the time had come for him to look for a wife. He reached over to his shelf, took a book written by Lessing and began to read Friedrich Von Logau's epigram. Turning the pages he saw the words: *"How do you aim to turn a white lily into a red rose; kiss a white Galathea, and she will blush and smile."* The young man wrote the epigram on a small piece of paper, folded it, and placed it in his wallet. Later in the day he rode off on his horse to visit a minister and his family. He stayed for a while, and when he left told them that he was also going to visit an acquaintance of his parents; an old

121

military colonel whose niece was taking care of the ailing old man. The minister's daughter gave him a letter and asked him to take it to the old colonel's niece, her friend. The young scientist, his name was Reinhard, rode for several hours over hills and through valleys and arrived at his destination in the evening hours. Just then a young woman opened the door and walked outside. Willi read from the book:

Finally, Reinhard dismounted the horse. Holding onto the reins of his mare, he looked at the pretty appearance. He did not utter a word, bowed, and handed her the letter of the minister's daughter. But, alas, it was not the letter; instead, he handed her the epigram he had written down earlier, "How do you aim to turn a while lily into a red rose; kiss a white Galathea, and she will blush and smile." He held the letter and his wallet in his hand, and only discovered his error after the woman had already taken the note and read it. She kept it in her hand and looked at the confused and blushing Mr. Reinhard with wide open eyes and quivering lips. Silently she handed him the note and took the letter intended for her. When she saw the seal on the letter her face lit up, she looked beautiful, and full of goodness. Her dark eyes flashed intelligently, and quickly reading the letter, laughed, and said in a mischievous voice:

"I must confess, dear Sir, this has been a most peculiar event. A stranger on a horse falls from the sky holding onto the weak fence-post of my garden. He hands me a writing with a man of the cloth's seal, the bible, cup and cross. In this letter my friend from the valley, the minister's daughter, reminds me not to forget to send her seeds of my radishes. If you are willing to defend yourself and explain where you hail from, then you are welcome in this house. And I, who am presently talking since my uncle is sick with arthritis and has remained in his room, want to talk seriously and sensibly with you about the future development of your strange path of life." The charming woman was illuminated by the rays of the setting evening sun as well as of a bright inner light, and the appearance quickly allowed the surprised Reinhard to regain his composure. He told himself that here and nowhere else could he try out the epilog of old Von Logau, and only now did he realize its deeper meaning and its far reaching work and complication with which the attempt would be associated.

Every evening Willi read from the books and both he and Leny were overwhelmed with a strong patriotic feeling. For brief moments their thoughts wandered from the uncertainty of the occupied island to their beloved homeland.

NOT EVEN THE HIPPOCRATIC OATH IS HONORED

The longer the Japanese occupied the area, the worse the conditions became. Once the Japanese imported their own occupation currency, food became more and more expensive and scarce. Thoughts were constantly on having enough food to survive. The natives did not trust the new paper currency, they were accustomed to the Dutch silver coins, which, to them, represented an actual value. The exchange rate from Netherlands East Indies currency to Japanese money was ten-fold. Most money exchangers were Chinese. The Japanese confiscated everything; there was no more new fabric; medicine, watches and paper became even more expensive. Matches were no longer available, so they reverted back to starting fires with steel, flint and tinder. After the imported powder milk was used up their two little girls were no longer able to drink milk which they would have needed so badly at that age. Flour that used to be imported from Australia was no longer obtainable, and a year after the Japanese occupation, bread could no longer be bought or made. The young family ate rice three times a day, and they desperately tried to find food rich in vitamins. Often, so often they thought of the year in the mountains, the daily fresh vegetables and all the meat from hunter Wongso. Their diet became identical to that of the natives; they ate as many vegetables, hot peppers, dried fish and other typical native products as possible so that at least they would not become ill with vitamin deficiencies. All of them had already lost much weight, but they were still healthy. Some items could be bought at the black market, but prices were very high. Medicines were virtually not to be had, and often they asked the natives for advice on how to cure minor ailments.

In the meantime, Mrs. Vrede, the Dutch woman Willi and Leny had known in Tawangmangu, had also been moved to Bandung. Her two young boys were still living with friends. For some time she was in the hospital, but the Japanese no longer allowed her to be treated so she was brought to Bandung where Willi and Leny were able to take care of her. The woman was getting worse, Leny went to check on her daily. The last Dutch physicians had been arrested and were in concentration camps, radiation treatment was no longer available to them. The patient became increasingly worse, she suffered immensely, and they knew that something had to be done. They decided that there was only one thing to do, they had to get help. Willi made up his mind to seek out the Japanese chief physician of the Borromaeus Hospital in Bandung where they had radiation equipment. They were hopeful that the doctor would help. So, one day Willi left in hopes of being able to talk with a physician who could help. As soon as he entered the hospital he was approached by an angry Japanese soldier.

The man stomped his foot and yelled at Willi, who said, "I am a Swiss citizen and I want to see the doctor." He showed the man his passport. After mumbling some words Willi could not understand, the soldier left. Willi waited a long time. Finally, the soldier came back, motioning Willi to follow. The Japanese doctor was sitting at a desk, dressed in a white uniform. He motioned to Willi to sit down. Willi immediately explained the desperate situation to the doctor and the discussion went back and forth. The man did not seem to be very interested, and did not show any concern or compassion for the woman who was dying from cancer. Willi knew that he had to convince this man of medicine that the patient needed to be admitted to the hospital for radiation treatment. Finally, the doctor agreed, and told Willi to bring her in a few days. Willi was relieved, thanked him, and got up to leave. Just as he reached the door the doctor called him back and asked him the nationality of the woman. Willi's heart began to beat, but he knew that it was impossible for him to hide the fact that the woman was a Dutch citizen. He thought of the Hippocratic oath also this doctor must live by, and told him that she was a Dutch citizen. The doctor's face darkened and he said, "No, she cannot come here, and she will not get the treatment; the more Dutch that die of natural causes, the less we will have to kill."

It was the end of the conversation, Willi was not allowed to say another word, and was ordered to leave. Leny was distraught when she found out what had happened. They talked late into the night and made a decision. She was going to hire two native nurses to take care of Mrs. Vrede day and night. The next day she made all the arrangements and was able to find two qualified women to take care of the patient. Leny stopped by each day, talked with her, read to her, and tried to make her as comfortable as possible. Once a week she paid the women. She always rode her bicycle, it was their only way of transportation other than walking. They had to be sure that if the Japanese stopped her for an inspection they would not find the money on her. So she always took a bouquet of flowers, and hid the money inside the bouquet, just in case. Often Willi went with her, but after a few days he was no longer able to go. One of his Javanese acquaintances who worked with him at the museum warned him that the secret police were watching him, and he should no longer go to Mrs. Vrede's house. Her husband was still a prisoner of war, and nobody knew where he was or if he was even still alive. She became increasingly worse, the pain she had to endure was becoming unbearable. Willi and Leny now faced the difficult task to find a way to get pain medication. The only thing that helped at this stage of the disease was morphine, other pain medications were unavailable. Prescriptions were no longer obtainable and they knew that they had to try to get it on the black market. Willi contacted his old assistant from Balikpapan who had also come to Java. He was a strict, but not fanatic Moslem, and an excellent business man. This very affable and intelligent Sumatrese agreed to help them obtain morphine. Willi knew that he could trust the man; also, he had helped him out several times with money. They still had an emergency supply of old silver money with which they offered to pay him. Two weeks later the man brought sixty ampoules of morphine at three guilders each. The nurses knew how to administer the medicine, and Mrs. Vrede finally had some relief from the terrible pain she had endured for so long.

HAMRA AND BARDI

On July 26th, 1943 to their greatest surprise and joy, a telegram arrived from Switzerland. It read: *"All are well and healthy, how are you?."* It was the first news they received from Switzerland in a very long time, and they were thankful that their loved ones were well.

During that time Leny hired a young woman to help with the household chores and the children. The "kokki" came from a nearby village. She had a young daughter about nine years old, her name was Bardi. Bardi and the girls spent hours playing together. She and her mother still spoke the old Javanese dialect, and before long, the girls picked up the ancient language. Leny often gave Hamra extra money so she could pay her rent. The woman was kind, loyal, and every morning at dawn she and Bardi came to the house, and every evening after all her chores were done she bid Leny good night, and asked if she could please come back the next day. The Japanese forbid the natives to work for Europeans, but few of them heeded the warning. Hamra was devoted and hard working, she cooked, cleaned, and took care of the children. Bardi taught Agnes how to weave, and they made beautiful baskets of palm fronds or grasses. One day, a Javanese friend came by for a visit. Suddenly he stopped talking and listened intently.

He looked at Willi with a surprised expression on his face and said, "I am hearing children talking in high Javanese." Willi motioned him to follow. They went to the back porch. There were Agnes, Bardi and Ruth, and Agnes and Bardi were chatting away in high Javanese.

They no longer had gas for cooking so all the meals had to be cooked on coals. As soon as Hamra arrived in the mornings she started the coals which remained simmering until the last meal of the day had been cooked.

During that time there was an outbreak of bubonic plague in the native villages. One day Hamra and Bardi did not show up at dawn. Leny immediately knew that something was wrong. She also knew that Hamra did not have a husband, and as far as she knew, had no family other than her young daughter. She became extremely concerned and began to ask around. Several times she walked over to the nearby village to find out if anyone knew Hamra. She continued her search for several days. After about three or four days she again walked down another dirt road lined with trees and shrubs. A small brook with flowing brown water ran alongside the narrow path. She had to cross over a bridge to reach the village. Several dogs came running up to her and barked at the strange white woman. People stuck their heads out of their huts, curiously glancing out, and wondering why a white woman was coming to their village.

Leny approached the first hut and asked a woman who was feeding some chickens, "Do you know a young woman with a little girl, her name is Hamra?"

The woman shook her head and said that she did not know her. Finally, an old woman hobbled up to Leny and said, "I know Hamra, she is ill." She pointed down the dirt road and showed Leny where Hamra could be found. The bubonic plague had become an epidemic, but Leny knew that the disease was mostly spread by rats in unsanitary areas. She followed the directions the old woman had given, occasionally stopping and asking the people for directions. Finally, she arrived at the hut. In a tiny room on the floor on a mat was Hamra. Leny immediately realized that she was very sick. Bardi sat on the floor next to her mother, a sad look on her face. For a moment Leny looked at the two. She softly spoke Bardi's name. The child raised her head and her little face lit up with a bright, relieved smile.

She jumped up and ran to Leny. She began to cry and said, "Njonja," you have come to help us. Please, please help my mother, she is so sick." Without hesitating, Leny gathered the meager belongings, and with Bardi's help, the three slowly walked back to the house, Leny and the child supporting poor Hamra who was very weak and sick. At home there was a big, empty garage. Leny turned it into a comfortable room for Hamra and Bardi and the two quickly settled in the clean room. Leny nursed Hamra back to health and with proper care and food she was soon on her feet again. She did not have the bubonic plague, but had been so ill that she might have died from lack of care if Leny had not found her when she did. The two remained with them until the war ended.

BLACK MAGIC

Hadi, Willi's Javanese friend who had warned him that the Japanese Kempetai spies were watching him, also worked at the museum. During that time the Japanese had organized an exhibit to show their accomplishments in occupied Java. The exhibit was held at the museum, Hadi was in charge. Willi recommended that he organize a display on geology and on the discoveries of primitive man of Java. It was a great success and Hadi was commended in the local newspaper for his accomplishments. At the museum there also was a Japanese lieutenant who beat and slapped people at any given opportunity, for no reason whatsoever. This was done to intimidate and embarrass the Europeans as well as the natives, and all of them had at one time or another been slapped in the face by the cruel Jap. It was the same man who had brought his sword down on Willi's arms. Everyone avoided him as much as possible. His name was Tomai and before coming to Java he was in China where he apparently sustained a severe blow to his head which made him crazy. He was then sent to Java as a military spy. Willi and the other scientists had no choice but to accept his degrading treatment; he had a gun, and a human life was of no value to him. One day he came to see Hadi and declared that he would now take over the exhibit, that it had been his idea anyway.

Hadi bowed his head and said, "At your service." Tomai started to leave the room, but Hadi called him back and said that he wanted to tell him a story. In a quiet voice he spoke, "I am a simple, peaceful Javanese and am sitting in front of my hut. A pot of rice is cooking on my hearth and I am hungry. A Japanese officer walks toward me, armed with a Samurai sword and a pistol, and says, 'That is my rice and I want to eat it all.' I bow my head and tell the Japanese that the rice is his. He is armed and I do not wish to fight. I also tell him that the rice will stick in his throat."

Tomai understood the Malay words, shrugged his shoulders and left the room. Willi paid very close attention to every word Hadi said, and asked him what he meant when he told the Japanese that the rice would stick in his throat.

Hadi replied, "This is 'guna-guna,' black magic. The throat of the Japanese will swell up, he soon will be unable to utter a word, but when he comes close to suffocating, I will remove the spell."

Willi looked at his friend carefully and saw that the intelligent man was serious. What did this mean? As a scientist, Willi was skeptical when it came to superstition, black magic and mysticism. More and more he heard many strange stories and wasn't certain what to make of them. Two days later Tomai came to the office again. He was hoarse and had a scarf tied around his neck. A week later the lieutenant was unable to button his collar and could no longer utter a word.

Hadi looked at Willi and winked, his look silently saying, "You see, it works." The Javanese employees of the museum whispered that Tomai was seriously ill and could no longer swallow, but not a single person felt sorry for the annoying and arrogant man. A few days later Willi heard that he had to be admitted to the marine hospital in Surabaya and that he was near death.

A few days later Hadi said to Willi, "Only you and I know what is actually wrong with Tomai. I will not let him die, but I had to retaliate because he took away my beautiful exhibit." About a month later, Tomai reappeared. He had lost a lot of weight and had become more placid. He had recovered from the mysterious throat affliction. Willi was still not certain what to make of the incident, but he had witnessed the whole episode from the onset. All he could do was shake his head in disbelief. He knew that few of his friends would believe him if he told them the story.

A few weeks later he was talking to his old assistant from Sumatra who had supplied them with morphine for Mrs. Vrede. He told him how an enemy could be killed from a distance. Each day a needle or sharp bamboo stick was inserted into a doll resembling the enemy, then a curse was placed on the doll. The method always worked, he said. Willi had heard similar stories before, especially during the time they lived in the mountains of Java. He was told that the word "guna-guna" was never to be uttered thoughtlessly as it would cause a Javanese great panic. The same applied for "hantu," which meant bad spirit and which would also greatly agitate a native.

Another strange story occurred while Willi was working at the museum in Bandung. His secretary was a young Menadonese woman. Her name was Botur, and Willi and Leny knew her parents quite well. They were Christians and sided with the Dutch. The family had four children and a busy household with people always going in and out. One day mother Botur noticed that someone had stolen her valuable diamond ring. She went to see the Shaman, a fortune teller and psychic; she wanted to find out who had stolen her ring. The Shaman told her that the person who had taken her ring was a frequent visitor to her house, and she would recognize the thief when he came to the house the next time. He would request a glass of water, and the moment he lifted it to take a drink, it would break in half. Many people came to the Botur house, they drank the water, but nothing happened. Then, after a few weeks, a relative of the family stopped by for a visit. He asked for a glass of water, raised it to drink, and the glass broke in half. Mrs. Botur told him that he had stolen her ring and to bring it back to her immediately. The perplexed thief rushed home and brought her the valuable ring. Neither Willi nor Leny could comprehend this story and could not search for an explanation because they simply could not understand the totally different world. The Botur's were good Christians, but if they wanted to find out something, then they went to see the Shaman.

Work at the museum continued more or less the same. Heinrich had an assistant, Putan, who guarded the famous discovery site where the skulls of Java man had been found. It was in Saringan on the shores of the Solo river. From time to time Putan searched the banks of the river for artifacts. Over the layers where the remains of primitive man had been found were also old graves dating back to the Hindu era. These graves contained many riches which he collected and sold. He was not doing too well during the Japanese occupation and nobody bought his treasures. Heinrich asked Willi to help the man when he came to Bandung. One day Putan visited Willi and brought with him a basket filled with many artifacts he had found in Sangiran. There were cut carnelian beads, blue glass beads, small quartz globules, three gold nose rings and three carnelian cameos, one with a carved wild pig, and two with carvings of crabs. Two of the nose rings depicted Hindu horror masks, and one was a figure of the god Wododari. Putan told him that he had found the artifacts at the foot-ends of the graves inside clay pots. He also frequently found gold bracelets, ear rings and finger rings. Most of the gold treasures he sold to a Chinese who melted them down. During the Dutch government it was forbidden to sell gold artifacts, and, therefore, all the gold items were immediately melted down. Willi bought the decorative beads, the three gold nose rings and the three cameos. They were very reasonable and he paid Putan with silver coins who was able to exchange them at a good profit rate on the black market. He now could buy enough food to feed his large family for several weeks. Willi and Leny had always saved money. Willi earned a good living from 1938 until the Japanese invaded. They were able to live very reasonable, food was cheap, housing was provided by the company, as was their medical care, so they put quite some money aside. When Leny left Borneo the end of 1941 she took most of the money with her. They had mostly saved silver coins. The money had to be used sparingly, but a certain amount was set aside so they could occasionally buy artifacts for their collection.

Back in Switzerland their families were desperate to find out how they were doing and where they were. Willi's parents received the following telegram:

Bern, August 30th, 1943.

Mr. Mohler, Gelterkinden.

We have just been notified telegraphically by the Consulate in Tokyo that the family Dr. W. Mohler is well and healthy in Bandung. Please send us payment in the amount of Swiss Francs 15.40 to cover the costs of the Swiss consulate in Tokyo. An invoice is enclosed.

TOTAL DOMINATION AND ARREST

Many nights they were awakened from a deep sleep by loud pounding on the doors of their neighbors' homes. Women and children began to scream, and they could hear the blows when the men were beaten. After a while the cars drove off and it was quiet again. Terrorized Willi and Leny asked themselves when their turn would come.

On December 13th they were sitting in the living room, Willi was reading from one of the books he had borrowed from the library. The girls were still awake when suddenly there was a commotion outside, cars drove up, men's voices were heard, then loud stomping of booted feet, and, finally, banging on the front door. Willi told Leny to remain seated and to hold the children. He went to the door and opened it. He was pushed aside by a group of Japanese soldiers who stomped into the house. The officer in charge screamed at Willi that he knew that there was a radio transmitter on the roof. Willi said that he knew of no transmitter on the roof and that he was renting the house. Several soldiers began opening all the drawers and cabinet doors. Everything was thrown on the floor. All the curtains were pulled down, the men checked to see if anything was sewn in the hems. The armoires were emptied, items were thrown from shelves, and dishes roughly pushed aside or thrown on the floor. They were definitely looking for something. All the items their Dutch friends had given them in Tawangmangu for safekeeping were still in their house. Willi and Leny had decided rather than hiding them all around the house in obvious places such as the hems of curtains, they would keep everything in one place. Along one of the walls in the living room stood a large, brown, wooden ship's trunk they had brought with them from Switzerland. It now contained all the personal belongings of their Dutch

132

friends who had been arrested and who were in concentration camps. The Japanese officer in charge put his boot on the old ship's trunk as he interrogated Willi. He had a short stick in his hand and several times pounded the edge of the chest with it. Willi's heart was beating, but he tried to look calm. He knew that if they found the items with the names of Dutch people, they would probably all have been killed instantly. Over and over the Swiss were told that if they associated with or helped the enemy, they would be executed. The wooden trunk was never opened. There it stood, in the middle of the room, the soldier had his boot on it, yet they completely overlooked the chest. The Japanese continued to search a while longer, but could not find anything. The house was in shambles, every room was littered, they had emptied everything on the floors. The soldiers had systematically emptied every piece of furniture in the entire house, but they completely overlooked the old wooden trunk in the living room. Maybe they thought that it was too obvious a place to hide something in. After a while they pushed Willi out of the door, into a car, and drove off. Agnes and Ruthie were terrified and clung to Leny. She tried to calm the children and told them that their daddy would soon be back. She also told them to remain on the couch, she would be right back, and quickly followed the soldiers outside. She demanded that they tell her where they were taking her husband. The officers were obviously annoyed and consulted with each other for some time. Finally, they told her where they were taking him. Hamra and Bardi were hiding in their room. The moment the cars drove off Leny called to them and told Hamra that she had to leave for a while, and to stay with the two frightened children in the house. Then she got on her bicycle and pedaling as fast as she could, went to the home of the Swiss consular representative to inform him what had happened. Then she went to her friend Lisa's house. There, just minutes before, the same had happened, her husband Peter had been arrested in a similar fashion as Willi had. They too had moved from Tawangmangu to the city a few months earlier. Leny did not stay very long. They decided to go to the jail where they were holding their husbands the first thing in the morning. They hugged, told each other that things would be all right, and Leny went home. The children were getting tired and she tucked them in. Both had been crying, missing their daddy, and she sang their prayer song and told them daddy would come home soon. She tossed and turned all night long, she could not sleep, and prayed for Willi's safety.

Willi was driven through dark streets. After about twenty minutes the car stopped and he was pushed out. He was shoved through the door of a building, down a hall and into a large, empty room. There he had to take off all his clothes except for his undershirt and underpants. His belt, socks and shoes were taken, as were his wedding ring and watch. Then down another hallway to another door. He was shoved into the room and the door was locked behind him. The room was dark. Peter arrived at almost the same time. There were a number of prisoners in the small room, most of them natives. There were some Dutch and some Chinese, some had already spent months in the dungeon. Some of the men had long hair and beards. The cell was about nine by fifteen feet; at one time it had been a small bedroom of the Salvation Army. Now it was their jail. The men could not go outside, they had to urinate in a tin can in the middle of the room. The can had overflown and the stench was unbearable. Willi's eyes and throat began to burn.

Early the next morning Leny and Lisa rode their bicycles to the prison. It was a messy place, they heard people screaming. The Japanese were very upset when the two women showed up, asking them what they thought they were doing there. Leny angrily told them that they were there to find out what had been done to their husbands and they wanted to bring them food. The soldier they had spoken to walked off and left them waiting. They waited so long standing up that Lisa became dizzy and had to sit on the floor. She had a chronic heart condition, the excitement made her very weak. Finally, it seemed an eternity, the soldier came back, and said that they could bring the men food. It was to be in special containers, but fruit were forbidden. The reason? Fruit contained vitamins. Java had an abundance of fruit, but the Japanese wanted the Europeans to get as little healthy nourishment as possible. The women were then told to leave and were never to come there again. The food was to be sent by a native. Leny and Lisa immediately went to see the Swiss representative again. They reported to him what had happened. It was decided that they would prepare the food, but he had to make the arrangements to have a trustworthy Javanese deliver it to the prison every day.

Willi found a small corner in the cell and sat down on the filthy floor. He dozed off but did not sleep. As soon as the sun came up he looked around. Some of the men were so weak that they could barely talk. Most of them suffered from malnourishment edemas. They were covered with parasites, had sores and skin rashes, and many of the natives had dysentery or gonorrhea. Thousands of bed bugs crawled out of the walls and sucked their blood. All night long more men were thrown into the cell until there were twenty-three inside the tiny room. They lay on wooden boards. The soldiers humiliated them, taking great pleasure in placing the food in the urine spill in the middle of the room. The food had to be eaten with fingers, there were no utensils. The days wore on, nothing happened. They did not get enough to drink which soon resulted in tremendous pain in Willi's kidney area. Sometimes he heard women screaming as they were being tortured. He never saw any of the women. The Japanese tortured them by inflicting burns with cigarettes, or pulling their arms up behind their backs until the bones snapped.

Leny and Lisa took turns cooking the food for the men in prison. They made a large amount and the most nourishing food possible. Every day at around eleven in the morning a native knocked on the door, took the food, and rode off on his bicycle to deliver it to the prison.

Willi and several other Swiss men were released from the prison after ten days; he felt as if he had spent ten days in hell. Others were kept much longer. After their husbands had been released, Leny and Lisa continued to send food until the last prisoners had been set free. The last two were Anders and Eggman. Anders had just arrived in Bandung a couple of days before he was arrested. Eggman, who had been the chief geologist in Balikpapan, was arrested shortly after Willi and Peter had been taken by the Japanese. The two men remained in the terrible hellhole of the old Salvation Army building for ten months. Willi and Leny tried everything in their power to have their friends released, but to no avail. All of the Swiss men, not just in Bandung, were arrested more or less at the same time for the same reason; they had helped the Dutch who were being tortured and mistreated in concentration camps. Alfred Lang, who had gone to Kopeng at the foot of the volcano Merbabu, and who organized assistance for women and children, was also arrested. He was taken to Salatiga, interrogated, mistreated and tortured, and was also incarcerated for ten months. The Japanese forced him to drink tremendous amounts of water, he then had to lie on the floor, and the soldiers took turns stomping on his stomach until the water came splashing out of his mouth. He had to endure terrible, unmentionable things, but the older man later rarely spoke about what had happened to him. When Anders was finally released he was totally distraught and suffered tremendously. His brown eyes had an empty, terrified look. The tall, lanky man was very skinny, his bones stuck out sharply. His whole body was covered with sores and open wounds. Willi and Leny immediately took in their old friend and nursed him back to health. He was in total shock and begged them to give him a blanket, so when the Japanese arrested him again, he would at least have a blanket with him. When Eggman was released he had a bad case of dysentery. His wife was able to slowly get her husband back on his feet again. Only a few weeks later the Japanese arrested him again. Eggman had to bring a Eurasian woman money from the company. Her Dutch husband had been arrested and was somewhere in a concentration camp. When Eggman stopped by the woman's house, he chatted with her a bit. He told her that according to Radio Saigon, the war would not last much longer. The next day the Japanese arrested him again. The woman had an affair with a Japanese officer who was with the Kempetai and she told him what Eggman had said. The Swiss government, after almost a year, finally realized what was being done to Swiss citizens in occupied Netherlands East Indies, and protested, and only then were the Swiss released. Eggman would probably not have lasted much longer. He had a terrible case of bacterial dysentery. The Japanese did not care, to them the more Europeans that died, the better. In Tawangmangu Willi's old friend Jakob, and on the other side of the mountain Christian, had also been arrested, and were incarcerated for ten months, as were Otto and others. An old friend Willi and Leny had known in Balikpapan, a geologist from Poland who also worked for the company, was arrested in Palembang. He was tortured for so long that he took his own life, leaving behind a wife and daughter. The long time consular representative, who had owned a watch and jewelry business in Bandung, was also incarcerated. The reason? He was a member of a Masonic lodge. Following a visit by the German consul of Tokyo, all the Masons on Java were arrested, and without any further reason, thrown in jail. After McArthur took back the Philippines, the Swiss government finally became aware of what was happening.

A PLEA FOR HELP

Only a few weeks after the last Swiss were set free, things again became very critical for Willi and his friends. A Dutch colleague, who was in a prison camp near Bandung, sent a plea for help. He asked them to send him twenty-five thousand guilders in small currency. Most of the people in the prison camps were starving to death, if they could somehow obtain money, they could bribe the soldiers and buy food. Some Japanese as well as the natives would do anything for money, including selling food to the prisoners. Of course, Willi and the others knew that having any contact with the prison camps was considered to be assisting the enemy which was punishable by death.

During the war months, all the company employees tried to stay in touch with one another. They had schemed a way to receive and pass on notes to each other without ever being detected by the Japanese. One area the Japanese stayed away from were the cemeteries. The men, and, of course, they were all Swiss since all the other Europeans were in a concentration camp, now routinely attended funerals. Nobody bothered them, and they knew several natives they could trust whom they paid to pass the notes from the camps and bring them back. The corpses of the deceased were wrapped in reed mats and were on horse drawn carts. The cart drivers handed the notes to Willi and his friends and took the notes along with the money back to the camps. This way, friends and families were able to stay in touch with each other. Another Swiss friend, his name was Emil, carried letters from the men's concentration camps to the women's camps. He always carried a small leather pouch with a leather strap, in it were the letters. One day several months earlier, he and Willi were on a train together, Emil's bag was filled with notes from the men and he was on his way to a women's camp in west Java. The two men had to get up and walk forward in the train, when, by accident, Emil dropped his leather bag, and all the letters fell out. The two quickly bent down, grabbed the notes, stuffed them back, and continued walking. Fortunately, nobody saw the incident, at least not any Japanese, and the natives always sided with the Europeans and kept still. Unfortunately, some time later the Japanese did find out what Emil had been doing and he was arrested, tortured and beaten and then incarcerated. He was another Swiss who had to endure the terrible torture of being forced to drink large amounts of water and then the soldiers jumped on his stomach.

The plea for help from the Dutch colleague was also received at the cemetery. Willi and the others had to move fast. First they had to find a person whom they could absolutely trust. They knew of a Dutch woman who had not been arrested because she was having an affair with a Japanese officer. Her husband was somewhere in a concentration camp, probably also starving. Willi and his friends pressured the woman to assist them to find a trustworthy Korean or Japanese who could deliver something for them to the prison camp. They told her that in return they would not mention anything about her affair after the war was over. They had to take such drastic measures because they knew that the lives of hundreds if not thousands of people depended on their being able to get the money to them so they could buy the food needed to survive. The woman knew that the men were serious and her reputation would have been ruined if anyone found out about the affair after the war was over. She hooked them up with a Korean soldier who was of the Christian faith. Now the men decided that they had to find a way to get more money and to send one hundred thousand guilders to the camp; the risk would be the same and the more money they could get to their friends, the more people could be helped. All of them donated a portion of the emergency money they had received from their company at the onset of the war, they borrowed over forty thousand from a friend for which Willi signed an "I owe you" note, and the rest of the money was borrowed from a Chinese money lender. Finally, they had a hundred thousand guilders in small bills. They told the woman to let the Korean soldier know that he could come to Willi's house. A few days later the soldier arrived on his bicycle. They offered to pay him twenty-five thousand guilders to be given to him after he had safely delivered the money to their needy friends in the prison camp. The man refused to accept any money, he did not approve of the inhumane treatment of the Dutch by the Japanese and assured Willi and his friends that he was glad he could help. He had a piece of fabric with him into which he tried to tie the money. The piece was much too small so he walked over to one of the blue curtains hanging from the dining room window, cut a large enough piece off with his knife, wrapped the money in it, and placed the big bundle on his bicycle. He slung his gun over his shoulder, climbed on his bike, and told Willi and his friends that he would be back the following day to tell them that the transaction had been successfully accomplished. He smiled and waved, and rode off down the street.

The next day they anxiously waited for the Korean soldier to report how things had gone, but he did not show up, nor did he the next day, nor the day after. A week went by, and he had still not returned. Everyone was getting sick from worrying. What could have happened? They feared the worst. If he had been caught carrying the money, he would have been questioned as to why he had such a large amount of money on him. Probably they would have tortured him, and, if he had talked, he would have given them away. Or, what if he had decided to keep the money for himself? The suspense became unbearable. They were worried sick and could talk of nothing else, each day their hopes that the money had reached their friends in the camp waned. The days turned to weeks, three weeks had already gone by and still no word from the Korean soldier. They were no longer able to sleep, listening for the tiniest sound in the night if cars were approaching. The Japanese usually came at night. Wherever they went, they looked over their shoulders, was a spy following them, were they soon going to be arrested, were they going to be shot? The situation was totally nerve wrecking and the anxiety increased from day to day. One day, late in the afternoon, there was a tapping on the door. Willi got up and went to see who it was. There he stood, alert, cheerful and happy. He told Willi that he had successfully delivered the money to their friend, but had been ordered to transport prisoners of war to Sumatra that same day and had been unable to stop by. Willi, Leny and their friends thanked God that the transaction had gone well and were grateful to know that their Dutch friends in the concentration camp could buy the food they needed to survive. They never saw the Korean soldier again, but thought of the kind man often without whose assistance they could not have helped their Dutch friends.

The few Swiss men who were in Bandung continued to help where they could. They were able to get cans of lard which they smuggled into the women's camps nearby. Their helper was a Chinese. The camps were surrounded by fences. The man had built a contraption on the inside of the fence; he was employed by the Japanese and worked in the camp. He placed large bamboo tubes through openings in the fence. A special time had been arranged when the guards were on the other side of the camp. The men crawled through the bushes behind the fence and the Chinese pulled the cans through the tubes into the camps. The women needed the fat and the Swiss men were able to smuggle quite a large number of cans of lard into the camps on many occasions. Fortunately, they were never caught or there would have been serious consequences. Several times there were close calls when a Japanese soldier came too close, but the Chinese was smart and always had a kitten with him to make the soldier think he was looking for his pet.

CONSTANT FEAR

Willi continued working at the museum, but leaving the house became more and more dangerous. The Swiss were no longer allowed to gather in groups of more than two, but they continued to visit each other anyway. The girls were growing, Agnes was five and Ruth three years old. Both children had blond hair and a very light complexion. One of Willi's and Leny's greatest fear was that one of the children would be kidnapped. They heard of young children, mostly girls, being taken from parents and then used as child prostitutes for the Japanese military. One evening Willi was standing in front of the house, holding Ruth. A Japanese officer approached. He talked with the child, stretching out his arms to see if she would go to him. Willi's heart beat faster as he clutched his child close to him. He was terrified for he knew that the moment the Japanese had her, she might be taken from him. Ruthie was a very friendly child, and was generally not afraid of anything or anyone. Willi prayed that she would not go to the soldier. He could feel her little arms tightly around his neck; she was afraid of the stranger in uniform. Thank God. The soldier kept on motioning her to go to him.

Suddenly, Ruth turned her head, frowned at the man, and let out a bark, "Arf, arf." She was barking at the soldier. To be called a dog was a great insult to a Japanese and Willi had no idea how she knew that. The soldier was taken aback for a moment, angrily turned his heels and walked off.

Several weeks later they had another frightening incident with the child. From the time she could walk she was fascinated by all kinds of creatures and frequently discovered a beetle or caterpillar in the yard. On that particular evening, Willi and Leny were in their living room with friends who had stopped by for a visit. It was still quite early, around four in the afternoon, and, as always, they were discussing food. Ruth was playing on the porch,

Agnes and Bardi were in the back weaving baskets.

Occasionally Ruth came inside, declaring, "Ular, ular."

Willi said to her, "That is nice, Ruthie, now go play some more." She walked off, but returned a short while later, still saying, "ular." This was the Malay word for caterpillar, but it also meant snake. Willi and Leny thought that she had seen a small caterpillar, there always were many around the yard. Finally, after she came in for the fourth time, the grown-ups decided to see what she was talking about. There on the porch in a corner was a large cobra; it was coiled up, its impressive head swaying from side to side, ready to strike. From that day on they paid very close attention to what Ruth said and were thankful that she had not approached the dangerous reptile.

Willi and Leny again had some friends over one evening. The girls were playing in their room and it was getting time for them to go to sleep. Leny went to tuck them in and give them a good-night kiss, but Ruthie was not in the room. Agnes did not know where she was. Leny ran into the living room and alerted the others. They searched the entire house. Hamra and Bardi had already retreated to their room, they had not seen her either. Willi and Leny became frantic, the child could not be found anywhere in the house, she was not in the garden and she was not with Hamra or Bardi. When Willi reached the front yard, he saw that the gate was open. By that time it was pitch dark outside, it was around seven in the evening. They split up and walked in different directions. Willi walked down the street calling her name. He had walked about three blocks when he saw something white ahead of him. As he came closer, there sat Ruth on the side of the road in her white pajamas. Willi picked her up in his arms and as quickly as he could, went home and alerted the others to come in, that he had found her. It was not safe to be outside at night. In her hand Ruth was clutching a firefly; she told Willi that she had gone out of her room and was on the back porch when she saw it. She followed it around the side of the house, out the front yard, and was finally able to catch it when it rested on a branch on the side of the road. She had gone quite far and when she looked around, did not know where she was so she sat down by the side of the road, hoping that someone would find her. Willi and Leny made her promise that she would never again walk off, and that when she wanted to catch something, she had to come and get her parents.

Willi stopped keeping a diary altogether. They heard that a Dutch prisoner of war in Bandjarmasin had been keeping a diary which the Japanese managed to get a hold of. In the diary the man mentioned several names of people who had helped bring them food, and Dr. Weiss, the Swiss missionary doctor, was one of them. The Japanese went to his house, took him, his wife and nurse into the front yard and decapitated all three right there and then. They did not kill the children. In the confusion, the youngest, a three year old boy, wandered off and could not be found. After the war he was discovered living in a village. A native woman had taken the frightened and lost child into her care. Willi and Leny were not certain how many more people had been executed at that time in Bandjarmasin.

Another sad story they heard happened to one of their Dutch friends. The woman and her little four year old daughter were in one of the concentration camps. Whenever the prisoners were outside they had to line up while the Japanese held inspections. When a soldier walked by, the prisoners had to bow their heads. The small child did not want to bow, the soldier lifted his gun, aimed, and shot the child dead while she was holding her mother's hand.

Bandung had a beautiful animal park, but in 1944 all the animals in the zoo had starved, including five orangutans, numerous other primates, rhinoceros, deer and many more. Money to buy food for the animals had run out and they were left to slowly starve. The zoo keepers tried as long as possible to keep the animals alive, but they were no longer being paid and one after the other left. Willi met a man who told him that all the animals had died, and since he was always interested in collecting skulls of animals for the museum in Basel, he asked the man to get him a couple of the skulls of the orangutans. The following day the man arrived with a sack containing not just the heads, as Willi had asked, but the entire dead animals. The stench was unbearable. Willi managed to prepare the skulls, but the terrible odor made him sick for days.

Time went by slowly. There was no end of the war in sight, but they somehow survived. Food was a terrible problem, money was beginning to run out, and their diet became even more monotonous. Leny still had several bed sheets and table cloths left, and every couple of weeks she took one of the pieces of fabric and went to the market. There she bartered for hours to exchange the fabric for money to buy food and other items they needed to live. Even soap could no longer be bought. There was a cheese factory in Bandung which the Japanese had also taken over. In general, the Japanese did not eat cheese, but their food rations always contained some. Hamra had an agreement with several Japanese who lived nearby to exchange rice and vegetables for cheese. It was a wonderful treat and a good source of calcium.

Just down the street lived a group of Japanese, they were mostly civilians who worked in offices. Agnes and Ruth often went there to play. A river ran along the back of the yard, overgrown with vegetation. One day the men cut all the bushes down with sables and the girls watched the activities with interest. The men never bothered the girls. At the house was a small dog and the children often played with it. Soon it had puppies and the girls went to see them daily. One day the puppies were all gone. They looked around and then spotted the little animals in the shallow water of the river, their lifeless bodies slowly moving in the current. The girls just stood there, staring at the little corpses, tears running down their faces. They could not comprehend how anyone could do such a thing. One of the men saw the children and realized what they must have felt. He called to them to come to the house. Then he gave them a gift; a tiny can of condensed, sweetened milk. The girls took the can and ran home. Willi opened it and the girls spooned out every drop of the sweet milk. It was an unforgettable event which both remembered for the rest of their lives; the small can of sweet milk they received during the war. It was the only time they could remember that they had milk during that time.

For breakfast, lunch and dinner they ate rice. For breakfast the rice was cooked with duck eggs and spices, somewhat resembling oatmeal, for lunch and dinner the "kokki" made various rice dishes with vegetables when they could scrounge some together. They rarely had any meat, and only from time to time Leny was able to buy dried, salted fish at the market.

One night, it was after midnight, there was an incredible explosion near their house. An ammunition warehouse blew up, shattering the windows of the house. Ruth was not awakened by the loud bang, but Agnes was instantly awake and was terrified. For several nights she would not go into her own bed and slept with Leny and Willi. Then, only a few weeks later, a storm swept through the area, lifting the entire roof. Water came gushing down the walls and all the furniture had to be moved to the center of the rooms. Until they were able to have the roof repaired, the girls slept with their parents.

In the early spring days of 1945, Willi and another Swiss friend, Erwin, began a new hobby. They were raising the caterpillars of the Atlas moths (Attacus atlas). Each day Willi checked to see if one of the pupa had hatched; Ruthie was always close by. The caterpillars themselves were about six inches long and about three quarters of an inch thick. The body was smooth and Ruth often carried one of the harmless caterpillars on her arm.

Erwin was another friend who lived with them in Bandung. Before the war began he owned a watch and jewelry business. He had lived in Java since the early 1930's. Soon after the Japanese invaded the area, his entire inventory was taken from him. Shortly after that, a few officers went to his home and demanded he hand over his watches. He told them that he did not have any, they had all been taken from him already. The soldiers became enraged, they beat him so severely that all his teeth were knocked out. He was fortunate to survive the beating and kicking. He lay motionless on the floor, his attackers thought that he was dead and left. Erwin also grew up in Basel. He was a tall, handsome man. He was not married and was in his forties during the war. His parents were very affluent who had moved to Switzerland from Germany. They owned an import/export company. Erwin went to America in the 1920's, from there he moved to Mexico where he lived on a hacienda. As he was the oldest son in the family, he took over the jewelry business and moved to Java.

ANTICIPATION OF PEACE

On May 29th, 1945, a very strange thing happened, which especially impressed the natives. From that day on, they were convinced that the war would soon be over. The birthday of the Japanese emperor, Tenno Heika, was being celebrated. Willi was at the museum standing by a window looking out at the celebration activities on the lawn in front of the building. The museum had obtained a new flag, a rare event because of the fabric shortage. Young, uniformed apprentices hoisted the new Japanese flag while all the employees were gathered around, looking up at the flag with the rising sun. A high ranking Japanese officer was giving a speech, when, in the middle of the ceremony, the flag somehow became loose, and slowly slid down the flag pole until it lay in a heap on the ground. Not a sound was uttered. A Japanese soldier quietly picked up the flag and carried it into the museum. The very superstitious natives began to whisper. Rumors spread through the city that there had been a sign that the Japanese were going to be defeated and the war would end. Rumors spread very fast among the natives, even without radios or newspapers. If one asked a native the source of the news, he always answered, "kabar angin," news from the wind.

The end of June Jakob arrived in Bandung from Batavia with the young daughter of the Swiss missionary who had been killed by the Japanese in Bandjarmasin. He was bringing the girl to stay with Willi and Leny for a while until she was able to continue the trip to live with another family somewhere in the mountains where it was safer and quieter.

The end of July Willi noted a larger than usual number of marine soldiers wearing white uniforms. He wondered if it meant that Japan had lost the majority of its marine. Nobody knew what was going on, and the uncertainty was becoming unbearable. There was an office in Bandung where Swiss citizens could get information. It was kept a secret, they all had to use great caution going there. A radio was in the office, and even though only one station could be heard because the rest had been blocked, everyone was eager to receive even the tiniest bit of reliable news. They had to be extremely careful because it was still forbidden to listen to radios.

On that day, Willi was standing in front of the building when a tall, older man with gray hair wearing a hat approached him and asked, "Are you also Swiss?" They began to talk, and it turned out that the old man grew up in a small town very close to Willi's hometown. He was born in 1874, and during his youth had run away after committing a minor offense. He had taken his brother's military identification certificate and then joined the Royal Netherlands East Indies army. He started to cry when they spoke of mutual acquaintances, and for a short while both forgot that they were in an occupied country living among foreign races. The man's name was Adolf Meyer and he lived with his Sundanese wife near Bandung. He owned a house with a garden, but told Willi that he had problems with looting gangs. They had attacked him and his wife, and when he tried to defend himself, they had almost severed his left hand. Meyer wanted to leave, as everyone else did too.

Another Swiss national holiday arrived, but the small group of Swiss could not celebrate as it was forbidden to meet in groups. Willi, Leny and the girls went to visit friends. At around one in the afternoon the air alarms sounded, a few hours later the sirens went off again, but nothing happened. Their friends told them that they heard a rumor that the Japanese army was deteriorating and that Russia had declared war with Japan. After the visit they rode home. In honor of the day of independence, Willi told the children the story of William Tell.

The next day at the museum two of Willi's Javanese friends told him that there would be a lunar eclipse and to observe it carefully because with the eclipse, the war would end. At night he and Leny went into their back yard and looked up at the dark sky. The moon turned darker and darker until it was completely in the earth's shadow. It turned dark green to almost reddish until the shadow disappeared, and then the moon once again shone in its full beauty in the cloudless tropical night. They stood quietly in the back yard, looking up into the sky, wondering if there would soon be peace. Was the prophecy of Djojobojo coming true?

A few days later, on August 6th, Willi wrote in his diary that they had reached the zero-point as to the entire war situation. They knew absolutely nothing for certain, all they heard were rumors and speculations. It was a frustrating situation to have to live with such uncertainties and not knowing what was actually happening. From every direction there were rumors and speculations, but nothing was ever confirmed, and the whole situation became even more confusing. Only a few days later he wrote down his thoughts:

It seems impossible, but maybe the rumors are true that the Japanese have been defeated. We heard on the grape-vine that Stalin has declared "them" war. Some people said something about an atomic bomb. What are they talking about and what is an atomic bomb? Not even the physicists and chemists among us can conceive the meaning of this. Is it true? It is about time that it is finally going to end. Food prices have gone up tremendously, one egg costs ninety cents, a kilo of pork forty guilders, and one gram of Emitrin powder (medicine) two hundred fifty guilders. We used to pay five guilders for a whole pig.

Willi's entries in his diary the next several days were all written in Swiss dialect.

August 11ᵗʰ, 1945. Early in the morning we heard that the war is over and that Japan has surrendered. The Potsdam ultimatum has been accepted.

August 12ᵗʰ, 1945. In Bandung more than one hundred people have been arrested for spreading rumors. We all feel very ill at ease. The situation is very uncertain and we still do not know what is going on.

August 22ⁿᵈ, 1945. Today, at 7:00 p.m. there was finally an official announcement on the radio that Japan has lost the war and has capitulated. The Japanese in our neighborhood are alert and happy, and are laughing and singing, they are apparently also glad that this terrible war is over. We had anticipated that there would be a wave or hara-kiri among the Japanese, but this did not happen. We had silently hoped that this would rid us of the feared and cruel Japanese Kempetai.

THE WAR ENDED BUT FIGHTING CONTINUED

Toward the end of August Mrs. Vrede was getting worse. The two nurses were still with her around the clock, and every possible moment Leny went to see her. Some time ago the morphine had run out, so instead, their source brought cobra venom in ampoules. According to the pharmacists and the nurses, the venom had the same effect as morphine and it relieved pain. Unfortunately, one day an ampoule was left on the patient's night stand by mistake. When she saw that it was cobra venom, she became agitated and thought that someone was trying to poison her. The nurse on duty could not calm her down, so she rode her bicycle as fast as she could to get Leny. The two women rode back to Mrs. Vrede's house where Leny was able to assure her that they had checked with the pharmacists who assured them that the cobra venom was safe to be used and would help ease her pain. She stayed with the patient for some time to calm the frightened woman. She died on September 11th, a month after the war officially ended. After the cobra venom Willi was again able to obtain more morphine and until the patient's death, his source brought them a total of 900 ampoules while they were taking care of the dying woman. It had been heartbreaking to watch her deteriorate daily. They still did not know where the husband was. Some women and men had already been released from the prison camps, but there was no sign of her husband. Her two sons were still with acquaintances, they had suffered tremendously to see their mother so ill, and everyone, including Mrs. Vrede, agreed that it was best for the boys to stay away. During the time of her death, the Japanese had disappeared from the city. All over there were native gangs causing much disorder. Willi had to obtain a death certificate to make the funeral arrangements, but not a single doctor would come to the woman's house. Willi searched out every doctor he knew of, but to no avail. Many patients who were coming from the concentration camps were given priority, and many Dutch physicians were still somewhere in the prison camps or they themselves were too ill or too weak to go to the deceased woman's house. Finally, he found a physician who agreed to sign the death certificate without seeing the deceased; Willi's description had convinced him that the woman was dead. Then Willi rode his bicycle to the outskirts of the town to the Pandu cemetery to have a grave dug. After a long search he found a Chinese who was willing to provide a casket and horse-drawn hearse. The man gave Willi detailed instructions as to how they were to proceed so that the funeral procession could get through the city without hindrance, and without being attacked or shot at by the looting gangs. Everyone was told to bring their bicycles to the funeral. They gathered at the house, the casket was carried out and placed on the hearse, and the funeral procession walked slowly to the end of the street. As soon as the small group of mourners turned into the next street, the horses began to trot and then gallop. Everyone jumped on their bicycles, and the entire funeral procession rode as fast as they could through the streets until they reached the cemetery. They hoped that they would not be bothered or shot at if they went fast. The funeral had to be held without any ceremony, partly because there was no minister, and partly because the cemetery had turned into a dangerous place for Europeans. Willi and Leny and the others placed flowers on the grave and said good-bye to their friend who had suffered so much during the past years.

Slowly more and more Japanese were again seen. A very strange situation followed. The Japanese were still armed and nobody had yet seen any Allied soldiers. The gangs of native bandits rampaged through the city armed with Dutch rifles, swords, spears and knives. They shouted "merdeka," freedom, and robbed and plundered everything. Everywhere skirmishes broke out between the Japanese and the natives.

On September 25th, 1945, Willi wrote the first letter to his parents since December 1941. It arrived a month later.

Dear parents,

Finally it is possible again to send you a letter, and to let you know how we survived this terrible war. First I want to tell you that Leny, the children and I are well. We hope the same of you and all the other relatives. How are grandfather and grandmother? Agnes already has her permanent teeth and has to start school in the spring and we hope that this will be in Switzerland. Both Agnes and Ruth speak fluently Swiss-German, Dutch and Malay and they even picked up some Japanese. We received the last telegram from you in January. Since the end of 1941 until now we have not received a single letter from you. On January 15th, 1942, I left Balikpapan with other Swiss. Leny and the children had already left in November (before the war started here) for Java. Until the Japanese invaded Java I was in Tjepu (an oil place in east Java), but I left there on February 27th, 1942, and we went to Tawangmangu near Solo where our families had been living for some time. We moved to Bandung in February 1943 where I worked in the museum. Bandung is a city of about 150,000 inhabitants and is surrounded by volcanoes. Life in Bandung was difficult for us, we were constantly surrounded by the Japanese secret police who accused everyone, whether Dutch or neutral, of being spies. The war here was against races, and the Japanese aimed to slowly kill off all the Europeans in a typical Asian fashion. I will write more about that another time. On December 13th, 1943, I was arrested with other BPM Swiss after the Japanese police searched and ransacked our entire house. We were indicted on "underground actions and assistance to the Dutch." You will have a hard time comprehending this in our free Switzerland that someone is thrown in jail for helping poor hungry European women and children. After ten days of incarceration three of us were set free, for lack of proof. I was emaciated, covered with parasites, my clothes were full of ticks, and a rash covered my entire body. Other than that I was healthy and quickly recovered. We tried several times to get away from here but it was not possible. Even our consular representative spent more than four months in jail. What the Japanese monsters did to some of our other compatriots you will hear later, several Swiss were even decapitated. Well, the Japanese have now been punished. For the time being we are staying in Bandung and are anxiously awaiting the arrival of the Allies. As soon as it is possible we will come home to Switzerland. By the way, we lost everything in Balikpapan, and arrived in Java with a couple of suitcases and some clothes. We had enough money and enough to eat, and are not the only ones who lost everything they owned. At least we are still alive. I hope this reaches you in best of health and I will write soon again. Please write us soon, our address is: Carel Fabritiuslaan 8, Bandung, Java.

A strange situation was developing in Java and Willi did not know what to make of it. Not a single Allied soldier had been seen. Many homes of the Europeans were either still occupied by the Japanese or natives. The Indonesians considered themselves as rulers, and Europeans were confronted by people carrying pointed bamboo sticks. They were questioned and inspected to see if they were carrying weapons. Every native was armed with at least a knife or dagger. The Indonesians were carrying guns taken from the Japanese. The biggest hatred was between the Eurasians and natives. The entire "merdeka" movement had been initiated by the Japanese and their currency was still in circulation.

As they had not received any news from home, Willi wrote another letter on October 10th:

Dear parents, on September 24th I wrote you my first letter and am wondering if you received it. In the meantime much has become clearer to us, and I can advise you that we will be coming home the first chance we have. We are planning on spending Christmas with you, finally, after having been gone for seven years. We will remain in Switzerland for several months, so we can fully recuperate, but I am not sure yet of the exact plans. One thing is certain, I have a secure position with the company for the future. One problem are my clothes, I lost all my warm clothes in Balikpapan. Well, I am sure that this problem can also be solved, and maybe you can make some arrangements for me for clothing cards. I can inform you that we were never seriously ill during the war, the children are both well and so is Leny. I am healthy too, just very thin. Please do not worry about us and we will soon be able to tell you everything in person. We are looking so much forward to our reunion in our beloved Switzerland. Love, Willi.

On October 10th the situation had reached its peak. Indonesian mobs walked through the streets with guns, swords and spears, detaining the Japanese and taking their swords. The airfield Nadir was taken over by the local mob. At around 11:00 in the morning Willi heard gun shots in the city, close to their house. The Kempetai then went into action and in a short time were able to control the situation. As soon as shots were fired, the natives ran away. In the afternoon the situation was completely under control and the airfield was taken back. In one street four armed Japanese soldiers drove a group of Indonesians ahead of them, the natives were running as fast as they could. Willi was standing nearby, watching the activities. Everywhere he saw posters which read, "we are ready to die for freedom." He heard that the British High Command had ordered the Japanese police to restore calm and order in the cities of Java and the Japanese heeded the command thoroughly. Any person on the street who had a weapon was shot dead. It soon became known that the Japanese shot without warning, even if a person only carried a bamboo pole. Willi was returning home from an errand one day when he witnessed such an incident from up close. He was on his bicycle when he encountered two Indonesians who each had a pointed bamboo stick in their hands. They approached Willi in a threatening manner. Two Japanese soldiers came from the opposite direction with guns slung over their shoulders. They quietly approached the two, drew their guns, aimed, and shot the two dead without uttering a word. With their shoes they pushed the dead bodies to the side of the road, called a passing Indonesian on a horse cart, and said, "angkat," remove.

The Japanese drove through the city on a small armored tank, one soldier manned the canon. They were heading toward the city limits to the airfield Andir. The Indonesians had barricaded the road with large oil drums. The soldiers called out something and the people quickly removed the barriers. After the Japanese passed through, the Indonesians again set up the barriers at the same location. A group of spectators gathered. A short while later the soldiers with the tank returned. The Indonesians laughed defiantly, waiting for an order. Not a word was uttered. Two shots rang out. Many people sank dead to the ground, others lay bleeding in the street. In a few days order was again restored in the city after the Japanese had relentlessly killed the mobsters and looters. Many innocent people had been killed by the looting gangs. Willi's old Chinese friend Chang was also killed during those days. They had been friends for years and he lived next door to Willi and Leny in Bandung. A group of Indonesian rebels arrived, went to his door, and without warning, he was hacked to death. His wife and two children were able to flee by climbing over a wall. A grotesque situation developed, and they had to be thankful that the despised Japanese were still there to protect them.

Finally, they were able to read in the newspaper what had happened in Nagasaki and Hiroshima. The atom bombs saved the lives of thousands of Europeans who lived in the areas the Japanese had occupied. Later Willi heard of Japan's plans that after the final war victory, all the Europeans were to be taken to the swamps of Borneo and killed or left to die.

On October 14th a notice went around the city that upon nightfall, Indonesia would declare war with the Dutch, Eurasians and Ambonese. The Europeans were again under Japanese protection. They were amazed at the irony of destiny. The Indonesian radio was broadcasting that each Indonesian would find his enemy that night; this was a call for a massacre of Europeans. Still, Willi had not yet seen a single Allied soldier. There continued to be occasional battles between the Indonesians and the Japanese. The mob gathered in the streets, and as soon as the soldiers showed up, they ran away. Many local natives were also attacked by the fanatics. The Japanese were ruthless. Willi saw one soldier force an Indonesian to swallow six bullets, turn around and shoot another man with his pistol.

Still every day Willi went to work at the museum. One morning all the Japanese scientists congregated there. They were disarmed except for their Samurai swords; all the paleontologists, geologists and mineralogists who Willi had worked for. All of a sudden a mob of about one hundred Indonesians gathered in front of the building; they were armed, and were out to kill the Japanese scientists. Willi knew the new museum director quite well, his name was Ali, and asked him what he thought of the situation.

Ali said, "You can see for yourself, our people want to kill the Japanese who have tormented us for three years."

"Ali," Willi said, "if this entire mob enters our beautiful museum to kill all the Japanese, everything will be destroyed. Who is going to clean up the mess and all the blood?" Ali thought for a moment, nodded his head in agreement, and went to a window to talk to the mob. Willi quickly walked to the group of scientists and told them to follow him. He took them to a back door and let them out. He knew that the men had not joined the war of their own free will. The old professor Okada's lips quivered as he shook Willi's hand, nodded, and Willi saw the skinny legs with the varicose veins quickly follow the others out the back door. They were able to go to a collection site the British High Command had assigned them. It was a self-internment, since the Allied troops sill had not arrived in Java.

Meanwhile, in Switzerland, Willi's parents received the following letter: *Swiss Political Department, Division of Foreign Affairs, B.21.318. Neth. Ind. BO.*

Bern, October 18th, 1945. Dear Mrs. Mohler, In response to your inquiry of October 10th, we regret to have to inform you that unfortunately we have no news regarding our compatriots in Java, even though we have for some time now been trying to obtain information. Recent developments may be the reason for this. As soon as we are able to obtain news about your son, we will immediately advise you. Respectfully, The Chief of Foreign Affairs.

The situation became more and more precarious. Europeans were murdered and molested. The gangs came from other areas of the island. Finally, the Swiss again had a representative at the consulate who at the same time was also a Red Cross official. He stayed at the best hotel in Bandung, and the first thing he did was hang the Swiss and the Red Cross flags from the building. Both flags were taken down immediately by Indonesian guerrillas and burned; the people had vowed to never again tolerate a foreign flag. The Swiss official complained to Willi about the incident and the man did not know to whom he should protest. Willi felt that they certainly had more important concerns than to worry about a burned flag, they wanted to leave and go home. He knew the secretary of Sukarno and asked the man if he would write a short note of apology about the incident and have it signed by Sukarno. This was done, and so the youngest republic apologized to the oldest that eager freedom fighters had burned the Swiss flag without knowing what they were doing. That problem was thus solved. Shortly after the incident, Willi received a letter from the Swiss consulate reminding him that he had not paid his military taxes for four years, and that he was to pay the taxes before returning to Switzerland. They had just received notice from the British that they would soon be able to be evacuated. He owed the Swiss government five hundred guilders in military taxes, but had no way of obtaining such a large amount of money. Most of their money had by then been almost completely depleted. Then Leny had a great idea. She still had one linen bed sheet left and fabric was still in great demand. She soon found an eager buyer, and after bartering for a long time, sold it for exactly five hundred guilders at the black market. Willi took the money and paid his military taxes. At least now they could plan their return to their homeland with a clear conscience!

November arrived, still they waited for news that they could leave. On the 2nd they heard greetings from their families over the radio. For the first time in years they heard their families' voices and were thankful that everyone was well. The following day Willi heard that three company employees, two Swiss and a Dutch, had been murdered in Lares, Sumatra, and two daughters of one of the Swiss men were missing and had probably also been killed. Another Swiss, an engineer, had been seriously injured in Surabaya. Then one by one the Europeans began to leave. The wife and daughter of Willi's Polish friend, who had committed suicide after being tortured by the Japanese, were flying to Singapore, and from there continue on to Europe by ship. Heinrich, his wife and daughter were also able to leave. His valuable material of the Java man was safe. More and more of their old Dutch friends were set free. Willi and Leny were still safeguarding their friends' valuables; it was still hidden in the wooden trunk. One by one they came by, thankful that their valuables were safe and to have them back. Most of them had lost everything else they owned and only had tattered and torn clothes on their backs. Leny and Willi gave away some of their clothes even though they were by then in pretty bad shape, but they were in better condition than some of the clothes their old friends wore.

On November 10th they received notice from the Swiss consulate that they could leave Bandung by plane on the 14th. Only a few personal belongings could be taken; arrangements had been made to have all the trunks taken to a building where they would be stored under consular protection and forwarded at a later date.

EVACUATION FROM THE WAR-TORN ISLAND

On November 14th, 1945, Willi and Leny woke the girls up early in the morning. Hamra and Bardi were already up, both were crying silently. The girls hugged their long-time servants as Willi placed their few small suitcases by the door. Leny had given Hamra everything they no longer needed or were unable to take back to Switzerland. They ordered a taxi to take them to the airport. From all over the island families arrived, there were twenty-five Swiss men, women and children who boarded the English transport plane, a Dakota, at 9:30 in the morning at the air field Andir. The plane took off flying in a north-westerly direction, and in twenty-five minutes was already over the coast of Java. Clouds covered the Java Sea. They flew along the shores of Sumatra, crossing the island near the Musi Delta. At 11:00 they flew over the estuary of the Sumpur river and then over the Strait of Banka. About an hour and a half later they crossed the Lingga archipelago and the equator. The plane descended slowly over the Riouw archipelago, and at 1:30 in the afternoon they landed in Singapore. They walked across the runway to a waiting truck and were taken to the hotel Seaview. They were tired and somewhat dazed, and still could not believe that they were actually finally out of harms way and on their way home. Everyone enjoyed the peace and safety of the city. Things were well organized. The British immediately arranged activities and parties for the children who were taken on outings to battleships, were given toys, played games, and received gifts and candy. Singapore was a hustle and bustle of thousands of refugees, all trying to find a way home. Willi immediately went to see the Swiss consul to find out what they had to do. The man sat behind a large desk. On it was a huge pile of

Malacca dollars. He asked Willi how much he needed. Willi told him that he needed no money, he had enough, but wanted to leave for Switzerland with his family right away. The consul informed him that he had been instructed by the Swiss government in Bern to send all the Swiss to New Zealand or to Australia; the Swiss government would pay for the entire trip. He also told Willi that there was no work in Switzerland, and if he wanted to go there, he would have to pay for the trip himself. Willi was getting irritated. He told the man that he would take care of the trip himself, his company would pay for it anyway. The consul then invited Willi to sit down and chat with him for a while, but Willi declined. He felt that he was in the wrong place and left the consulate as fast as he could. He thought to himself that it always was the same story.

After a restful night and a good breakfast they went to the Raffles hotel. There they met their old friends Christian and Flori who had also just arrived. Other families coming from Sumatra had also gathered at the BPM office. All around they met old friends and acquaintances, some they had not seen since 1941; it was a joyful reunion, and they told each other how they had survived the war. After a delicious dinner they went to bed early that evening; seeing so many new faces and running into old friends had made them tired. The next day they stayed at the hotel. A relief organization handed out clothes and shoes to the refugees; finally they had decent clothing and shoes to wear. One day they went to the Raffles museum. Willi and Leny were fascinated with the beautiful collection of artifacts, and decided to return if they had the time. They had to be back at the hotel in the afternoon to meet a special visitor. Lady Mountbatten was visiting the group of refugees. She asked the families how they were doing, where they came from and where they were going. She spoke with Willi for quite some time. She told him that she had just been to Java and did not understand what was happening there either. Sunday was spent at the hotel again which was right on the beach. They still could not quite believe that the nightmare of the last few years was finally over. They enjoyed the safety of the area and thanked God that they had survived the war. The reality finally began to sink in that they were really on their way home and out of harms way. On Monday they returned to the Raffles museum once more where they spent the whole day. There were interesting items from Malacca and Indonesia, and Willi was particularly interested in the ethnographic artifacts and weapons. Fortunately, the museum had not been damaged during the war. On Tuesday, while going on a walk, Ruth discovered a large spider. Its body alone was about six inches long. It was a

Nephila maculata and she found it in the gardens of the hotel. Willi sketched it in his diary. On Wednesday morning they again went to the beach. Then, in the afternoon, all the youngsters were taken through the city on a long-boat. The next day Willi sent a telegram to their family that they were in Singapore on their way home. Later in the evening, again for the first time in years, Willi and Leny went to see a film, and felt that they were finally beginning to live a more or less normal, civilized life again. Most of that Friday was spent at the beach. The view from the hotel was to the south toward the islands of the Rious archipelago. There were many ships in the harbor. They watched the sun go down, and enjoyed the beauty of the last rays reflecting on the still water of the ocean. On Saturday the children were again taken to a British battle ship. Once more a long-boat picked them up at the hotel to take them to the ship which was a great adventure. On Sunday Otto and Rosa left for Switzerland via Colombo. The Schmidhof's and Winter family stopped by the hotel for a visit. On Monday English sailors came to visit the children, who were again taken on an English battle ship. The girls left at 2:30 in the afternoon and did not return until after dark.

When Willi asked one of the sailors around 5:30 where the children were, he said, "Oh, they are at a party aboard the ship and will probably not return before seven." At around exactly that time they heard chatter and laughter, and the girls arrived, carrying candy. Both their faces were covered with chocolate smears, something they had never before tasted. And again the next morning they went to the ship. Willi and Leny watched with smiles on their faces as the little children climbed aboard the long-boat, laughing and singing, and having a good time. The British were extremely caring and wanted to provide as much fun for the children as possible. They knew what the youngsters had gone through during the last several years. The long-boats were about twenty-five feet long and able to transport twenty men. They were powered by propellers and traveled both on land and in the water, riding over a gang-way right into the hull of the ship.

On November 28th they were told that they could leave the following day or the day after on the Dutch ship the "Niewe Amsterdam." Shortly after the announcement they were told that the plans had to be changed because the Dutch had declared that they would only take on Dutch citizens. This greatly annoyed the British R.A.P.W.I. (Relief of Allied Prisoners of War and Internees). The Dutch seemed to have already forgotten that they could not have survived the war without the assistance of people from other countries, or without the Swiss who had helped their Dutch countrymen during the hard times of the occupation. Willi and Leny were disappointed, but knew that sooner or later they would be able to leave. They decided to make the best of the time, so they took the girls back to the beach again. They discovered all kinds of interesting sea creatures and found brittle stars, shells and crabs. The next day Will signed them up for the next available flight to Colombo because there just seemed to be no ships available for them to leave on from Singapore. Then, on December 1st, they were notified at four in the afternoon that they could depart for the airport at six the following morning for a flight to Colombo, Ceylon. Early that morning they took off from the Strait Johore on a Sunderland air-boat. They flew along the Malacca coast, then toward north Sumatra, then they were over the Indian Ocean. At 5:30 in the evening the coast of Ceylon came into view and they landed at the Royal Air Force station Koggala at 6 at night. They had traveled for twelve hours straight and were exhausted. The men were taken to barracks at the air force quarters, women and children were taken to hotels. The next day they left at 1 p.m. to go to Galle where they were to take the train to Colombo. Upon arriving at the train station, they were told that they had to return to Koggala because of some difficulties. After a long wait they were finally taken to Colombo on a large military truck. It was a long drive on a winding road along the coast lined with coconut trees. Leny had Agnes on her lap while Willi held Ruth. Cramped together on the floor of the truck the refugees held on to their meager belongings. They arrived after ten at night and were taken to barracks near Mount Lawinia. They were so tired that they immediately fell asleep. The next morning they were up early and went to the beach. Willi collected sand samples which contained foraminifers to add to his collection. The barracks were right on the beach. The waves crashed on land with tremendous force. The sound was heard day and night. Right next to the barracks stood a building which looked very familiar. Willi and Leny remembered their short stay on the verandah of the hotel seven years earlier where they had stopped for a nice cold beer and a cup of tea on their way to Borneo. The next day, it was December 5th, they went to the city where they received more clothing and shoes. Ceylon was a beautiful island, the view was spectacular. Coconut trees lined the shores, and fishing boats with large white sails moved gracefully over the high waves. The next day the announcement finally came that they could leave the following morning.

SEA VOYAGE HOME

On December 7, 1945, they embarked on the "Tamaroa," a 12,000 ton mutton ship which used to transport meat from Australia and New Zealand to England. During the war it was converted into a military transport ship. When the refugees boarded the vessel the sea was rough. Leny became sea sick right away; she was also three months pregnant. All the men had to sleep on one side of the ship in large quarters, women and children were in cabins. The captain told Willi that the ship moved at fifteen knots per hour and that the voyage would last twenty-two days. On the third day the weather turned better and the sea was calm. Willi and the girls watched the flying fish for a while. Every few days they had to turn their watches back. On the sixth day the ship entered the Gulf of Aden east of Perim near the entrance into the Red Sea. On the eleventh day at sea they entered the harbor of Suez early in the morning where they anchored. Everyone disembarked, and they were taken by long-boat to Ataka, an American relief warehouse. They had an elaborate reception, and were given food and refreshments while the military band played. German prisoners of war, who had been in the Rommel army, waited on the refugees during dinner. Then they were taken to a large room with long tables and were given winter coats, hats, caps, gloves, shoes and more. Willi and Leny selected warm coats for them all, some sweaters, pants and dresses, shoes and socks, and a warm, cozy robe for each girl. One was pink and the other one light blue with animal prints. The Germans then carried the sacks back to the ship. At the harbor Willi saw many sunken ships, only the masts and chimneys were visible. They left in the late afternoon, and entered the canal around five, arriving in Port Said the next morning. Dealers in small rowboats came to the ship, a rope with a basket was used to pass

161

merchandise and money between the ship's passengers and the merchants. The girls each got an orange. Willi explained about the canal, and told them that Ferdinand Lesseps had been its inventor, and that it was built in the mid 1800's. The weather was improving and Leny felt a bit better. Every afternoon Willi took the girls on deck where they were given a cup of tomato juice which they thoroughly enjoyed, and which they drank out of their own little hand-crafted Djokja-silver cups from Java. For the rest of their lives, when they tasted tomato juice, it reminded them of their afternoon visits on the deck of the large ocean cruiser. On the fifteenth day the ship passed Malta. There was a Christmas party for the children. Christmas day was the eighteenth day at sea. In the morning the Sierra Nevada was visible to the north with its snow covered peaks. It was the first snow Agnes and Ruth had ever seen. They enjoyed a delicious Christmas dinner. It began with tomato soup, followed by goose, pork, cauliflower, potatoes, pudding, nuts and oranges. It was the best meal they had eaten in many years. Later in the evening of Christmas day Willi showed the girls the Rock of Gibraltar which rose from the ocean in the far distance. On the twenty-second day at sea the lighthouses of the Irish coast lined the shores, in the late afternoon they were near the coast of England, and they arrived in Liverpool late at night. It was December 30th. The next morning everyone debarked the ship, but Willi, Leny, the girls and a few other Swiss waited and waited and froze. It was extremely cold. They had to wait from nine in the morning until five in the evening when they were finally taken to a guest house by the Red Cross. All the Danes, Dutch, French, Norwegians and Swedes were greeted by their countries' representatives in the morning and taken to hotels, all except the Swiss. An eerie fog hung over the city and when they arrived in the small room, the beds were ice cold, the water frozen in the wash bowls. Agnes and Ruth trembled from the cold. The four huddled together in the bed to keep warm. The next day Willi bought a hat, and later they took a taxi to the city. They were notified at night to continue their trip to London the next morning. On January 1st, 1946, they boarded the train and arrived in London at 3:30 in the afternoon. As they got off the train, the Swiss consul was there to greet them, and he took them to a very nice guest house, Charles Street number 33, in the center of London. The consul then escorted the small group of Swiss to the hotel Dorchester where they were treated to a fine dinner. Willi found it amusing that the telephone number at the hotel was Mayfair 8888. For the first time in many years they truly enjoyed a civilized atmosphere. Willi was quite curious why all of a sudden the Swiss government had such an elaborate reception for them. Later he found out that a few days earlier, several other Swiss had already arrived from South East Asia, and had experienced the same neglect by the Swiss government. One of them, it was their old friend Erwin, wrote an article in the Zurich newspaper about the "always helpful Switzerland" who helped other countries and organized relief aid. Swiss citizens, though, were less interesting, and one could not improve the Swiss "image" by assisting its own citizens. The article certainly had its effect, and Willi, Leny and the girls enjoyed the next few days in London. They saw Buckingham Palace and the changing of the guards. Everywhere they went they could see the tremendous destruction of the city. Entire sections of houses were gone. Willi found out that according to official reports, one million homes had been damaged, of which about 40,000 were completely destroyed. In the afternoon they applied for a French visa and exchanged money. They visited Madam Tussaud's wax museum and on January 3rd left London at ten at night. They spent the night aboard ship in New Haven. The following day they left on the T.S.S. Isle of Guernsey, and arrived in Dieppe at noon. The city was a jumble of ruins; it was completely destroyed. The trip continued by train in the afternoon heading for Paris. Everywhere they saw the destruction of the war. Late at night they arrived in Paris and went directly to the hotel De Reynolds near the Place d'Etoile. They were exhausted from the long boat and train trip, and went to bed right away. The following morning a waiter knocked on their door and brought black coffee and a delicious French bread. Willi asked the waiter to bring their breakfast in about an hour, with milk and butter for the children, as well as cheese and jam. The waiter gave Willi a strange look, and told him that he had just brought them their breakfast, nothing else was available. Several hours later Willi went to the Swiss embassy where they were organizing the return to Switzerland of the many refugees. He was told that they had to go through a quarantine in Pontarlier. He protested, and told them that he now wanted to go directly home with his family. They were not about to be quarantined somewhere; since leaving Indonesia they had been traveling for six weeks. He was told that he would have to pay for the trip himself, so he borrowed a thousand Swiss Francs from the embassy and bought their tickets to Basel. The next day they climbed aboard the train that would take them home. It was the last stretch of the long and exhausting journey. Their few small suitcases were with them in the train compartment, but the conductor said that they could not have their luggage with them, and took them to one of the cargo trains. When they arrived in Basel their suitcases had been cut open with a knife, and the few items they had been able to save during the war were all gone, including the clothes they had been given by relief organizations in Ceylon and in Suez. Essentially, they had what was on their backs or in their hand luggage. Willi also lost the bronze arm ring mold he had found in Dago during the war. He had put the artifact carefully wrapped in cotton into a cigar box. The thieves must have thought that the box actually contained cigars, and when it did not, probably threw it out of the train. Willi checked later with the rail company if the item might have been found alongside the tracks somewhere between Paris and Basel, but nothing ever showed up. Somewhere in that countryside is an old Hindu-Javanese mold, or maybe someone found it and has it somewhere in his or her house, not aware of what the item actually represents. Along with the mold some precious artifacts they had wrapped in some clothes also disappeared.

HOME AT LAST

At the train station in Basel were Willi's and Leny's families, and everyone hugged and cried. The Swiss government then treated the returning refugees to a excellent dinner at the hotel Fluegelrad near the train station in Basel. Willi and Leny ordered bratwurst, hashed brown potatoes and a salad, something they had not had since 1938. The waitress told them that they could have a veal steak or even a pork chop, but they preferred the Swiss sausages. When Leny's father drove up in front of their house, the whole street was lined up with family, friends and acquaintances from their home town. Welcome home banners were hung, people waved, and there was much laughter. Ruthie did not like all the hugging and kissing, she kept wiping her cheeks, and tried to hide behind Leny. Who were all these strangers? she thought. She had never seen her grandparents or the rest of the large family. Willi's mother cried and cried, and his father had a happy smile on his kind face. Shortly after they arrived, he took Willi aside for a moment and handed him an invoice. It was for a thousand Francs and had just arrived. It was for the money Willi had borrowed in Paris just a few days earlier. Here the government was certainly prompt to request payment of money borrowed by a Swiss family who had just been evacuated from South East Asia. Of course, Willi repaid the government immediately. They quickly settled in their beloved homeland. For some time Willi had difficulties having his salary transferred from Holland to Switzerland. They had just lost everything during the war, but the Swiss clearing house only allowed Willi to receive three hundred Francs a month for a family of four, with a third child on its way. But alas, Willi thought, we are, after all, only Swiss. Willi was given ten months leave by his company and eventually was able to receive his full salary.

Right after their arrival, Leny's family arranged a celebration with all the trimmings of Christmas, and with all the aunts and uncles, grandparents and cousins present. There even was a Christmas angel; one of Leny's cousins dressed up as the angel and handed the two little girls presents. Each received a doll, chocolates, clothes, coloring pencils and paper, books, and hand-knit woolen stockings. It was the only thing the girls did not like, they had never worn stockings before, and the wool made their legs itch. Delicious meals were prepared, but it took Agnes and Ruth a long time to become accustomed to the food; it tasted very strange, they were used to eating rice and spicy foods. Now all of a sudden they had to eat mashed potatoes, sweet puddings and other strange tasting foods. Willi and Leny often glanced at their two little girls at the big dining table, their spoons playing with the food, their little cheeks as round as those of a hamster, filled with the strange tasting food they could not swallow. Their grandmother filled the glasses with milk but it made them gag, especially since it was warm, and usually had a skin on it. Willi's grandparents, both in their late eighties, were thrilled to see him again, and to meet their great grand-daughters for the first time.

Slowly they recuperated from the deprived war years, and were putting on a little weight. They spent a long vacation in the mountains, in Zernez near the national forest. Their old friend Erwin was also staying there, at the same hotel, the Baer and Post. Every morning Ruthie and Agnes went to their uncle Erwin's room, and he gave them fresh croissants loaded with sweet mountain butter, cheese and jam. After breakfast they went on long walks in the snow, went on sleigh rides, and built snow men with the fresh fallen snow. After a few weeks in the healthy mountain air the children had rosy cheeks and round little arms. The whole family had definitely been affected by what they had gone through, and suffered from some form of occupation complex. Shortly after they arrived in Switzerland, Willi and Leny went to a pharmacy and bought all kinds of medications to treat intestinal problems and minor ailments; all medicines they no longer were able to get during the war, and which they would have needed so badly. Also, one day Willi went for a walk in the country-side with one of his old friends. They had walked for a while when Willi heard a car approaching on the winding hillside path. Without hesitating a second, he ran as quickly as he could into the forest to hide behind a tree, calling to his friend to hide also; for a moment he had forgotten that he was in Switzerland. In occupied Java only the Japanese had cars, and almost always it was the Kempetai who beat the Europeans for no reason. Whenever possible, they avoided them because they knew what was in store. The disabling feeling of fear at the sight of police remained with Willi for the rest of his life. At each routine police traffic control or upon encountering a police officer he was gripped by fear which only waned once the policeman had spoken to him.

On February 5, 1946, Willi submitted his war losses replacement request to the Swiss Political Department in Bern. He had been told to submit a request for the losses incurred in Balikpapan, Borneo. Once he was informed that the request was to be written in English, and submitted to the United States of America; then he was told to submit it in German to the Swiss government. Willi also found out that Japan had deposited all its assets, millions of dollars, in Swiss banks before the war, and that Switzerland would not release the money until the losses the Swiss citizens had incurred had been compensated. So he submitted the replacement request to the Swiss Political Department in Bern, as he had been told to do. Their lives had been spared, but they had come out of the war zone with essentially only the clothes on their backs, they had lost thousands of Francs worth of belongings, and were anticipating to finally be compensated by Bern. Many years later Willi told his daughter Ruth:

About seven and a half years later, on June 10th, 1953, I received a letter indicating that further information was needed to complete the investigation. The Swiss government wanted to know, for example, where the household goods we had lost had been purchased, if the items had been new when purchased, and the letter also stated:

"We request that you provide proof of purchase for the lost items as well as their value by submitting receipts or certified notifications by persons who were familiar with your household in Balikpapan. At the same time you are to provide the exact time and names of persons responsible for the loss of your property." Ridiculous! I received the letter in Venezuela. I attempted to provide the information requested by the Swiss government, but it could simply not be done. I could not even furnish a list of the many scientific books I had lost because the authors and titles would have had to be looked up in a Swiss library, and we were living in South America at that time. Also, I had no receipts for all our household items and valuable personal belongings; they had been destroyed at the same time that our house was destroyed by bombs. I was not there when the Japanese conquered Balikpapan and demolished the entire area, and I certainly could not provide the names of the persons responsible. As to witnesses who were familiar with our household, all I knew was that our old servants were living somewhere in the jungle of Borneo

*or New Guinea, and I did not know their whereabouts or if they were even
still alive. Finally, I wrote the following to Bern:*

*"I have a question regarding the details you requested in order to process
this case. Is it likely that any compensation will ever be forthcoming or is
this detailed information requested to provide the government with statistical
data regarding war losses?" Various letters arrived from Bern which we
received via the Swiss embassy in Caracas. Finally, on July 23rd, 1956, I
received notification from the Commission of the Japan Compensation that
we would receive twenty percent of the actual loss amount as a first installment
from which a processing fee of a half percent was deducted. It took ten years
and eight months for us to be compensated less than forty percent of our
entire losses, and we never received another cent. We did not pursue it further
because it was much too frustrating. Also, the thousands of Francs worth of
treasures we had collected could never have been replaced anyway, including
most of the books I lost.*

The assistance Willi and the other Swiss had provided the Dutch citizens
in the concentration camps, especially the money they had been able to
smuggle to them which had saved many lives, had been registered by the
Dutch, and the Dutch government wanted to present them with a medal of
honor. All of them declined because they felt that it was not necessary to
give them a medal for helping fellow human beings. The company then gave
each of them an engraved silver cigarette holder with inscription:

*"In appreciation for assisting our families in Netherlands East Indies
during the Japanese occupation."*

Along with the cigarette case they each received a check in the amount of
5,000 guilders. When Willi received the money after the war, the Dutch
government had deducted 1,400 guilders for war capital gains. Willi talked
with the tax authorities in Holland about the tax, and told them that it was
ridiculous to deduct capital gains taxes.

After a lengthy discussion, the tax official looked at Willi, and asked,
"Would you have received the money if there had not been a war?"

Of course, Willi had to say no.

"So, it is war time capital gains," the tax man said logically. Willi was
speechless. Even war time aid during a time of great suffering and at great
risk of loss of life had to be taxed!

The next ten months they spent recuperating in Switzerland. On June 27th
their third daughter, Irene, was born in Basel.

RETURN TO JAVA

On November 22nd Willi had to return to Balikpapan to resume his work, and to help in re-building the oil place. Leny and the children would follow later. The plane was scheduled to leave Schiphol, the airport of Amsterdam, at seven in the morning. Shortly after take-off it developed engine trouble and had to turn back. The flight had to be rescheduled. The next day, it was still early in the morning, the plane took off. Willi sat by a window so he could look at the view below. He saw the peaks of the snow covered Alps, then they flew over Lyon, Monaco, Cannes and Nizza, and at around 9:30 he saw Corsica. About an hour later they landed at the English airport in Rome. The flight continued two hours later. At 6:30 in the evening they landed in Cairo, Egypt, and Willi was taken to a hotel by a company car. At one in the morning he was awakened, driven back to the airport, and the flight continued at 3:30. About five hours later they landed in Basra. Willi had just enough time to stretch his legs and eat something before they continued the trip. At 5:00 in the evening the plane landed in Karachi, Pakistan. Willi had a nice dinner, rested for a few hours, and at 2:30 in the morning they took off, heading for Calcutta, India, where they arrived two hours later. The passengers ate breakfast and left at 7:15, they landed in Bankok, Thailand at around noon, ate lunch, and then landed in Singapore at 6:30 in the evening. Again Willi was driven to a hotel where he spent the night. They left the following morning and arrived at Kamajuran in Batavia at around eleven. He was taken to the BPM company lodging, showered, rested, and then met an old acquaintance, Haaring, and several others he had known before the war.

On December 4th he flew to Bandung where he had several meetings with Haaring and others regarding company material. On behalf of the museum of Basel, Willi arranged exchanges of the original material the Japanese had sealed and declared to be Swiss property after Willi interfered during the war, informing the authorities of its existence, mainly the index cards of foraminifers. His friend Werner was going to take the collection back with him when he returned to Switzerland. Shipping would have been too risky. Willi made an inventory of all the items which he then mailed to the museum in Switzerland.

Bandung was completely destroyed and he took many pictures of their old house. Not much remained. The living room was covered with debris and there was a large hole in a wall. The stove was in a corner, and all that remained of the children's room was a pile of bricks and dirt, the rest was all burned. Standing among the ruins made Willi shudder, and he was thankful that they had managed to survive and get out in time.

What was left of the children's room after the house was destroyed

He had also gone to Bandung hoping to find their luggage which they had to leave behind when they were able to be evacuated a year earlier. Also, he wanted to look up the old gentleman he had met during the war who had served in the Netherlands East Indies army a long time ago, and who was now spending his old age in Bandung. Willi finally found him, he was old and tired, his savings had dwindled, his home was destroyed, and he wished to see his homeland one more time. When he saw Willi he started to cry, and wanted to hear all about his beloved homeland. Willi spent several hours with the old man, telling him about his family and acquaintances he had met in Switzerland. He told Willi about the horrors he endured a year ago, shortly after Willi and his family were able to flee the area. He was attacked again, and still had a large scar above his right eye. The blows he sustained on his head left him blind in one eye, but slowly some of his sight was returning. When he was attacked he was beaten on the head with a sword, and his attackers left him for dead which probably saved his life. They took all his possessions and then they set his house on fire. When Willi returned to the hotel that evening he wrote his parents a letter asking them to arrange to have some clothes sent to the old Swiss, he needed shirts and overalls. He sent the old man's address so they could mail the package directly to him. Willi knew that he would eventually get back on his feet, but felt that he needed some help now. Mr. Meyer was still due quite an amount of his pension from the Dutch government; it was still being blocked. He was going to use the money to rebuild his home.

A few days later Willi was walking in the city when a policeman approached him. It was one of his old assistants from Balikpapan who had become a Dutch police officer. They talked for a while, and he told Willi about an apparent theft at the offices where their luggage had been stored which had been under consular protection. Arth, the policeman gave Willi the address of a Mrs. Kendel who seemed to have stolen goods in her home, and he told Willi that he might find some of his possessions there. Willi went to the lady's house right away. She was about fifty years old, of mixed heritage with a German name. She was extremely skeptical, and did not want to let him in her house, so he told her that he would return the following day with the police. Then she quickly agreed to let him in. What Willi encountered was beyond his imagination. All the furniture of the representative of a Swiss pharmaceutical company was in the house, and there were cases filled with books. He took a closer look, and found thirty-two books with his name stamped on the inside. In one of the bedrooms there were piles and piles of suitcases, one entire room was stacked full. Then, in a corner, Willi saw an old, familiar hand carved chest from Formosa which looked just like the one they had left behind. He took look another look to be certain, and told the woman that the chest belonged to him. He recognized it, and remembered every detail of the elaborately carved chest they had bought so many years ago. The woman proceeded to lecture him that she had received the chest many years ago from an uncle and that it was not his. Willi turned it over, and there, on the bottom, in red letters, was his name. He had written his name on every item before they were evacuated. He showed the woman his passport which convinced her that the chest was his. He took it and the books with him. Before leaving, he asked if he could see the other buildings, which, after first hesitating, she allowed. He looked around. On shelves were small barrels with dyes, all with the pharmaceutical company's logo. There were several more suitcases and boxes filled with medicines. All the material had been stored under consular protection at the buildings. Now all the items were at this woman's house. An entire burglary story now unfolded itself. The Swiss citizen Neider had robbed the consulate and the entire pharmaceutical company inventory as well as all the luggage the Swiss had to leave behind when they were being evacuated. He had already gone through everything, and had taken all the valuable items. Anything he could not take he hid in Mrs. Kendel's house. After a long search, Willi only found the books and the chest; all his valuable kris and other artifacts, including a very valuable painting by the Swiss artist Theo Meier, were no longer there. Willi informed the Swiss Political Department by letter about his discovery of the stolen goods. The matter was delayed for such a long time that when months later officials went to pick up the pharmaceutical company's inventory at the house of Mrs. Kendel, it was all gone. He had also informed the pharmaceutical company directly about the stolen goods, and they had gotten in touch with Neider who was back in Switzerland.

The company was surprised about Willi's discovery of the stolen goods, and he received a letter which stated in part:

"Neider did not appear to be untrustworthy... however, our impression of his character was not a hundred percent positive, and it is quite possible that you are correct in your characterization."

Legal proceedings had begun against Neider in Switzerland, but the stolen goods had already been disposed of. Leny was asked to be present at a house search, along with several of their friends, but nothing was found that belonged to them. Neider had taken the majority of the items to Holland where he sold them. During the war he had also taken items from Dutch and German citizens for safekeeping; he had sold everything. Willi heard in Bandung that Neider and two Germans had participated in the thefts. All three had walked around with the Swastika on their sleeves. An official of the Swiss consulate in Batavia, who had known Neider for a long time, helped him transport the stolen goods weighing about 3,000 pounds from Netherlands East Indies to Switzerland where, on top of that, he was able to import all the stolen items duty free because of his so-called "connections." More complaints were filed for embezzlement of personal property. Neider recriminated, and about a year later Willi received a letter from Neider's attorney. In the letter it stated in part:

"You have made detailed and positive accusations, and at the same time filed a complaint of theft. As a result of your actions, my client was arrested in Zurich. All the actions were found to be without proof, the case was discontinued, and Mr. Neider was released."

The attorney further wrote:

"Please inform me how you intend to compensate Mr. Neider for the irreproachable embarrassment."

The attorney left it up to Willi whether he wanted to pay a full amount or in monthly installments. Willi was not sure how many people received the same letter, as the man had stolen from everyone who had been in Java during the war. It was quite incredible, not just did they lose all their household goods when the Japanese occupied and bombed Balikpapan, they also had all of their personal belongings stolen by another Swiss who had the audacity to request compensation because Willi reported his thefts. He ignored the letter. Three years later he received a short notice from the Swiss consulate in The Hague, where they were living at that time, advising him that there was a document for him of the Swiss Justice and Police Department regarding the Neider case. It was eight pages long, and there were eight plaintiffs from Switzerland, Austria, England and Indonesia, but the statute of limitations had expired in the meantime. It was for informational purposes only. The suit of the Swiss consulate in Batavia was upheld because of "surreptitiousness of false documentation according to Article 23, para 1, StGB." Willi and Leny were never compensated, none of their stolen goods were ever found or returned to them, and Willi did not know what happened further with the case. His collection of the Hindu-Javanese kris, the many other artifacts, the beautiful painting by Theo Meier and more are probably scattered around Europe, their owners quite likely unaware that they had bought stolen goods. He did hear once many years later from a friend who thought that the painting was somewhere in England. Willi found out later that a Gurkha officer had cut the painting from its frame and took it. They were able to save a few rare items which they had carried in their hand luggage. Other than that, all the artifacts they had collected piece by piece were gone.

On December 20th, 1946, Willi visited the Haaring's for tea. Dr. Haaring wanted to leave for Europe the following April or May and wanted to fly, but his wife was terrified of flying, and she wanted to go by ship. Willi had to take care of additional business in Java and meet with several people. One of them was an American who was with the Ministry of Agriculture in Washington. He told Willi that America was very interested in vegetable oils and rubber. The American government was adamant that the Dutch monopoly in the archipelago be given up, and the market be opened to other nations and to the free market. America fully supported the Indonesian republic, and this represented a threat to the Dutch. Willi was convinced that the republic of Indonesia was going to win the war, the more the rest of the world became aware of the problems of Indonesia, the stronger the republic's position would be. He also felt that the Indonesians were provoking many of the incidents to make the rest of the world aware of the situation, and that maybe then some of the great powers would intervene. Of course, this would have been of disadvantage to the Dutch. Fighting was still going on and he often heard shots nearby.

BORNEO REVISITED

Willi returned to Balikpapan the end of December. He left Balikpapan on January 15th, 1942, and now, five years later, was returning. He could not believe his eyes. Everything had been destroyed. For the time being he lived at the BPM Pasang Graham, the hotel which more resembled barracks than a hotel. All over the area there were grenade splinters, steel helmets, old guns and piles of debris, and in some more remote areas the remains of hundreds of fallen Japanese covered the ground. Nothing remained of their old house, Klandasan number seventy-two. All that was left of the beautiful ficus trees were the stumps. The huge factories were piles of ruins and rusted iron. Huge oil tanks which had contained up to 20,000 tons of oil had collapsed like card houses, and even the metal plates had melted in the fires. Thousands of natives who had worked for the Japanese during the occupation had been killed, so the Allies would have no workers. Willi tried to leave it all behind and in the past; new buildings were being constructed, and the debris was removed. Jakob had also returned. The two old friends did many things together, they drove around in the jeep and went target practicing. A total of five Swiss were already back in Balikpapan. Willi was expecting Leny and the children to join him in June, and he was anxious to have his family with him again. He often thought of the girls chasing butterflies and bugs, and in his mind saw them playing outside year in and year out.

His old assistant, Deloten, was also back and began working for Willi again. The two men talked about Silatus, whose mother, living in Java, had known that her son had died in Borneo long before official notification had been received. Deloten described to Willi the day Silatus died. It happened exactly as his mother had said. The date, the hour, the thrashing of his head from side to side, it all happened as she had visioned, and he died at the edge of a tapioca field in the arms of Deloten.

Abdul Menar, Willi's old Sumatrese assistant, had also returned. He told Willi about the massacre on February 24th, 1942. He had been one of the many natives who was forced by the Japanese to watch as the seventy-eight Dutch were shot, decapitated or stabbed to death at the beach. He took Willi to the area where the massacre had taken place. Right away Willi found human bones which had washed ashore. The two men gathered all the bones they could find, and later they were officially buried at the memorial cemetery at Stal Kuda on the outskirts of Balikpapan. Menar told Willi what had happened on that sad day. One of the medics of the company hospital, his name was Rijder, was a very tall Dutch man. He had two sons, about twelve and fifteen years of age. The Japanese began shooting at the prisoners who were standing waist deep in the water. Rijder kept lifting his sons out of the water after having been hit numerous times, and his two children had already been killed. He was hit over and over, but kept lifting the lifeless bodies of his children out of the water. Many bullets had already entered his body, but he continued to lift up the boys. Then one of the Japanese soldiers waded into the water, and with his bayonet stabbed the blond giant to death. There also were several clergy, and one of the priests spoke the rites and tried to console the victims until he too was shot dead. The massacre continued until every person was dead and the ocean's water turned red from the blood. Menar also told Willi what happened to many Indonesians. The Japanese had deep and long tunnels dug, and told the natives to go inside where they would be safe and protected. The natives did so in good faith, believing that they would be protected from the bombs. As soon as all the people were inside, men, women and children, the Japanese blocked the entrances, and all the people perished. They slowly starved to death. Willi also saw horrifying photographs depicting human thighs and other body parts. The photographs had been taken in secrecy, and it authenticated the fact that toward the end of the war the Japanese had killed and eaten young Indonesian girls, and had committed cannibalism in Balikpapan.

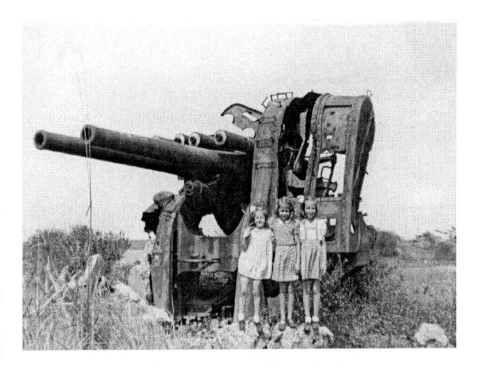

An abandoned canon near Balikpapan, Borneo, 1947
(From left: Ruth, friend Tieneke, Agnes)

AN ABANDONED JAPANESE CAMP

During the months they were recuperating in Switzerland Willi had frequently visited the museum. One of his old friends, an anthropologist, asked him if he could try to get him some Japanese skulls. One day in Balikpapan a lumber merchant told Willi that way up near a tributary of the Bay of Balikpapan near the native village Miangau was an abandoned Japanese camp full of swords and other military remains. There he could find as many skulls as he needed, they were scattered all over the place.

On January 22nd Willi and Jakob left early in the morning on a small motor boat, accompanied by four Indonesian guides. The expedition would take them into one of the most remote regions of Borneo's east coast. It could only be reached by boat and on foot. At first they had to cross the northern part of the bay. Flying fish shot out of the water, flew through the air like birds, and then dove back into the water. On the muddy shores, between the mangrove roots, they saw jumping mudskippers. The men passed many small islands, and then entered the mouth of the Sepaku river. All along the shores were scorched Japanese ships. Kingfishers flew over the water's surface and flowering jungle trees emanated a sweet, exotic fragrance. On a branch of a tree Willi saw birds the size of a dove with shiny blue feathers and orange-red beaks. The river became narrow, and the small boat barely made it through all the pieces of driftwood and debris of sunken Japanese ships. After a while they had to leave the small boat behind, and continue the trip in a rowboat which an "orang pasir," a native from the jungle, had loaned them. The Pasirese were of Malay and Dayak lineage and were the inhabitants of central Borneo. Some were Moslems and some were believers of animism.

Toward evening they pitched their tents on the banks of the Miangau river. The sun and the humidity had exhausted the men and they soon fell asleep. They arose when it was still dark, and at six in the morning when the sun came up were already on their way to climb the twelve hundred feet high Gunung Parong mountain. Three of the men carried their food and water, one remained with the tents. The small group followed an old, narrow path which took them through the village Miangau, and about thirty minutes later they were at the abandoned Japanese camp. Everywhere there were skeletons, skulls, weapons and decaying uniforms. The natives told Willi that the Japanese fled to the north after the Australians landed in Balikpapan, and had come to the hard to reach, remote area. A short time later the heads of the Japanese started to swell, and most of them died; they probably died of malnutrition and beriberi. The dead were buried, and the few remaining men soon also died. The hordes of wild pigs had grubbed everything up, and the remains were scattered all over the jungle ground. Untouched since the war ended were disintegrated lean-to's made of palm fronds, dug-outs, machine guns and swords. Along the banks of the river were steps which had been built by the Japanese. Willi decided to collect the skulls on their way back. The path continued to the river's upper course past magnificent geological outcrops; gray clay alternated with shoals of the finest sandstone. At one of the locations the natives cut grinding stones for use in their huts and kitchens. Life in the almost untouched jungle region was full of beauty. Numerous hornbills, some were as large as turkeys, flew overhead in pairs. The fluttering wings sounded as if an old locomotive were passing by. Willi found out that the bird was called "burung anggang." The Dayak hunted them for meat, but mainly for their colorful feathers and beaks which were often worn during ceremonies. Small and large apes romped in the trees above them, and their calls and screeches echoed through the jungle. Beautiful butterflies floated through the warm, still, humid air. Especially noticeable were shiny blue butterflies with small tails on their wings, and dragonflies with silvery blue wings. In the thick jungle the men came upon a group of natives gathering honey from tall trees. At first the men were very shy, but as soon as they were certain that Willi and Jakob were neither from the government nor the military, they became very friendly. The timid natives offered them honey; it was as clear as water, and tasted like the multitude of sweet smelling flowers of the tropical jungle. The men spoke a language among themselves Willi could not understand, but he was able to converse with them in Malay. The natives showed them how to reach the peak of Gunung Parong. The last ascent was extremely steep and laborious, and the wall of the limestone stratum glowed in the bright sun. They had to cross over rubble and through a couloir, and finally reached the top. The peak was over a monoclinal layer. Large gray butterflies with black spots flew around the steep limestone slopes drinking the water that ran from the crevices. The vegetation on the stratum was very abundant. Flowering orchids hung from the trees, and numerous fern species covered the ground. Willi saw shrubs with long, sharp thorns. The two were not the first Swiss who had reached the peak. Rusted nails pounded into a tree, and a board with the words, G. Parong, were from the time a Swiss topographer surveyed the area. He used the towering peak as the triangulate point. This had been in the 1920's, and they were on the limestone mountain on January 23rd, 1947. After inspecting the area they descended through the couloir and began their hike back. At the abandoned Japanese camp Willi selected four nice skulls and placed them in a sack. A very nervous native carried it, they still had to hike for about ten hours before arriving at the camp site by the river. After eating rice cooked over an open fire with vegetables and dried meat mixed in, the two men fell asleep right away. Around midnight Willi was awakened abruptly by a terrible noise. He sat up in his tent. The natives were hollering, banging on metal and poles. The noise was so loud that Willi crawled out of the tent, and asked the men what was going on. One of them told him that the spirits of the Japanese would not let them sleep; they kept floating out of the sack, so they had to drive them back inside with loud noise. Willi took a piece of string, tied it around the opening of the sack, and soon everything was quiet. All they could hear were the sounds of the insects on the outside of the mosquito nets. Early the next morning they were ready to continue their journey back. The rowboat quietly drifted down-river. It was again a journey full of surprises and beauty. A group of Proboscis monkeys jumped through the branches of the trees on the banks of a small river. They were called "bakatan," and lived in mangroves and jungle vegetation along the rivers. Around sunset they often came close to the water to prepare for roosting in the tree tops. The monkeys fed on young foliage and fruit and were known to die in captivity. The men stopped the small boat to observe the fascinating animals. What a strange appearance they were, their faces almost resembled faces of clowns with long fleshy noses. The faces of the adults were of a bright yellow-orange color, the juveniles had bluish faces. The females had pointed, upturned noses, the males' proboscis were round and fleshy, and hung down. They watched the interesting apes for quite some time. Willi had seen them many times already, but each time he watched the creatures with fascination. It was quite a large group, the big male occasionally glancing down making sure that his family was safe. Hornbills flew overhead with groaning sounds made by their wings. Up in a tree at the river's bank Willi saw a solitary reddish-brown male orangutan. The boat drifting quietly down the river did not seem to disturb him in the least. The Malays called them "mawas." Since 1932, the orangutan was on the endangered species list of the Animal Protection Ordinance. It is non-destructive on vegetation. The Dayaks hunted the orangutans with blow pipes and, unfortunately, the young were captured for sale. The price for a baby orangutan was five guilders. After drifting down the river for some time they reached the ocean again. Nipa palm nuts, "nipa-nipa," drifted on the water's surface, and the natives fished them out of the water. The small boat soon reached the first small island in the Bay of Balikpapan, and they were home before the sun went down.

Many years later Willi told Ruth what happened with the Japanese skulls he had collected in the jungle of Borneo: The Japanese skulls were now in Balikpapan, but I had to figure out how to get them to Basel, Switzerland. This was not going to be an easy task because it was forbidden to possess or transport human remains. The prohibition especially applied to the Australian cemetery which was later transported back to Australia. I had an acquaintance whom I had known since before the war who worked for customs. I explained the skull situation to him, that I had obtained them in the jungle for the museum in Switzerland.

He had a perfect solution and said, "The next time you travel to Switzerland, bring me the trunk with the skulls before you leave. On the trunk write in large letters - used material".

This worked great, and the declaration was certainly correct. I took the trunk with me to Switzerland and delivered the skulls to the museum. Later, after an article had been published, my anthropologist friend was contacted by the Japanese to find out how he had obtained the skulls. He asked me what to say, so I told him to just say that they had been bought from a Chinese in Indonesia. The Japanese decided it would be useless to investigate further.

On Ruth's sixth birthday, on January 25, 1947, Willi's grandmother died. She was eighty-six years old, and Willi had been thankful that he had still seen both his grandparents alive after the war, and both had met their great grand-daughters, Agnes, Ruth and Irene. The children had spent much time with the old couple at their farmhouse in a nearby village. Willi had been very close to his grandfather, a farmer and forester, who had taken Willi on hikes through the countryside from the time he was a very small boy, and who had taught Willi much about animals, plants and nature.

THE TURMOIL CONTINUES

On January 27th the telephone connection with Sanga-Sanga was disconnected and the pipelines were disrupted. All the Europeans were arrested by extremists, and fights broke out in both Sanga-Sanga and Samarinda. The Dutch were nervous and again there was talk of evacuation. There were no official reports, and it annoyed Willi that again everything was a secret. He wanted to be kept abreast of the political situation, and not again have to experience uncertainty and hear nothing but rumors.

Balikpapan was slowly being rebuilt. Willi was still living in the barracks, as were all the other men. He talked often with his old Indonesian workers who had remained in Balikpapan during the occupation. One of them told him that the Australians attempted to land seven times, each time they were driven away by the Japanese until Balikpapan was completely destroyed. The native village Klandasan was totally destroyed and was no longer there, as were all the homes on the hills where the Europeans had lived. The eighth landing was successful. The Australian cemetery was proof of the tremendous loss of life the conquest of the important oil place had cost. The Dutch were still very nervous because, even though the war was over, the area remained dangerous. Many freedom fighters and bandits terrorized the region. There were only a few geologists to start up the work again. The Indonesians did not trust the Dutch, and the Dutch viewed each Indonesian as an extremist who had his pockets filled with hand grenades. A couple of days after the unrest in Sanga-Sanga notices circulated, informing the employees that the rebels had been driven away, were being pursued, everything was under control, and the employees should not be concerned. The note said verbatim:

"The disrupters have been driven away and have been arrested. BPM employees have contacted the main office. The action can be viewed as successful, and there is no need to be alarmed."

An Indonesian friend told Willi that at dawn on the 25th, twenty of the thirty military garrison attacked Sanga-Sanga. The leader was a Menadonese officer of the Netherlands East Indies army. The police joined the mutiny and coolies were armed with hand grenades. Women also participated in the revolt. All the Europeans, about one hundred twenty-five, including women and children, were arrested, but were not mistreated. Looting began, private homes were robbed and the company store, the "toko" and other stores, were pilfered of goods worth about 20,000 Guilders. The military enforcement had to be transported by sea from Balikpapan to Sanga-Sanga where the uprising took place. Battles ensued, and about five hundred Indonesians fell; the coolies could not properly handle the grenades. The Dutch lost six people, one civilian was shot and killed during the revolt. He tried to defend himself and was shot in the back. The police commissioner was murdered, and four Dutch soldiers died during the fighting.

Willi and Jakob continued their exploration during their free time, mainly to discover more interesting plants and animals. Everywhere they went they found remains of the war, canons and guns, air defense bombs, hand grenades and ammunition. After the attack on Sanga-Sanga it was feared that the rebels would attack again, this time from the jungle near the barracks where they lived. Everyone had a gun and ammunition. To numb their fears, many young Dutch men drank large amounts of brandy, and frequently there were destructive outbursts when the men got out of hand, and they began to destroy furniture. One night things were really getting bad, the intoxicated men picked up the beds of others who were sleeping, and carried them outside. They laughed, screamed, and went into a frenzy. Suddenly Willi heard a shot, and the turmoil instantly stopped. He got out of his bed into the hallway. Several of the men came up to him and asked if he knew where the shot had come from.

"The shot was fired from the bordering jungle, go to bed, turn off your lights, remain quiet, and nothing more will happen because it is pitch dark outside," he advised the totally flabbergasted residents of their primitive, wooden hotel. The men quickly sobered up. A short while later a young Swiss topographer knocked on Willi's door, and said, "I just could not stand it any longer, so I fired a shot out of my window toward the jungle." Willi had suspected it. The young man always returned from work in the humid heat dead tired, and told Willi days earlier that he would fire a shot if the noise became too loud. It did have its effect. When the men went off to work in the factories the next morning, Willi and the topographer cleaned the gun barrel, and disposed of the shell. They wanted to make sure that the police would not notice what had happened in case they checked the guns.

IN THE HANDS OF EXTREMISTS

The oil refineries of Balikpapan had been completely destroyed during
the war, and a new plant had to be built. They needed river gravel for the
concrete which could not be obtained in Borneo. Willi recommended to the
engineers to use limestone. They agreed, but first of all needed some material
to test its solidity. The disadvantage was that the former limestone quarry
was on the other side of the bay deep inside the jungle. The area could be
reached by barges up a small river, but it was feared that extremists, armed
with weapons to fight the Dutch, were in the area. Willi offered to investigate
the region, and to bring back some sample material. He took eight coolies
and a barge with him. They arrived in Riko, a tiny settlement near the river,
around four in the afternoon. An older couple lived there whom Willi knew
from before the war. They were happy to see him. The woman wore the
white cap of the Hadji, the Mecca pilgrim of special status. She always called
Willi her son. The couple lived in a large house on stilts with their children
and children's children, and invited him to share a meal. He spent the night
in his tent near the edge of the small jungle village, and early the next morning
set off to cross the river alone. He had with him his geologist's hammer, his
Swiss passport, money and cigarettes in case he needed to pay someone. The
limestone quarry was overgrown with vines, but he could see it quite well; it
would suffice to build the entire new plant. Near the river was an overgrown
boardwalk, and next to it several large piles of limestone that had already
been cut before the war. He intended to take it with him on the barge. Nearby
were some huts by the river's edge. Willi looked at them carefully, but they
seemed to be abandoned. The path, he noticed, which was built before the

185

war, looked as if it had recently been used. He glanced around, all he heard were the sounds of the jungle, so he walked over to the limestone piles and, bending over, took a good look at the material. After he finished his inspection, he decided to return to the river. All of a sudden he was surrounded by three Indonesians; it seemed as if they had appeared out of nowhere. The men were armed with sharp knives, and they had long hair and beards; they were the guerrillas who had sworn that they would let their hair grow until Indonesia was freed from the Dutch. These were the fanatics who killed anyone of white color, and it was said that they were ruthless. The men ordered Willi to follow them to their leader. They took him to one of the huts near the river, pushed him through the door into the dark interior, and handed him over to a woman. It was immediately apparent to Willi that she was the leader of the group. The woman began to interrogate him. About five more Indonesians were in the hut, sharpening their knives, but did not participate in the interrogation. The first question Willi was asked was if he was a policeman. He showed the woman his Swiss passport, and told her what he was doing at the limestone quarry. He explained that he was a doctor "tanah," an earth doctor, and offered her American cigarettes. She took them greedily, and the spell was broken, for she offered Willi a cup of tea. He began to feel a little more at ease, the dim figures sharpening their long knives did not make him feel too comfortable. After a while she told him that he could leave, but he said that he wanted to take the limestone piles down by the river.

She looked at him for a moment, and then asked, "How much will you pay, and with what kind of money?" Willi offered to give her half a guilder in silver money per pile. She agreed. He went down to the river and called for the barge to come from the other side. Soon his helpers began loading the limestone. For each pile Willi gave the woman a silver coin, and after they had completed the trade, he advised that she and her men retreat further into the jungle. More limestone was needed, and the Dutch would first secure the area with military. After the limestone was loaded on the barge, he returned to Riko, and visited his friends Hadji Arpan and his wife. He also decided to hire a young Menadonese as overseer, he had known the man for some time, and he seemed to be very trustworthy. The people from Sungei Riko were afraid of the Dutch government "nica" and the military because unfortunately, they often harassed the natives. Just to be on the safe side, whenever Willi spent the night somewhere in the jungle, he always placed one of his kris on top of his mosquito net, as his old friend Pandirdjo from Java had suggested many years ago. The next day he went to inspect an area near Sepaku where a new road was being built. The vegetation was lush, and swarms of mosquitoes descended on him. On the road to Ulu Kaman he saw the foot prints of wild pigs and deer, and saw a "banteng," a wild ox which was only about five paces from him. The animal looked up from its grazing when it spotted Willi who stood very quiet, snorted a few times, and then walked off into the bush. Willi spent the night in his tent again, and started on his return trip the following day. In the brown water he spotted a large water snake as it gracefully swam to shore. The boat moved quietly down-stream. As soon as it approached, crocodiles sunning on the banks slid silently into the water. Willi again saw many Proboscis and other monkeys. He stopped at Riko to say goodbye to the old couple. Hadji Arpan gave him four tail feathers of the Argus pheasant. After his return, the limestone from Riko was found to be favorable to use as building material. The area was occupied, and a large quarry with machines and runway was built at the site. The military encountered no rebels, and the factory was built.

SLOW ROAD TO NORMALCY

On March 7th the police searched for a wounded rebel at the Marconi station on the road to Klandasan. A few days earlier, several Indonesian rebels were sighted and pursued. A battle followed, and four Indonesians who had taken part in the Sanga-Sanga revolt were shot. One of them was wounded, and managed to escape into the hills. Others fled to the north. The police did an extended search, but did not find the injured man.

Willi spent much time outside, and his skin turned into a dark tan. His lab was still quite small, but he was scheduled to move into a larger building in a short while. Many of his old Indonesian assistants were working for him again, and others had come looking for work. Willi felt bad that he could not give all of them a job yet, but offered to find them work in other departments.

The men, though, always answered the same, "I will wait until I can work for you." The natives always asked him about the "njonja" and the "noni". Willi hoped that Leny and the girls would soon be able to join him, he did not like being alone. Also, the office had informed management in The Hague that a house was available, and that travel arrangements could be made for Leny and the girls to come to Borneo. Slowly the area was being re-built, and goods could again be bought. Willi had enough to eat, and he was especially happy when the company provided its employees with soap; each person received two bars of Palmolive soap a week. This was quite a luxury, especially having had to live for a number of years when soap was no longer available. One of the few things that the Japanese had not destroyed was the water supply system.

He was scheduled to leave for Batavia, Java to attend several meetings, and on March 15th left on the company Catalina. The plane flew over the Telakai river and then the Barito area. He looked out of the window, and saw below the low-land hills covered with "alang-alang," the sharply pointed grass which grew to about three feet tall and which was very abundant. Wherever trees were eroded, the "alang-alang" grass took over and was extremely hard to control. The dried grass was used to cover roofs, and the roots were consumed by the natives. The plane landed at Kamajuran at three in the afternoon. Willi was driven to the hotel Des Indes where he met several of his old colleagues. Most of the men who had been together during the Japanese occupation were back. He was scheduled to fly to Bandung, but had to cancel the last minute, so he rescheduled the trip because he had so many meetings to attend. A couple of days later he heard the disturbing news that a Dakota had disappeared between Batavia and Bandung, and that his old friend Haaring of the Mijnbouw museum in Bandung was on board the flight. It was the same flight Willi had initially been scheduled to take.

On March 19th he heard on the radio that the Dutch government requested that the "Commissie Generaal" immediately sign the "lingga djati" agreement. He thought with amazement that the Dutch were actually still convinced that a military enforcement would put an end to the unrest. He felt that the only proper solution would be that the Dutch sign the agreement. The Dutch seemed to be relying much too much on their old laws, trying to resolve the issue themselves, but there were too many differences between the Dutch and the Indonesians. The "lingga djati" was finally signed on March 25th. Willi returned to Balikpapan on an old B-25 bomber which was quite an experience. They left Kamajuran at seven in the morning. The flight over the volcanoes was beautiful and impressive. The plane landed in Surabaya at nine. From there they left for Bandjarmasin, and landed in Balikpapan in the late afternoon.

He resumed his work at the lab. On April 1st he read in the local paper that the search for the missing Dakota continued. The search party consisted of Dutch, Indonesian and Red Cross personnel. Willi was very concerned about his old friend Haaring, and he feared the worst. He kept thinking of his wife who was so terrified of flying.

A couple of days later several men at the barracks hotel were drunk again. They drank the Jenever until they were inebriated, and were so out of hand that they destroyed furniture. That night they broke doors, dishes and other items which during those days were very hard to replace because of the shortages. Later, at work, the men boasted of their heroics in the "underground actions" which really annoyed Willi. The soldiers did not seem to know how to act in a quiet, dignified manner. The noise the drunken men made often lasted until two in the morning, and many times Willi was very tempted to shoot out of the window to put a stop to it.

During the evenings he read or wrote letters.

On April 7th, 1947, he wrote his parents:

Thank you for your letter. I was happy to hear that you inherited the old family bible of 1701. I have written to Adolf Meyer, and he wrote me back that he had not yet received the package you sent, but will let me know as soon as it arrived. He also asked me to thank you and all the others for their assistance, he really needs the clothes. Last week I had to make another trip into the interior, this time west of the Bay of Balikpapan, to hire workers for a quarry. Best regards to all.

On April 8th the newspaper, **Het Nieuws** of Balikpapan had the following article:

The missing Dakota has been found in the Preanger mountains on April 6th, 1947. The rescue team found the wreckage on Sunday afternoon on a hill of the Burangrang. The plane caught on fire and it seems unlikely that there are any survivors. On Saturday the military rescue team was unable to reach the wreckage due to bad weather conditions. A new team was sent out on Sunday which reached the site at 11:30 in the morning. Only the totally burned remains of the plane were found. The Dakota had left Kamajuran on March 13th at 9:00 in the morning on its way to Bandung. There were two pilots on board and twenty-four passengers, all of them perished.

It was confirmed that Willi's friend Haaring was one of the passengers who had been on board the plane, and he was saddened at the terrible tragedy of the plane crash, and the loss of his friend's life and the lives of the other passengers.

Flori arrived on April 18th, she was on her way to join Christian in New Guinea. Willi was sorry that his old friend was so far away. He spent as much time as possible with Flori catching up on how she and Christian had spent the last several months in Switzerland recuperating. He told her how much he was looking forward to having his family with him soon. He accompanied her to the airport, and wished them well. The days wore on, May arrived, and he was still without his family. On May 1st he wrote another letter to his parents:

A couple of weeks ago a card arrived from Adolf Meyer in Bandung telling me that he received your package which you sent off on April 7. He wrote

*that you sent him four pairs of pants, three shirts and seven pairs of socks,
and that he thanked you and everyone else "a thousand fold" for the clothes
he needed so badly. He is still having problems with his eye, and can not see
out of it yet.*

*I am happy to inform you that in a few days I will be moving out of the
barracks and into a house. It is in Klandasan where we used to live before
the war. Our old house was completely destroyed and nothing remains of it,
even the beautiful trees were shot down. New houses are now being built. An
old friend told me that our little Gibbon ape we had a long time ago which
had stayed with one of the "djongos" was shot by Japanese soldiers. It had
been playing in our old neighborhood when one of the soldiers spotted the
little monkey, aimed his gun, and killed it for no reason. It did not bother
anyone, and had adjusted well to more or less fending for itself. The "djongos"
had kept an eye on it, and used to bring it bananas. What a useless act of
cruelty toward an innocent little animal. I was also told by the same "djongos"
that the white heron I had rescued at the beach many years ago, which also
remained in the neighborhood, was shot on that same day. Apparently the
soldiers were bored so they began to shoot at any animals they spotted.
Anyway, the war is over now, new houses are being built, and I am so happy
to be moving into one soon. Until Leny and the children get here I will be
sharing the house with a couple of young topographers. I have already bought
pots and pans. Things here are more or less quiet, and removal of the debris
and ruins of the old factories is going very slowly. Things seem to be taking
much longer than initially thought. It is still hard to get workers and material.
My love to all.*

Willi was anxious to be moving out of the barracks and into his own
home. The "hotel" he had been living in was infested with rats, and every
night he was awakened by the varmints. The animals scurried around the
room, and on occasion had even hopped onto the beds. Willi slept with a
large pole next to his bed, and had already killed several of the ugly critters
when they entered his room.

Around mid-May he received a letter from Leny telling him that she had
been notified by the company that she could leave for Indonesia the end of
May or beginning of June. She was concerned about traveling with three
small children by ship, and would prefer to fly. Willi decided to make all the
arrangements from Borneo, and to send a telegram to company headquarters
requesting that flight arrangements be made immediately for his family. The
house on Klandasan 142 was reserved for him, and he was scheduled to

move into it on the 19th of May. He had already gone to the house several times. The walls were still bare and there was no furniture, but he planned to wait until Leny arrived to furnish the house. For the time being he would only get a few necessities.

One day one of his workers showed him an edition of the Communist newspaper "Suara Buruh," the paper of the workers. On the front page in red letters of the May 1st issue was a picture of a worker with a hammer and sickle and a photograph of Stalin. One picture depicted a plowing "tani" in a Javanese "sawah", a farmer in a rice field, and below the photo it said: *"If we want to win the revolution we have to mechanize the rice agriculture."*

Finally, Willi was able to move into the house. He hired a "kokki" and "djongos," a married couple. His name was Mas Senen, hers Sukjem. Shortly after he moved in, Mas Senen approached him one morning, and asked about a kris that had to be somewhere in the bedroom. Willi had purchased a kris a while earlier, but Mas Senen had not seen it nor did he know that Willi had bought a Madjapahit kris because that had been several months before. Mas Senen told him he had seen a blue flame late at night coming from Willi's room, and knew that there must be a very powerful kris in the closet. He described the area where he had seen the flame which was exactly the height in the closet where Willi had put it wrapped in an old towel. He fetched it from his room, and showed it to the "djongos." Mas Senen greeted the kris according to Javanese tradition while sitting on the floor with his legs crossed. He checked it, and told Willi that it had great powers, that it was very old, but he still had to find out where it came from. It should only be cleaned on a Friday during the month of "sura," the first month of the Moslem calendar. The blade was detached from the handle. It was then inserted into a five centimeter wide bamboo container with an opening. The blade was placed into a liquid consisting of water, lemon juice "djeruk nipis" and pieces of pineapple, and left in the mixture for two days. A brush made of banana leaves removed tiny rust stains. If a kris was well taken care of then it would never have any rust. After two days the acid liquid was removed from the blade, and rubbed with a piece of "warangan," the mixture of arsenic sulfide. It was of reddish to reddish-orange color. The "warangan" made the regular metal turn black and the meteor or nickel iron, "pamor," turned a metallic bright color. The remainder of the "warangan" was left on the blade and could not be wiped off with a piece of cloth. A rice paste had to be used called "dedek." The blade was carefully pulled through the paste which removed any traces of the "warangan." Following the cleansing the kris then received an offering of flowers and incense. Just prior to the offering Mas Senen spoke the following words, addressing the spirit of the kris:

"Setulu reku kai wesiadji to we ne mangan," which freely translated meant: honorable holy spirit, I am bringing you nourishment. The kris was covered with fragrant flowers and a new "sarong," a piece of white, new and never before used fabric. Later Mas Senen hung it vertically on a wall in the bedroom. Willi was delighted that he had a "djongos" who was so knowledgeable about old traditions and customs, and found it of tremendous interest how a kris immediately brought a Javanese and European together. He spent hours asking him all kinds of questions about kris and other local customs. Also, it was of great interest to him to be able to compare the rituals he had seen before in Java, and the similarities of the rituals of his two

Mas Senen cleaning kris in 1947

Mas Senen served the meals and tended Willi's clothes and the garden.

Sukjem, his wife, did all the cooking. Both were from Java. Mas Senen also told Willi many fascinating stories about Java, and about the meaning of dreams and the exegesis of day-to-day life. If a person saw a coconut falling from a tree, it meant that one would soon die. If a frond of a coconut palm fell to the ground, whether this was seen during a dream or in reality, then it was viewed as a warning that there will be an accident. If the mosquito net or the "sarong" tore, then it was a sign that the spouse was committing adultery. This was called "main-gila" which meant, "to act crazy." If a person dreamed that teeth were falling out, it meant that a family member would die. If they were the teeth of the upper jaw, a parent would die, teeth of the lower jaw meant that a sibling or other close relative would die. This was called "sudara." If a young woman dreamed of a cucumber, then she had an intimate relationship and was pregnant. If a pregnant woman dreamed of a lion, her child would be a son, if she dreamed of a dove, she would give birth to a daughter. If a man dreamed that he was catching a dove, then his wife would soon bear him a child. Javanese always viewed a dream as a warning, but it could be both good or bad.

The end of May Willi went on another trip into the interior. This time he went up the Manggar river. The shores were lined with mangroves. In the branches of one of the trees he saw an old, solitary ape, and when the boat drifted by it looked down and snorted at the people below, but did not move. The boat drifted by an abandoned village which had been taken over by the Japanese during the war. They had built numerous storage sheds. Everything was destroyed, even the coconut tree tops had been shot off, and everywhere Willi saw large holes in the ground where bombs had detonated.

On May 29th Sukjem and several helpers were busy preparing for the traditional "slamatan." The women cooked all day long. Then, in the evening, twenty-one "djongos" gathered at the house. Each was handed a glass of tea and some food. In front of the oldest person was a container with glowing coals on which incense was burning, and a sweet aroma permeated the entire house. A large glass contained sweet smelling water. The fragrances were the gifts "sari" to bring forth the gods to alert them that a person wished to speak with them. The guests sat in a circle, including Willi, while the oldest man narrated words in High-Javanese. Best wishes were extended to all the inhabitants of the house, for the "njonja" and the "noni", and that the "tuan" would soon have his family with him. After the words were spoken, a prayer was recited in Arabic. Willi then thanked everyone for coming and for wishing him good fortune in his new home. The guests each received food to take home and then departed silently. The ceremony had been much like the ones Willi attended before.

Two days later he sent a telegram to The Hague: *"Mohler urgently requests family travel arrangements be made within six weeks stop house arrangements have been made."* The days and weeks passed slowly. He spent all his free time studying the animal and plant life around him. In early June he found an agate snail near the house on Klandasan. The species had been imported during the Japanese occupation. Abdul Menar told him that the snail was wide-spread, and appeared in great quantities in Samarinda where thousands could be seen on trees, roads and in gardens. They caused tremendous damage because they ate the young banana plants. This snail did not exist in the area before the war. The rainy season had begun, and on June 10th about five inches fell in six hours. Near Pulu Tukung there were mud slides, and the main road in Klandasan was filled with rubble. Willi's office building was flooded, and the floors were covered with mud and water.

The Dutch were again becoming extremely excited; it reminded Willi of the time just prior to the invasion by the Japanese. Everyone was told to leave their homes and go somewhere else immediately, but they were never told where to go. Barbed wire was installed all around the factories, and the Dutch were whispering, "we will attack now." Nothing was done and nothing happened. Willi found out that one of the ships in the harbor brought fabric which was being sold on the black market. Another ship that had recently arrived with a shipment of rice was about forty tons short. It seemed that the rice had been stolen somewhere along the way. Corruption was getting out of hand, and the sad thing was that many Europeans participated and instigated the corruption. The rains continued and caused serious damage. A few days earlier, it was June 21st, Willi heard on the radio that the Dutch government had ceased all its relationships with the Indonesian republic.

On June 23rd Jakob almost had a fatal accident at the police station in Kp. Baru where he had to go to get a permit. He was standing in the lobby of the police station, waiting for his turn, when suddenly an Indonesian policeman went amok. He had been caught stealing, and when confronted, pulled out his pistol, and began shooting at random. He shot two other policemen, and Jakob was standing so close that the blood of the injured men splattered all over him. The other employees were able to subdue the assassin. His reason for the shooting rampage was that one of the policemen had called him a liar, and he had gone crazy. Willi was shocked when he found out what had happened, and was thankful that his friend was unharmed.

The end of June arrived and Willi was still alone. The company told him that he would be moving into another house, one on the Pantjur hill had become vacant, and it was bigger than the one he lived in. Willi hired another servant, her name was Sudjana. She was the granddaughter of Mas Senen and Sukjem, and would be the "babu," the nursemaid to watch the children, especially the baby Irene who was only a year old. Willi was becoming more and more anxious to have his family with him, he did not like living by himself. He had been asked by the company to give a lecture on geology, paleontology and exploration. About a hundred persons attended his presentation at the club. He was glad for the distraction.

The beginning of July he moved into the house on the Pantjur hill. More and more break-ins were occurring in the homes of the Europeans, particularly on that hill. Nine new houses had been recently built, and not one could be properly secured or locked. The police were not very effective, and the company security guards were not armed. The homes of those in higher positions had either a tall fence around the property or the men had bodyguards. Willi felt that it would have been the best thing to place barbed wire around the entire residential area, but it would probably have been considered to be too expensive even though there were huge piles of barbed wire lying around all over the place left over from the war. On July 21st all relations between the Dutch and the Indonesians ceased, and military actions were enforced. The republic was unable to guarantee peace and safety because the gangs of the T.R.I. (Tentara Republik Indonesia) did not heed the government's instructions, and a cease fire could not be achieved. The Dutch tried hard to avoid any interference by third parties because their superiority and monopoly in the archipelago would have been endangered; they seemed to be unable to accept the fact that Indonesia could be an independent republic, probably because all had been educated in the old-fashioned colonization manner.

TOGETHER AT LAST

Willi received a letter from Leny that the visa had not yet been granted, and that Ruth had the chicken pox. He hoped that everything would go as planned, and that the trip would not have to be delayed. He was getting very nervous and anxious to finally have his family with him. On July 25th he received notification from the office in Batavia that the visa had been granted and forwarded to the Dutch embassy in Bern. He was very relieved, and decided that he would never again travel without his family. A week later there had been no additional news from Leny. He was getting frantic, had they been able to leave the end of July and where were they? He could hardly stand it any more. He had no appetite and could barely eat. Jakob stopped by in the evenings, and tried to cheer Willi up. He knew how hard it was to be alone; Emmi was not joining him in Borneo, she and the children were staying in Switzerland so they could attend school there. On August 2nd Willi received a telegram:

"Departed July 30th Amsterdam family Jung, L. Mohler and three children."

The long awaited news that his family was on the way had finally arrived, and he was elated. On August 4th there was a cease fire in Java, the battle had lasted all of two weeks.

On August 6th at 10:30 in the morning another telegram arrived, it read:

"Air plane 6/8 on its way carrying Mrs. Mohler and three children."

Immediately he departed for the airport, and at four in the afternoon the DC-3 landed at the airport Sepinggan with his family on board. The children looked well and had grown much. Willi was so happy to have them finally with him again. Leny and the children were enthusiastic about the trip, everything had gone well except that Agnes and Irene became ill during the trip with chicken pox. From Amsterdam they flew to Cairo where they spent the night. On the second day they flew to Baghdad, Iraq, landed and had lunch, and continued to Karachi where they spent the night again. On the third day they flew to Calcutta, and then to Bangkok where they remained overnight. From there they continued on to Batavia. Because Agnes and Irene had the chicken pox the company doctor told Leny that they had to remain in Batavia for a few days until the children were no longer infectious, and he could treat them before they went to Borneo. Arrangements were made to remain at a hotel for several days and Ruth, the only one who was well, was thrilled to have the freedom to roam about the hotel gardens where she discovered fascinating insects and reptiles. During their trip, the plane had not been permitted to land in Singapore out of protest against the Dutch military actions on Java and Sumatra. As expected, Leny did not notice anything of the war which was over quickly.

The girls were happy to be home, they ran through the garden and searched for butterflies and beetles. The whole family was introduced to Mas Senen, Sukjem and Sudjana, who immediately became very protective and fond of the entire family.

During August the break-ins increased, and on a daily basis the homes of company employees as well as those of the natives were broken into, but the company did nothing about the situation. They did put up signs, but it was quite apparent that most of the thieves were illiterate, and would not have heeded warning signs anyway. One night a thief broke into the home of one of their neighbors. The man heard the thief, went to investigate, and when he confronted the intruder, he was stabbed, and had to be taken to the hospital. The thief managed to escape.

For some time a rumor was going around in Balikpapan similar to the one during the war that when the company constructed all the new buildings, human heads were being sacrificed at the new sites. The rumor stated that the company ordered that before construction could begin, human heads had to be sacrificed to the gods at the construction sites, and that the heads had to be of Indonesians. That type of sacrifice was called "djulik." It was also said that apparently a company car drove around at night transporting heads of native children, and that headless bodies had been found. Late one night one of the company cars was stoned because the natives thought that the car was on a head-hunting expedition. All of the rumors, were, of course, utter nonsense. Unfortunately, the people were becoming suspicious, and Willi felt that it could well be possible that it might result in actions against Europeans. Some functionaries of the republic might have been responsible for spreading the rumors and accusations.

A few days after their neighbor had been attacked in his own home, the thief was apprehended. He told authorities that he had acted in self-defense because he had been attacked first.

One day in September one of Willi's workers brought him a "kantjil," a musk deer which had been caught in the Telakai region. The incisors of the little male protruded from the side of its mouth. The animals lived in the hills and the mountain regions, and were mostly solitary. The little deer that was given to Willi was already quite accustomed to humans and ate out of their hands, mostly bananas, peels and all, cucumbers, grass and vegetables. Even though it was not shy, it was extremely alert, and listened intently every time it heard a sound, its ears moving from side to side.

On September 12th, 1947, Willi wrote his parents a long letter describing how the family, especially the children, were doing:

The children have adjusted well, and I think the change of climate has been good for them. Two days ago Irene took her first steps. On Saturday I took Agnes and Ruth to work with me. My new office building is on a hill overlooking the ocean, and the area is surrounded by a tropical jungle full of beetles, butterflies, birds and even monkeys. When it turned too hot the girls came inside, and were allowed to look through the microscope and draw pictures. I have taken the girls to the beach several times already, and they become very excited when they see the beautiful colored fish, snails, shells and sea urchins. You should see them when they chase a large crab which they can mostly catch. They have to let it go again, though. Yesterday Ruth caught a cicada as large as a small bird. One of our cats jumped on it, and managed to eat the "tonggeret." When I came home from work she came running, and complained that the cat hat eaten her cicada. Both girls remember all their Malay, and are still fluent. We are getting enough food which is being delivered to our house daily. Leny is doing great, and has even put on a little weight. We hope that you are both doing well and send you all our love.

On September 14th one of the Dutch assistant geologists went hunting in Klandasan Besar. An Indonesian in uniform attacked him, and he sustained an injury in his hip from a bayonet. He was accompanied by two Dutch soldiers. When they reached the valley they encountered the solitary soldier armed with a gun and bayonet. He asked the three men what they were doing, and at the same time shot at one of them, but the bullet missed. He then attacked the geologist with the bayonet, stabbing him in the process. In self defense the geologist shot his attacker and killed him. The Indonesian soldier had belonged to the Dutch army, but had deserted some time earlier while on guard at an ammunition warehouse.

More and more of Willi's workers began to notice his interest in wildlife. One day one of them brought a pangolin, a scaly anteater, "trenggiling," which the man had caught near Balikpapan. When sensing danger, it rolled into a ball and wrapped its tail about it. It had very powerful claws. Underneath its broad, horny scales Willi found hundreds of parasites, mostly ticks. He removed them carefully with tweezers, and disinfected the areas. Some of the ticks he placed in alcohol for his museum collection. The animal managed to escape during the night, it was in the bathroom, and was able to crawl through a small drainage hole in the wall. Then one day one of the workers brought a tiny tarsier. Its eyes were huge, the ears close to its head and barely visible. It had a thick fur of silvery-gray color. It was given to Willi in a small box. When he brought it home the children were excited, but the little animal was curled up in the towel and slept. Willi explained to the girls that it would wake up at night as tarsiers are nocturnal animals. When Mas Senen saw the little animal he became very agitated, and told Willi that it had to be released otherwise bad things would happen to them. He said that it was a spirit, and that they could not keep it. Willi tried to convince Mas Senen that it would be all right, and could not harm anyone. Mas Senen stood his ground, and sometime during the night, when everyone else was asleep, he released it, for the next morning the cage was empty and the door open.

Sulandi often spoke of the prophecy of Djojobojo. He told Willi the continuance of the old prediction. It was as follows: After Java has been freed by Sukarno's proclamation of August 17th, 1945, the Dutch would again attempt to come to power. There would be military actions in July and August of 1947. By agreement of the "seven seafarers" (the United Nations?, Willi wondered) Java would be freed from the Dutch. New money will then be circulated, and Java will prosper, benefiting the rest of the world. This will occur during the middle of the Christian 20th century, "abat masehi," before World War III which will take place around the middle of the 20th century, and will last for only a short time. Only two countries will be affected by this war, and when it is over, Asia will be set free.

On September 29th Willi received a card from a friend in Bandung that Adolf Meyer had died in the Juliana hospital. The news saddened him. A unique compatriot had gone to the eternal hunting grounds, far from his beloved homeland which he had so wanted to see one more time. He was buried in Bandung.

October arrived. One day Willi, Leny, the girls and some friends traveled up the narrow river to go to Sungei Riko. Just below Riko the boat hit a submerged tree trunk. The jolt threw Willi overboard. He managed to hold on to the side of the boat with one hand, but the shutter of his camera broke when he hit the side. A couple of men pulled him back into the boat, and the trip continued. In the short time he had been in the water, a couple of leeches had already managed to attach themselves to his ankles, and with the help of Ruth and Agnes, they quickly began to remove the blood sucking parasites. As the boat approached, Hadji Arpan and his wife were waiting, excited to meet Leny and the girls. The children had a fascinating time roaming through the tiny native settlement and its surroundings. On the trip back they saw a number of porpoises. The natives called them "ikan dujung." Sometimes dead porpoises washed up on the beaches, and the natives collected the bones which were used as talismans to protect them from harm. If such a bone broke it was a sign that the owner needed to be cautious. Earlier that day Willi spotted an Argus pheasant in the underbrush near the village. Its call was similar to that of the peacock, but the animal remained silent when it heard a noise. It was mainly hunted for its plumage.

Leny wrote her family every week, telling them how things were going, and especially how the children were doing. On October 14th she wrote a long letter:

Dear loved ones, it is so hot today that I had to force myself to do anything at all. The heat and humidity are so severe that it drains us all of energy. Other than the heat we are doing well. Little Irene is walking now, and Willi is taking driving lessons. As soon as he passes his test he will get a company car. Jakob returned from a long trip into the jungle last Saturday. Every week-end he eats dinner with us at our house since he is now alone here as Emmi and the children have stayed in Switzerland. Unfortunately, he has malaria and is very thin, and we hope that he will soon fully recuperate here in Balikpapan. I will make sure that he eats healthy.

We had a small stable built for our "kantjil" with a fence, now it has enough room to run. Last week-end we went up a river into an area called Riko. It was incredibly beautiful and gave me a real concept of the jungles of

tł

Near Sungei Riko, 1947

roots anchored deep in the swamp. The trees are called "baku-baku," and there are palms called "nipa-nipa," and the natives eat the fruit. Some of the areas are completely impenetrable, and I can understand why some people refer to certain areas as "the green hell of Borneo." We saw no crocodiles this time, they were probably hiding so well that nobody could see them, but we did see several porpoises as they gracefully rolled through the water. The natives do not catch them because they consider them to be "orang," man, as they are mammals. When we arrived in the village, the chief and his wife greeted us, and invited us to their house. It is a large hut on stilts, and there is only one large room. The roof and sides are covered with palm fronds. Several generations live together, the old ones, their children and spouses, and the little children. After we had visited for a while we walked into the nearby jungle on a small path the natives use. We saw beautiful ferns and trees, and everywhere there were monkeys up in the tree branches. The most fascinating ones are the Proboscis monkeys with their large noses and red faces. This monkey is found only in Borneo. It had been a fascinating day for all of us full of new impressions and discoveries. All our love.

HUNTING WILD PIGS

On October 25th Willi and some friends left on a hunting trip to an area near Riko. Around four in the afternoon they climbed into a small prau, a Malay boat, and crossed the bay near Penadjam. Porpoises rolled in the water and at times came very close to the small boat. The rays of the evening sun illuminated the mangroves lining the shores and the inland hills with the "alang-alang" grass. As the boat traveled further up the river, they saw great numbers of Proboscis monkeys in the trees lining the banks. The monkeys, even though quite shy, had a very curious nature. As soon as a boat approached they appeared all over the trees, looking down at the people below. Willi noted that the monkeys seemed to be less shy during dusk than in the day time hours. After the sun set in the horizon it turned pitch dark. They put on their head lamps to find the way through the narrow river in the black night. Eyes of crocodiles reflected brightly in the rays of the lamps; at night there seemed to be more than during the day. The fragrance of flowering trees was intensified during the night. Occasionally, a native boat drifted quietly by, the people were on their way to catch fish. The lights attracted numerous nocturnal butterflies and moths and a myriad of other interesting insects. They left their boat in Riko, and continued by foot to Ulu Kaman. The small village of Riko was preparing for a celebration. Everywhere people were hustling about, getting ready for the feast. Dancers had arrived, and guests came from all directions to participate in the festivities. The people had on their festive clothes, and women adorned their hair with white, fragrant flowers. It was fascinating to see all the preparations and activities in the

---

otherwise quiet little village. The men watched for a while, and then continued toward the jungle. Ahead of them was a large limestone rock covered with jungle vines. The natives had placed an offering basket and burning flame on the rock; it cast a magical glow over the leaves of the vines. All around the mystical looking rock danced thousands of little lights of the fireflies. They stood still for a while to take in the glimmering apparition in the black jungle night. They entered the jungle deeper and deeper, but did not encounter a wild pig or a deer, the noise in the usually quiet village had probably scared them off. Willi saw a tiny tarsier, the small nocturnal animal with huge eyes, just like the one they had received a short while ago. They mostly live in pairs, and jump from tree to tree during the night in search of food. They feed on insects, frogs, lizards and fruit. In Malay they were called "kukus-kukus" and in Javanese "uwa-uwa." The little tarsier was so close to Willi and moved so slowly that he was almost able to catch it. Like Mas Senen, all the natives feared the tarsier because they believed that it was a spirit, and thus the animal was not hunted. After walking quietly through the jungle for hours, the men finally returned to Riko at around three in the morning. The natives invited them to sit down, so they watched the festivities and dances for a while. The music and dances lasted until five in the morning. They decided to go back into the bush and heard some wild pigs, but were unsuccessful in shooting anything. It was time to return to the boat, and slowly they started drifting down-river. Near Sungei Kanan they met a native who was checking his fish traps. He had just caught an eel, and offered it to them. He considered the eel to be half fish, half snake, and because of his faith, did not wish to eat it. The eel was called "ikan belut." It was about five feet long and its head was over two inches wide. Its underside was white, the upper part speckled yellow, brown and olive green; an excellent camouflage in the muddy waters of the jungle rivers. It had several fish and shrimp in its intestines. They took it along, Sukjem would make a fine dish out of the tender meat. They continued drifting slowly down the river when up ahead, they saw a native at the edge of the jungle. They tied the little boat to a branch, and climbed up the embankment to see what the man was doing. Lo and behold, he had just caught a wild pig in one of his traps. The native gladly gave them the sow, which was about one and a half years old. Willi and his friends were happy to take it because their own hunt had been unsuccessful. This way they did not have to go home empty handed. They gave the man some coins and a pack of cigarettes, and headed for home. They arrived in Balikpapan at around one thirty in the early afternoon, hungry and tired, but full of new adventures.

Willi was very busy at his lab. On November 6 he was walking around in the back yard after he and Leny had enjoyed their afternoon tea, checking his orchid plants on the trees when he heard a plane. He looked up into the sky, and saw that the plane was approaching from the Tarakan area and that it was a Catalina. As he was looking up at the plane in the sky there suddenly was an explosion, fire and black smoke encased the plane, and within seconds it fell burning from the sky. Willi watched in horror and disbelief. Later he found out that there had been no passengers on board, but the pilot and co-pilot both lost their lives. They never found out what caused the Catalina to burst into flames.

ANIMALS AND VAMPIRES

Almost every Sunday they went to the beach. One of the nicest beaches was at Manggar, and now that Willi had a car they were able to go more often. The beach spread out unendlessly, was of soft white sand, and almost every step they took a new treasure was found. The girls had already amassed a large collection of beautiful shells and small coral pieces. In mid-December they were told that they were going to move into a new house. It was the house next door because the company had decided to tear down the hill the brand new houses had been built on, flatten the area and build more factories. One by one the houses were torn down. For the time being they moved into the last house on the hill, it was nice and big, and had an extra bedroom and covered porch which led directly into a beautiful yard with big trees.

A comet appeared in the night sky close to Venus. At night, Willi, Leny and the girls went into the yard to observe it. They were in awe of the beauty of the sight; the increasing moon, Venus, the stars twinkling in the sky and the impressive comet. It had been visible since the ninth of December, but could only be seen three days later because it had been overcast. Mas Senen told them that the appearance of the comet meant that a disease would break out. There had been a cholera epidemic in several nearby countries, and the natives believed that it would come to Borneo. As a precaution, everyone had to be inoculated.

Agnes and Ruth arose early in the morning of December 22nd, just as the sun came up, and went outside to pick flowers. Their arms full of pretty blossoms they quickly went to the dining room where Mas Senen was setting the breakfast table, and placed the flowers all around Willi's plate. Ten years ago he had passed his doctorate exam, and the girls presented him with pretty drawings they had made. Leny had instructed Sukjem to cook a delicious breakfast with fresh eggs, freshly baked bread, and a large platter of fresh tropical fruit.

Just before Christmas they moved into their new home. A Christmas party was held for the children at the club. Willi's orchids were in bloom, and Leny had fun decorating the house with the children. A small casuarina tree was cut from the field below, and was placed in the living room. The girls made the decorations with dried seed pods, tiny cones and foil. The house looked nice, Leny had again decorated the living and dining rooms with flower arrangements made of ferns, blooming orchids and wild flowers. It was a nice Christmas. A large box was on its way from Switzerland, but had not yet arrived. Each day when a ship anchored at the harbor the girls wondered with excitement whether the Christmas box might be aboard. On new year's eve Willi and Leny went to the club. They had a delicious multi-course dinner which was followed by a formal ball. At three in the morning they strolled home; it had been a pleasant evening spent with good friends. As they were walking home they talked about all the break-ins in the neighborhood, and decided to get a couple of geese. A friend told them that they were good watch animals. A few days later they bought two geese, the goose was for Agnes, Ruth received the gander. Shortly after that whenever a stranger came into the yard, the animals made much noise, and the gander chased anyone who came near his goose. Only after the company increased police patrols did the break-ins somewhat decrease.

Agnes and Ruth were being taught school at home by Leny. They wanted the girls to be taught in German. Leny brought all the school books from Switzerland. Each day the girls had to learn arithmetic, reading, spelling and more. One morning during class Ruth heard scratching at the back door. When she went to check there was a black and white puppy, wagging its tail. Leny told her that she had to leave the animal alone, and not to feed it otherwise it would not leave. As soon as class was over, Ruth quickly went to the kitchen. She asked the "kokki" for a large plate of food, with rice and lots of meat. She then went back into the yard, and called the puppy. It was resting under some bushes, but as soon as the little dog smelled the food, it came out, and gulped down every bite. From that moment on the little dog was Ruthie's shadow, it followed her wherever she went.

One day months later Ruth was standing on top of the hill looking down to the village in the far distance. She spotted her little white dog who had been roaming the area as he frequently did. She whistled. Her little dog heard her, turned around, and came running toward home. He had to cross the road below, and then climb the hill to get to the back yard. He was already on the other side of the road when a jeep approached. The soldier saw the little dog on the side of the road. He turned the steering wheel of his jeep, drove through the grass, and ran over the little animal. Ruth stood rigid. She saw what happened. She was only seven years old, and started to scream. Willi and Leny came running out of the house, behind them the servants. She just stood there, crying and sobbing her dog's name over and over. Willi walked to the edge and looked down. There, in a small heap lay her little dog. Willi ran down the winding path as Leny took the children inside. When he reached the little dog it whimpered, and tried to get to him. Willi saw that both of the dog's front legs had been severed by the jeep, the bones were exposed. He knew that he had to act fast, nothing could be done for it, and it was in terrible pain. He took it away from the house, got his shotgun, and put the little dog out of its misery. Ruth missed the little dog for a long time. She just could not understand how anyone would want to hurt a little animal on purpose as the soldier had done. She remembered the Japanese men who had thrown the little puppies into the river when she was a little girl during the war. She just could not understand why people did such things. She always hid when she saw a soldier, and for a very long time did not want to have a thing to do with uniformed people.

One day in early February Willi had been to a late meeting and was riding in the back of the company car on his way home. It was already dark as it was after eight o'clock. He was looking out of the window when suddenly a meteorite lit up the night sky with a bright, strange looking green light. In a flash the falling star disappeared behind the hills. His Bandjarese driver had also seen the appearance, and with a frightened expression on his face, he said: "kujang." Willi asked him what that meant, and the terrified man said that it was a vampire. It took the driver a while to calm down, and then he explained the appearance. He told Willi that according to local belief, there were certain women who could detach their heads from their bodies, and only the intestines remained attached to the head. The ears grew very large, and the vampire was able to fly, and appears in the night sky as a bright light. It is in search of a victim, and hurls itself on a woman giving birth to suck her blood. Unless such an attack can be warded off with some magic remedy, the woman will die. The "kujang" was doing this out of revenge against the woman or her husband. Women who could turn into vampires could be recognized in that they did not have a groove between the upper lip and the nose. Willi had heard similar stories while living in Java, but, to him, what he had seen was a beautiful falling star.

THE WEDDING

On February 8 Sudjana, the nurse maid who looked after the children, was getting married. She was only fourteen years old. The festivities were going to be held at her parents' house in Parapatan. It was going to be a big feast and, as the bride was the granddaughter of Mas Senen and Sukjem, the Mohler's were invited. Unfortunately, Agnes was sick and could not go, so Leny stayed at home. Willi decided to take Ruth with him. They left with a gift for Sudjana, and drove to the small village where she had grown up. Willi found the house without a problem, they had been there before. The house was elaborately decorated. On each side of the doorway were two banana trees with fruit which had been cut and placed there for decoration and as an offering for Dewi Sri, the goddess of rice. "Gamelan" music was playing, and a "ronggeng" danced and sang to the music. It reminded Willi of the numerous child weddings they had attended in Java. They were greeted as special guests, and escorted into the house. A man was talking, and when he finished, rice was thrown into the air. The "ronggeng" gracefully took a veil, a "slendang," and the young groom stood up, and danced behind the "ronggeng" imitating the dance steps. The veil was handed to the main dancer, an older man, which he let flow around the necks of the men who were gathered around. Whenever a man was touched by the veil, he had to get up and dance. The women did not participate, and stood in the background. Sudjana, the bride, sat on a mat on the floor, dressed in beautiful clothes holding a fan, and she was surrounded by several women. Willi sat down on the floor in the men's section, Ruth joined the women in the back. Willi watched the dancing men, but every few seconds he looked over to where his little girl was sitting. Once when he glanced over, he saw her talking with one of the women, her little arms gesticulating, and she had a serious expression on her face. Willi could not hear what she was saying. Several women disappeared. His eyes went back to the dancing. When he looked over to where Ruth had been, the women had returned, carrying another fan. The next time he looked over Ruth was sitting on the mat next to the bride, her legs crossed, and she was fanning herself with a beautiful fan the women had fetched. She had a look on her face as if it were the most natural thing for her to do. Willi looked at his child, his blond Ruth, in the midst of all the brown faces, and it was quite a sight. The celebration was fascinating, the people danced, food was served, and they stayed until it began to turn dark. Willi gave Sudjana her gift, and then the two left for home. The festivities lasted for a whole week and cost the family about 2,000 guilders. Sudjana barely knew the groom, the parents and grandparents had arranged the marriage. After the wedding ceremonies had ended she returned to work. A year later Sudjana gave birth to twins. The babies were premature and died.

TARANTULAS, GEESE AND SNAKES

Willi also became interested in the remedies the natives used to treat all kinds of ailments. The end of February one of his friends shot a porcupine, a "landak," near Sungei Kendilo, and gave him its skull. The natives ate the meat. The quills were used to make hair pins and a medicine called "obat landak." The quills were placed on a rock, pulverized, and the powder mixed with water. The paste was then rubbed on afflicted areas. Women who had a cold, "masuk angin," (the wind has entered), put porcupine quills in their hair to treat respiratory infections. The porcupine quills also played an important role in Chinese medicine.

One of his assistants told him about soil consumption. In Java the edible earth was called "ampo." Women ate the earth because they believed it enhanced fertility, men ate it because they thought that it would make them strong. To Willi it seemed that "ampo" was eaten more as a tradition. Of the many people he spoke with none could give him an exact reason; of course, it could also have been that they did not want to reveal the true meaning. The soil had no taste or nutritional value. It was a clay, either of white, yellow, red, yellow-brown or gray-green color, and contained bituminous organic matter. The soil was carefully washed, left overnight, and then formed into small pieces. These were sprinkled with salt, rubbed with coconut oil, and then roasted. It was mostly consumed as a treat, and was sometimes eaten by pregnant women. Willi found out that it often caused constipation and disease. In Borneo the coal-slate and in Sumatra diatonatious soil were consumed by the natives.

In April on a day when it had been raining on and off Willi looked up from his work and glanced out of the window. He saw a large snake on the slightly elevated road in front of his office. It had probably crawled to higher grounds from the rain soaked wilderness area. Just then several coolies came down the path and also spotted the snake. One of them grabbed it by its tail as it tried to slither into the tall grass, pulling it out onto the dirt road. He thought that he was catching dinner, that it was a python. He was mistaken, for it turned out to be a large cobra. Fortunately, one of the other men was able to hit it over the head with a stick before it could turn around and bite its captor. This all happened with an incredible speed. Willi jumped up from his chair and ran outside. The snake was over six feet long, quite a respectable size for a cobra. Its poisonous fangs were more than half an inch long. By the time Willi reached the group of men they had already killed the reptile. He asked them if he could have it to add to his collection. When he came home from work he showed Leny and the girls the snake, and told them what had happened.

Ruth was turning more and more into a tomboy. She was fascinated with all kinds of creatures, and was always outside exploring the area. Only a few days after Willi had shown the children the cobra and how it had been caught, she was playing in the yard. She heard a strange noise and was curious, so she followed the distress call of an animal. She looked around, and saw that the noise came from a small tree in the yard. Carefully she approached, looking up into the branches. There she spotted a green snake. The rear part of a frog was in the snake's mouth, the head was still protruding, and the little animal made a pitiful sound. Ruth decided to save it. She tried to reach the snake. Its tail was just above her outstretched hand and she was only a couple of inches away. She figured if the natives could catch a snake by its tail, so could she. She reached and reached and almost had it when she was suddenly jerked back. Mas Senen pulled her away, scolding her, and he said louder than his usually quiet voice:

"Awas," be careful. The snake she had tried to catch by its tail was a poisonous species, the Dryophis, a green, slender tree snake. Its snout was long and pointed. It blended with its surroundings, and became almost indistinguishable from the twigs. It fed mostly on lizards and frogs. It was very poisonous, and even though its fangs were quite short, its venom would have killed a child. Mas Senen was very concerned, and told Willi and Leny what had happened. Ruth had to promise to never again attempt to catch a snake, and if she wanted to have one of her own, Willi would get her a young python. Leny agreed, but there was one condition, the snake had to stay outside, caged or not.

Mas Senen was the girls' guardian angel. When Willi and Leny went out at night, which was often several times a week, he sat in front of the children's bedroom window, a large knife and kris in his lap, and he faithfully waited until they returned home.

May 18th, 1948, was the official presentation of the silver cigarette holder in appreciation of the assistance the Swiss men had provided to Dutch prisoners of war during the Japanese occupation. The festivities were held at the main offices, and the men, about fifteen, were invited to an elaborate luncheon at the clubhouse.

Ruth was again exploring the nearby area when she caught a rare tarantula, Mygale javanensis. The arachnid was as large as a mouse. The giant spiders are poisonous, but Ruth was very skilled at catching animals, and knew how to be careful. Also, the tarantula was quite docile. The lecture about the snake had made her become more cautious. The tarantula's entire body was covered with hair. These spiders were mostly found in holes in the ground or under branches and trunks from where they emerged after the sun had gone down. They jumped on their prey, and fed mostly on small mammals and birds. Around that time the girls received another musk deer, a female. The two little animals got along well. There were notable differences between the two species. The female had spots and was light yellow-brown. Both animals had similar white stripes on the neck and chest. The female was taller than the male and somewhat longer. Also of difference were the colors the eyes reflected in a light at night. The male's eyes were green, the female's yellow. According to a friend who was an experienced hunter, he had observed two musk deer species in Sumatra and Borneo. One was larger, the "napu," which had spots, and the smaller one, "kantjil," had no spots. Both animals had been caught in the region of the upper Sungei Telakai. Around mid July both animals suddenly died. Everyone was devastated. A few days after discovering the two little bodies Willi saw a large green snake slither into the animal's run. He suspected that the snake had killed the deer, had been scared away, and now came back to feed. In some regions of Borneo the Dayak called the smaller species "blandok batang" which means, fallen tree, because the animals were frequently found near fallen trees. Willi prepared the two skulls for the museum collection.

Ruth with a snake in 1948

VACATION IN JAVA

On August 19th, 1948, they left on a four week vacation to Java. The company owned several nice bungalows on the outskirts of Bandung in an area called Tjumbu Luit. It had wonderful hiking places and a nice swimming pool. Small rivers meandered through the valleys, all around were rice paddies, waterfalls, and in the horizon the silhouettes of the volcanoes. There was a "kokki" and "djongos" at the house, and each day a truck delivered fresh meat, vegetables and other household needs. Willi had to attend several meetings in Bandung, and looked forward to seeing many of his old acquaintances. Politically, Bandung was more or less quiet, but still occasionally they heard gun shots near the house. Behind their bungalow at the edge of a wide lawn was a bamboo forest, a flower garden and banana plantation. The house had a large porch overlooking the lush gardens. Leny loved the bamboo; in the evening breeze the tall trunks gave off a melodious, rustling sound, at times it sounded like groaning when the trunks rubbed against each other in the breeze. After a couple of days, and after the children had become accustomed to their new surroundings, Willi and Leny took the girls to see their old house. Leny had not seen it yet either. She stood among the rubble, her hands covering her mouth, her head shaking in disbelief. How fortunate they had been to have gotten out of the terrible war alive. Agnes and Ruth could not quite comprehend what had happened to their old house which held so many memories for them. They looked at their old bedroom, and memories of frightening times came flooding back. As young as they were, they knew that they were now living in a much safer world.

A week later Willi left on an excursion west of Bandung with several other men of the company. All of them were heavily armed because of the general unrest; one of the men even had a machine gun. Before leaving they all had to sign a release form that they would not hold the military responsible if anything were to happen. Nothing happened on that day, and Willi returned in the late afternoon. They undertook many hikes and excursions, walked to nearby hills and volcanoes, and even found obsidian, the black shiny rocks which were formed from hardened lava. Whoever found the largest piece received a prize. They went to Batdudjidjar and Tjimani, and to Tago Gapu. On one day they hiked up another volcano, and came upon an andesite quarry. Workers cut holes in the rock into which dried wooden pegs were placed. The pegs were then soaked with water, expanding them, and the rock broke apart. The "tani" people were just like they had been before the war; they were friendly and enjoyed talking with Willi, Leny and the children. The four weeks went by much too fast, and on September 18th they left Bandung, and flew to Surabaya. Only ten minutes after take-off the plane developed mechanical problems and had to return to Surabaya. They spent the night at a hotel. Early the following day the flight continued over the Java sea, stopped over in Bandjarmasin, and continued on to Balikpapan.

While they were at the Bandjarmasin airport, Willi met two men he had known before the war, one was a Chinese the other a native from Bandjarmasin. The latter had known Dr. Weiss whom he had respected highly. The old Chinese joined the conversation, and told Willi that when the Japanese decapitated Dr. Weiss, his wife and nurse, they also killed his son. The son had owned a business which the Japanese wanted, so they just executed him, and took possession of the property. There had been many more victims at that time, one was an old Arab man who was close to a hundred years old. The old man owned several beautiful houses so he too was executed, and the J

Ruin of the house on Carel Fabritiuslaan in Bandung.

LAST YEAR IN BORNEO

The servants were happy to have the family back, and the house was spotless when they arrived. The children were glad to be home. Ruth immediately went to check on her animals. Mas Senen had taken good care of the chickens, geese, cats and other critters they had around the house. School began again the following morning, and Ruth, as always, had a hard time sitting still until lunch time. Classes began at nine in the morning, at ten thirty the girls had a break and ate a banana, and then they continued until noon. They had no school in the afternoon; it was too hot. Again they had to move to another house. The Pantjur hill was completely torn down, the swamp at the bottom of the hill was filled up, and new factories were built. The new house was in Klandasan, just minutes from the beach. It was so close that they could hear the roaring of the ocean waves from the house. Often, early in the mornings, the girls walked to the beach before breakfast to look for shells. Sudjana always went with them. On the week-ends Willi and Leny went along. Only feet from the shore were large shade trees. Tables and chairs were set up under umbrellas, waiters brought refreshing drinks, and a shower was nearby to rinse off the salt water from the ocean. Willi often thought of the tragedy that had happened at that site in February of 1942, and of the friends who had died in such a cruel manner. At around eleven in the mornings it turned too hot and they went home.

THE MAGIC KRIS

One afternoon in late November an old man on a cart pulled by a small horse approached the house. Willi and Leny were sitting in the shade of the trees, drinking tea. Willi looked up, and recognized the old man; it was the Buginese artifact dealer who used to come by their house before the war, and who offered his treasures for sale. He always had many beautiful old kris, hand crafted silverware, Dayak artifacts, Chinese pottery and more. His prices were reasonable, and he often sold Willi a precious item for a pack of cigarettes and a sack of sugar or coffee. He spread out his wares in the back yard. Willi immediately spotted a beautiful kris, its handle was made of ivory, and the blade was decorated with gold and silver. Mas Senen joined them and examined the kris. He placed the blade between his index finger and his thumb, starting at the handle until he reached the point. As he did this he said the words: "gunung," mountain, "guntur," thunder, "segara," ocean and "sat," ebb tide. The word spoken when he reached the tip determined its mystical powers. He then placed his left thumb nail on the blade to determine whether or not it would be favorable for its owner. If it felt cold to the touch, "dinging," then it was good, if it felt warm, "panas," then the relationship would be an unfavorable one. After a lengthy examination, Mas Senen told Willi it was very strong, and had the ability to stand on its point. Willi had heard stories before about kris being able to do certain things, but he was skeptical. He decided to purchase the rare piece, not because of its mystical powers, but because it was a beautiful piece of art. He was, though, interested to see it stand on its point, and asked Mas Senen to demonstrate it. He hesitated at first, saying that the experiment would be so strong that it might cause Willi harm because he was too young. They then determined that they were about the same age, thirty-seven years old, so Mas Senen told him that he would show him the power of the kris the following Friday. For the ceremony Willi had to provide a new white piece of fabric. Friday evening arrived, and Willi gave Mas Senen a piece of fabric which was spread out on the stone floor. He told Willi to sit to its north, Mas Senen sat south with his legs crossed. He removed the blade from the sheath holding the handle, and pulling the sheath away from it. This was necessary to inform the kris that there was no intention to fight. If a battle were to take place, then the kris was pulled out of its sheath. He greeted the kris in the same manner as he would a person, and beseeched it to manifest its strength by standing on its tip. Initially, it did not stand upright. He repeated the entire ceremony. Willi was watching his every move intently, and suddenly, in front of his eyes, the twelve inch long kris stood on its tip on a stone floor. At first it swayed lightly, and then stood still for about thirty seconds. Incredible what Willi had just witnessed. He told Leny about the experience, but she responded that he must have been hypnotized. Willi doubted it for he had watched Mas Senen's every move, and had been wide awake. After some persuading Mas Senen agreed to demonstrate it again in the presence of both Leny and Willi, and would let them know when he would do it again. Several days went by and then Mas Senen was ready for another demonstration. The experiment was called "djumahat legi," to make a powerful kris stand on its tip. Leny stood at the window looking out toward the neighbor's house and did not participate. They had arranged this beforehand to make sure that there was no hypnosis involved. The kris stood on its tip after the first attempt. Willi told Leny to turn around and to look. At first the kris swayed briefly, and then it stood still for half a minute. Willi knew that hypnosis had not been involved because Leny had seen what he saw. There was no explanation for the phenomenon, and they knew that few people would believe the story, but both had witnessed it with their own eyes. They just could not explain how the dagger was able to stand on its sharp point on a flat, smooth, terrazzo floor.

In December Willi had to go to Surabaya and Madura on a business trip, and was gone for a week. Only two weeks later, on December 19th, war broke out in Indonesia, but they did not notice anything in Balikpapan. Willi heard that on the outskirts of Bandjarmasin some activities were going on, and the military was trying to clear the area of freedom fighters and gangs. The extremists had been there for three years, ever since the war had ended. Postage stamps were changed, and the words Netherlands East Indies were stamped over with the word Indonesia. They spent a quiet Christmas with the children and friends. A new year's party was planned at the club, but the celebration was ruined at eleven at night when the guards were called in after everyone had gathered in the ballroom of the clubhouse. The guards were instructed to immediately make themselves available and be ready to leave. Nobody knew what was happening, the party broke up, and everyone went home. Nothing further happened.

ADAPTING NATIVE HABITS

Willi and Leny had planned on coming home in the early morning hours, so they were quite surprised at what they encountered when they arrived at the house. Apparently, whenever they went out, the girls got out of bed, and joined the servants in the back. They dressed up like the local women, wore sarongs and were in their bare feet. Usually at night all the servants from the neighborhood gathered outside, sat around a fire, talked and smoked. When Leny and Willi walked up to the back of the house they saw two small white-clad figures running off, the embers of a cigarette in their hands leaving small glowing trails in the dark night. Somehow the girls had convinced Mas Senen to make them each a cigarette so they could pretend to be smoking, just like all the natives did, adults and children alike. He had only rolled up some corn leaves without tobacco. The girls were adapting many of the native customs, and Willi and Leny were afraid that one day they would catch them chewing betel nuts as everyone else did. They had a long talk with the girls about the dangers of tobacco, and they had to promise not to get out of bed when their parents were not at home.

Ruth dressed as a native

MORE ENCHANTED PIGS

The end of January Willi and Jakob went hunting again because the fresh meat of a wild pig was always a welcome change. The men headed toward Taritip, a heavily vegetated jungle area. Near the edge of the jungle they came upon a large tapioca field, "ladang," owned by an old Bandjarese farmer. Often, wild pigs raided the tapioca fields and caused great damage. They walked up to the old farmer who was working in his fields, and talked with him, asking him if the pigs bothered his plants. The old man said that the pigs never bothered his plants, and never entered his garden. When Willi and Jakob looked around they saw that the old man was telling the truth for none of the plants showed any damage. They also knew that there were hundreds of pigs in the jungle adjacent to the garden. Only a few feet away they saw numerous footprints. Now they were curious. At first the old farmer hesitated, but then agreed to show them his magic remedy to ward off the pigs. All around his field, about twelve feet apart, he had placed sticks which were about three feet high. On each stick he had attached a white piece of fabric. This was the old farmer's entire defense to keep the very destructive pigs from his tapioca plants. He told them that from time to time he talked with the pigs when they came too close, and tells them to go back into the jungle. He seemed to have some strange power over the wild animals. They knew that wild pigs wandered into villages, and could often be seen foraging underneath the huts on stilts, but neither of them could imagine how some sticks with a white piece of fabric would deter them. All they could do was shake their heads in disbelief. There was no use to try to find an explanation, they were just not capable of understanding these things. Willi had already been told similar stories of controlling tigers and crocodiles. They chatted a while longer with the old man, offered him a cigar which he gladly took, and then continued into the jungle. They entered deeper into the bush, and came upon a small herd of wild pigs. Both aimed and shot. The bullets hit the animal, but did not bring it down. The injured pig ran toward Willi, ready to attack. Wild pigs were extremely dangerous animals in itself, but an injured wild boar could kill a person during an attack. Seconds seemed like an eternity. Willi aimed at the enraged animal racing toward him, pulled the trigger, and the beast fell to the ground just as it reached Willi. The two men, both shaken up from the experience, rested a few moments to recover from the scare. A short while later they were able to shoot another nice fat pig. On the drive home they almost ran over a marabou near Sepingan as it suddenly came onto the narrow path they were driving on.

FIGHT FOR FREEDOM AND INDEPEN-
DENCE

On February 18th, 1949, Willi attempted to explain the situation in Indonesia to his parents so they would not worry about them.

Dear parents, you must be hearing much about the present Indonesian situation so I will describe it to you briefly. The news is seldom objective which makes it hard to picture the actual situation. Last week it seemed that Holland was going to leave Indonesia, in other words, call in their troops. This would have resulted in chaos, and would have been precarious for both the Europeans as well as the Indonesians. Of course, Holland will have to relinquish the government to Indonesia. The federalists want to achieve independence through negotiations whereas the republic wants to achieve it, if necessary, by force. The republic is strongly supported by the Americans and Australians, but this seems to be more of an economic nature than out of freedom ideals. The Americans know very well that they can influence the Indonesians better in trade issues than the Dutch can. So you see, the main issues here are the economic interests. The Dutch do have a historic primary right because they did bring the country its prosperity. As long as there is oil, rubber, sugar, coffee, coconut oil, etc. there will continue to be interference from non-Indonesian powers. The Japanese had occupied the land during the war because of its natural resources. I am convinced that the Dutch are serious about giving up this land, but they want to do it in a peaceful manner. The military situation in Java and Sumatra does not look good for the Dutch, but we hope that when the actual Indonesian government has been formed, the tensions will ease. An immediate emancipation may not be the right answer and could hurt Indonesia. We are glad that we will not be going to Surabaya after all even though the city is quite safe. The surroundings, on the other hand, are very dangerous, and recently twenty homes belonging to our company in one of the resorts were completely destroyed. Fortunately, there were no casualties because the company will not subject its employees to any risks. It will still take a long time until the country has gained its freedom. Balikpapan is quiet and will remain so. If everything goes according to plans, we will soon be home. Love, Willi.

One day their gander went wild, he ran around the yard flapping his wings, honking loudly, he flew over the roof connecting the front of the house with the back, and then flew down the stairs leading to the road below. Willi and the girls ran after him, and were finally able to retrieve the animal. They could not understand what was wrong. Sukjem knew what it was though, and told them that a black ghost had visited the gander, and warned him that a bad storm was approaching. Willi looked up at the sky, it was clear, and there was not a single cloud in the blue sky. Later in the day the girls went to the beach with neighbors, and they drove the short distance in the tool car. All four children were sitting in the back of the small truck. They had been at the beach for about an hour when suddenly a water spout appeared just ahead. The group quickly ran to the car to head for home. By the time they drove the short distance back up the hill, roofs and tree trunks were flying through the air. Several large pieces of metal were hurled over the car. They were in the middle of a terrible tornado, which swept through the area with incredible fury, taking with it what was in its path. Huge Australian pines (casuarinas) were broken in half as if they were flower stems, half the roof of the nearby hospital was torn off, and garden furniture was lifted into the air and blown away. Sukjem had interpreted the gander's reaction correctly. Nobody was hurt, the children managed to run to the safety of the house before the storm hit full force. Its path went just east of the house which was not damaged. In one of the corners of the yard was a small tree under which Leny used to enjoy sitting in the later afternoon hours. When the storm passed, and they went outside, the entire tree had been uprooted and blown away. They looked around and walked down the street. On the other side of the road, in the middle of a large field, they saw it. The next day a gardener and his helpers carried the tree back, replanted it in its original spot, and it again became Leny's favorite little shade tree.

Willi had been scheduled to go to Surabaya, but the trip was postponed for a month. The areas around the city were very unsafe. Balikpapan was still quiet and not much was going on, but in May there was a big fire that lasted for over two days. An oil tank filled with airplane fuel near the Pantjur hill had caught on fire. They never found out if it had been sabotage.

FINAL FAREWELL

Their time in Borneo was coming to an end, and they were scheduled to leave for Europe in September. Willi did not want Leny to travel alone with three small children so they planned to go on their Europe trip together. Sometimes women and children went ahead of the husbands, but Willi and Leny preferred to be together. During that time Dutch airplanes were no longer allowed to fly over Indonesia since war had broken out between Holland and the republic. The security counsel forced the Dutch to return the Sultanate Djokjakarta. Willi felt that Holland was getting tired of war, and he often wondered why so many human lives had to be sacrificed. In the military cemetery in Djokja seven hundred young Dutch soldiers lay buried who had fallen since December 1948.

June 3rd was Willi's thirty-eighth birthday. As he was shaving he took a closer look, and discovered that he had some gray hairs by his temples. He mentioned it at the breakfast table, and both girls stated that it had nothing to do with age, but that he had only faded a bit. Their comment made him smile and they had a nice day. Shortly after his birthday he had to go to Surabaya for a couple of weeks to organize a new laboratory. He also spent a few days in Madura to survey the geology of the island. Contrary to Java, Madura was very strong and safe politically, which reminded Willi of mid-Java before the war. In Surabaya he met another old acquaintance from Java. The man had lived through terrible times, he had been in Tjepu during the Communist revolt when about three thousand people were killed. Willi hired the man to work for him while he was in Surabaya. He had to travel back and forth between Balikpapan and Surabaya for quite some time.

August had arrived and they spent many hours at the beach. In the afternoons a strong south wind made the ocean roar. The waves carried white caps to the shore, leaving a foaming mass piled on the beach. The children loved to play in the tall waves, they dove into the water, ran ahead of the oncoming waves, fell over, went under, and came up laughing. Every day a new shell or sea creature was discovered. Both Willi and Leny knew that the children would miss the beach. Indonesia was a paradise for children. Day in and day out they could play outside, and each day a new treasure was found or a discovery made. They were scheduled to leave for Surabaya the end of August where they would remain for about a month and then travel to Europe. By the time the plans were finalized it was September, and on the 19th they had to bid farewell to Mas Senen, Sukjem and Sudjana. They stayed at the Oranje hotel in Surabaya. The city was large, it was hot during the day, but turned pleasantly cool at night. Often Leny and the girls went shopping in the city, it was a nice change from the small-town life of Balikpapan. The hotel had a big, lush garden, and the weeks went by fast. On October 3rd, 1949, they flew to Batavia, and from there home to Switzerland.

EPILOGUE

I finished the first draft of my book in 1995, the fifty-year anniversary of the end of the war. My parents retired in their homeland in the early sixties. They built their dream house in Gelterkinden, Switzerland, where they are enjoying their retirement. In the year 2003, Willi celebrated his 92nd birthday; Leny turned 93. They still live in their lovely home, and are both doing well.

After Indonesia we moved to Holland for a couple of years, then on to Venezuela. In 1963, my father retired, and my parents moved back to Switzerland. Dad became active in local politics for some time, and was the expert on geological issues, the environment and ground water. For years he was a favorite local lecturer on fossils, history and geology of the area of his beloved Jura mountains of Switzerland. Each year, when I visit them, we go fossil hunting. Rarely have I known someone who knows every inch of his homeland as my dad does. Each walk through forests, hills and meadows is a fascinating tour through the history of time.

Agnes is married and has two sons. Irene has three children, two sons and a daughter. Another child was born in the fifties, a son, who is also married and has two boys.

I moved to America when I was in my twenties. I had been to America with my parents when I was a teenager, and decided then and there that some day I was going to live in the USA. I had never felt that I belonged anywhere; Switzerland was where all the family lived, but it was a vacation land to me. My teen years were spent in South America, but I really did not want to settle there either. I married in 1967. Ten years later I was a single mother raising two small children by myself. I now have two wonderful married daughters and, best of all, two adorable granddaughters and a grandson, and twin grandbabies on the way.

All the old friends, Christian and Flori, Jakob and Emmi, Hans, Alfred, Werner, Otto and Rosa, Peter and Lisa also retired in their homeland. They all lived to a ripe old age. Christian and Flori moved to Gelterkinden, and during the many get-togethers, family gatherings or dinners, hours were spent talking about the days in Indonesia. They lived just minutes from my parents. Christian was over 90 when he died; Flori lived in a nursing home where she died in 2002 at the age of 98. All the others have passed on, and are greatly missed. I was fortunate to be able to spend time with them, and to visit with them every time I went to Europe. Werner lived in Basel until he died, and when I was a young girl, we often met in his favorite restaurant. He gave me a beautiful old copper batik stamp from Java which I shall always treasure.

The widow of Silatus and his children moved to Holland. They have stayed in touch with my parents. One day around the 1970's my father received a letter from one of the Japanese scientists who had worked at the museum during the war, asking him if they could meet during their visit to Switzerland. My father, who holds no grudges, met the old man and his wife, and took them to see the beautiful Jungfrau in the Swiss Alps. They corresponded for some years.

The old trunk that held the belongings of so many Dutch prisoners of war until the occupation ended was given to me by my parents. Every time I see it I think of the day the Japanese searched my parents' house, the soldier with his boot firmly planted on its lid, never suspecting that it contained personal effects of Dutch prisoners of war. I look at the old chest which holds so many stories, and I treasure it.

I still had some questions when I finished my book, and asked my parents if they could provide the answers on a tape. At the end of the tape my father said:

*"Some words which also for you, Ruth, would be of interest. It concerns the dropping of the two atomic bombs on August 6th and 9th, 1945, on Hiroshima and Nagasaki. Every August we read articles in the newspapers about the terrible atomic bombs; that they were unnecessary because the Japanese had already lost the war anyway. I feel that only people who have **not** experienced the war can make such statements. Today, it is almost unimaginable what the conditions actually were in Indonesia during the time it was occupied by the Japanese. We had no news whatsoever from anywhere outside. Occasionally, we heard a bit of news from a few who had managed to listen to a radio, and it is well-known how dangerous that was. We never really knew anything for certain. On August 1st, 1945, we celebrated our national holiday with another couple, then we had an air alarm, nothing happened, and then at night I told you and Agnes the story of William Tell. We did not hear anything at all on August 6 when the first bomb was dropped. We still heard nothing on August 9th when the second bomb was dropped. We did hear, though, that the Russians had declared war with Japan. This gave us a bit of hope that the war would finally come to an end. On August 10th we*

still had heard no official announcements. After this rumor, though, we saw some Dutch and Indo-Dutch women walk around wearing the national colors of the flag of Holland, red, white and blue. The Japanese immediately arrested and incarcerated them. But, still at that time, we knew nothing for sure. This went on August 11th, 12th, 13th and 14th and for several more days. Everyone had a strange feeling that something had happened, but we were left in total uncertainty. Finally, on August 22nd, 1945, the Japanese radio made an official announcement that Japan had capitulated. It took that long until we heard what had happened. There was talk about an atomic bomb, but nobody could imagine what that was. Even one of our Swiss friends who was a physicist said that it was nonsense, that the bomb was probably a newly developed form of dynamite, and that there was no such thing as an atomic bomb. The Japanese who lived on our street were all acting happy, and we felt that they too, were relieved that the war had ended. Most of the Japanese who lived down the street from us were the so-called Sakura people, people who were working in the commercial and administrative sectors, and only few of them were soldiers. The situation then worsened in that the natives began to revolt and shoot at everyone. We never saw any Allied troops. Occasionally we saw an airplane in the sky. We were told that it was the British commander. As soon as the unrest began, he flew over the area, but never interfered. The situation worsened from day to day.

"I have to again state clearly that without the atomic bombs, hundreds of thousands, if not millions of people would have been killed because the Japanese land army had not been defeated. One has to remember that the Japanese had occupied a huge territory of South East Asia. Who do you think would have landed in those remote areas with their troops to fight the well armed Japanese? Also, later, during the war criminal cases, we heard of the plans of the Japanese to kill off all the Europeans. Why did the Japanese not capitulate after the first bomb was dropped? They felt confident, and only realized after the second bomb was dropped that they were losing the war. Without the bombs, the misery would have continued, and we would all have perished somewhere in the swamps of Borneo. We will forever be grateful to the Americans for ending the war, otherwise we would no longer be here. The bombs saved our lives."

Willi Mohler

Printed in the United States
17844LVS00003B/193-213